DAUGHTER OF THE SUN

A Tale of Adventure

JACKSON GREGORY

1st WORLD
LIBRARY
Literary Society

Daughter of the Sun

Jackson Gregory

© 1st World Library, 2007
PO Box 2211
Fairfield, IA 52556
www.1stworldlibrary.com
First Edition

LCCN: 2007901809

Softcover ISBN: 978-1-4218-4276-9
Hardcover ISBN: 978-1-4218-4178-6
eBook ISBN: 978-1-4218-4374-2

Purchase *"Daughter of the Sun"*
as a traditional bound book at:
www.1stWorldLibrary.com/purchase.asp?ISBN=978-1-4218-4276-9

1st World Library is a literary, educational organization
dedicated to:

- Creating a free internet library of downloadable ebooks

- Hosting writing competitions and offering book
publishing scholarships.

1st World Library Literary Society

Giving Back to the World

"If you want to work on the core problem, it's early school literacy."
- James Barksdale, former CEO of Netscape

"No skill is more crucial to the future of a child, or to a democratic and prosperous society, than literacy."

- Los Angeles Times

Literacy... means far more than learning how to read and write... The aim is to transmit... knowledge and promote social participation."
- UNESCO

"Literacy is not a luxury, it is a right and a responsibility. If our world is to meet the challenges of the twenty-first century we must harness the energy and creativity of all our citizens."

- President Bill Clinton

"Parents should be encouraged to read to their children, and teachers should be equipped with all available techniques for teaching literacy, so the varying needs and capacities of individual kids can be taken into account."
- Hugh Mackay

TO

ZINGARA

CONTENTS

I. IN WHICH A YOUNG AMERICAN KNOWN AS
"HEADLONG" PLAYS AT DICE WITH ONE IN
MAN'S CLOTHING WHO IS NOT A MAN 9

II. IN WHICH A SPELL IS WORKED AND
AN EXPEDITION IS BEGUN 27

III. OF THE NEW MOON, A TALE OF AZTEC
TREASURE AND A MYSTERY 41

IV. INDICATING THAT THAT WHICH APPEARS
THE EARTHLY PARADISE MAY PROVE
QUITE ANOTHER SORT OF PLACE 53

V. HOW ONE NOT ACCUSTOMED TO TAKING
ANOTHER MAN'S ORDERS RECEIVES THE
COMMAND OF THE QUEEN LADY 62

VI. CONCERNING THAT WHICH LAY IN THE
EYES OF ZORAIDA 70

VII. OF A GIRL HELD FOR RANSOM AND OF
A TOAST DRUNK BY ONE INFATUATED 82

VIII. HOW A MAN MAY CARRY A MESSAGE AND
NOT KNOW HIMSELF TO BE A MESSENGER 92

IX. WHICH BEGINS WITH A LITTLE SONG
AND ENDS WITH TROUBLE
BETWEEN FRIENDS 103

X. IN WHICH A MAN KEEPS HIS WORD AND
ZORAIDA DARES AND LAUGHS 117

XI. IN WHICH THERE IS MORE THAN ONE
LIE TOLD AND THE TRUTH IS GLIMPSED 129

XII. IN WHICH AN OVERTURE IS MADE,
AN ANSWER IS POSTPONED AND A DOOR
IS LOCKED 144

XIII. CONCERNING WOMAN'S WILES
AND WITCHERY.. 152

XIV. CONCERNING A DIFFICULT SITUATION,
RECKLESSLY INVITED... 167

XV. OF THE ANCIENT GARDENS OF THE
GOLDEN TEZCUCAN 176

XVI. HOW TWO, IN THE LABYRINTH OF MIRRORS,
WATCHED DISTANT HAPPENINGS 191

XVII. HOW ONE WHO HAS EVER COMMANDED
MUST LEARN TO OBEY... 204

XVIII. OF FLIGHT, PURSUIT AND A LAIR
IN THE CLIFFS... 214

XIX. HOW ONE WHO HIDES AND WATCHES
MAY BE WATCHED BY ONE HIDDEN................. 225

XX. IN WHICH A ROCK MOVES, A DISCOVERY IS
MADE AND MORE THAN ONE AVENUE
IS OPENED 233

XXI. HOW ONE RETURNS UNWILLINGLY
WHITHER HE WOULD WILLINGLY ENTER
BY ANOTHER DOOR 247

XXII. REGARDING A NECKLACE OF PEARLS
AND CERTAIN PLANS OF TWO WHO
WERE MEANT TO BE ONE 254

CHAPTER I

IN WHICH A YOUNG AMERICAN KNOWN AS "HEADLONG" PLAYS AT DICE WITH ONE IN MAN'S CLOTHING WHO IS NOT A MAN

Jim Kendric had arrived and the border town knew it well. All who knew the man foresaw that he would come with a rush, tarry briefly for a bit of wild joy and leave with a rush for the Lord knew where and the Lord knew why. For such was ever the way of Jim Kendric.

A letter at the postoffice had been the means of advising the entire community of the coming of Kendric. The letter was from Bruce West, down in Lower California, and scrawled across the flap were instructions to the postmaster to hold it for Jim Kendric who would arrive within a couple of weeks. Furthermore the word URGENT was not to be overlooked.

Among the men drawn together in hourly expectation of the arrival of Kendric, one remarked thoughtfully:

"Jim's Mex friend is in town."

"Ruiz Rios?" someone asked, a man from the outside.

"Been here three days. Just sticking around and doing nothing but smoke cigarettes. Looks like he was waiting."

"What for?"

"Waiting for Jim, maybe?" was suggested.

Two or three laughed at that. In their estimation Ruiz Rios might be the man to knife his way out of a hole, but not one to go out of his way to cross the trail made wide and recklessly by Jim Kendric.

"A half hour ago," came the supplementary information from another quarter, "a big automobile going to beat the band pulls up in front of the hotel. The Mex is watching and when a woman climbs down he grabs her traps and steers her into the hotel."

Immediately this news bringer was the man of the moment. But he had had scant time to admit that he hadn't seen her face, that she had worn a thick black veil, that somehow she just *seemed* young and that he'd bet she was too darn pretty to be wasting herself on Rios, when Jim Kendric himself landed in their midst.

He was powdered with alkali dust from the soles of his boots to the crown of his black hat and he looked unusually tall because he was unusually gaunt. He had ridden far and hard. But the eyes were the same old eyes of the same old headlong Jim Kendric, on fire on the instant, dancing with the joy of striking hands with the old-timers, shining with the man's supreme joy of life.

"I'm no drinking man and you know it," he shouted at them, his voice booming out and down the quiet blistering street. "And I'm no gambling man. I'm steady and sober and I'm a regular fool for conservative investments! But there's a time when a glass in the hand is as pat as eggs in a hen's nest and a man wants to spend his money free! Come on, you bunch of devil-hounds; lead me to it."

It was the rollicking arrival which they had counted on since this was the only way Jim Kendric knew of getting back among old friends and old surroundings. There was nothing subtle about him; in all things he was open and forthright and tempestuous. In a man's hardened and buffeted body he had kept the heart of a harum-scarum boy.

"It's only a step across the line into Old Town," he reminded them. "And the Mexico gents over there haven't got started reforming yet. Blaze the trail, Benny. Shut up your damned old store and postoffice, Homer, and trot along. It's close to sunset any way; I'll finance the pilgrimage until sunup."

When he mentioned the "postoffice" Homer Day was recalled to his official duties as postmaster. He gave Kendric the letter from Bruce West. Kendric ripped open the envelope, glanced at the contents, skimming the lines impatiently. Then he jammed the letter into his pocket.

"Just as I supposed," he announced. "Bruce has a sure thing in the way of the best cattle range you ever saw; he'll make money hand over fist. But," and he chuckled his enjoyment, "he's just a trifle too busy scaring off Mexican bandits and close-herding his stock to get any sleep of nights. Drop him a postcard, Homer; tell him I can't come. Let's step over to Old Town."

"Ruiz Rios is in town, Jim," he was informed.

"I know," he retorted lightly. "But I'm not shooting trouble nowadays. Getting older, you know."

"How'd *you* know?" asked Homer.

"Bruce said so in his letter; Rios is a neighbor down in Lower California. Now, forget Ruiz Rios. Let's start something."

There were six Americans in the little party by the time they had walked the brief distance to the border and across into Old Town. Before they reached the swing doors of the Casa Grande the red ball of the sun went down.

"Fat Ortega knows you're coming, Jim," Kendric was advised.

"I guess everybody in town knows by now."

And plainly everybody was interested. When the six men, going in two by two, snapped back the swinging doors there were a score of men in the place. Behind the long bar running along one side of the big room two men were busy setting forth bottles and glasses. The air was hazy with cigarette smoke. There was a business air, an air of readiness and expectancy about the gaming tables though no one at this early hour had suggested playing. Ortega himself, fat and greasy and pompous, leaned against his bar and twisted a stogie between his puffy, pendulous lips. He merely batted his eyes at Kendric, who noticed him not at all.

A golden twenty dollar coin spun and winked upon the bar impelled by Jim's big fingers and Kendric's voice called heartily:

"I'd be happy to have every man here drink with me."

The invitation was naturally accepted. The men ranged along the bar, elbow to elbow; the bartenders served and, with a nod toward the man who stood treat, poured their own red wine. Even Ortega, though he made no attempt toward a civil response, drank. The more liquor poured into a man's stomach here, the more money in Ortega's pocket and he was avaricious. He'd drink in his own shop with his worst enemy provided that enemy paid the score.

Kendric's friends were men who were always glad to drink and play a game of cards, but tonight they were gladder for the chance to talk with "Old Headlong." When he had bought the house a couple of rounds of drinks, Kendric withdrew to a corner table with a dozen of his old-time acquaintances and for upward of an hour they sat and found much to talk of. He had his own experiences to recount and sketched them swiftly, telling of a venture in a new silver mining country and a certain profit made; of a "misunderstanding," as he mirthfully explained it, now and then, with the children of the South; of horse swapping and a taste of the pearl fisheries of La Paz; of no end of adventures such as men of his class and nationality find every day in troublous Mexico. Twisty Barlow, an old-time friend with whom once he had gone adventuring in Peru, a man who had been deep sea sailor and near pirate, real estate juggler, miner, trapper and mule skinner, sat at his elbow, put many an incisive question, had many a yarn of his own to spin.

"Headlong, old mate," said Twisty Barlow once, laying his knotty hand on Kendric's arm, "by the livin' Gawd that made us, I'd like to go a-journeyin' with the likes of you again. And I know the land that's waitin' for the pair of us. Into San Diego we go and there we take a certain warped and battered old stem-twister the owner calls a schooner. And we beat it out into the Pacific and turn south until we come to a certain land maybe you can remember having heard me tell about. And there—It's there, Headlong, old mate!"

Kendric's eyes shone while Barlow spoke, but then they always shone when a man hinted of such things as he knew lay in the sailorman's mind. But at the end he shook his head.

"You're talking about tomorrow or next day, Twisty," he laughed, filling his deep lungs contentedly. "I've had a bellyful of manana-talk here of late. All I'm interested in is tonight." He rattled some loose coins in his pocket. "I've got money in my pocket, man!" he cried, jumping to his feet. "Come ahead. I stake every man jack of you to ten dollars and any man who wins treats the house."

Meanwhile Ortega's place had been doing an increasing business. Now there was desultory playing at several tables where men were placing their bets at poker, at seven-and-a-half and at roulette; the faro layout would be offering its invitation in a moment; there was a game of dice in progress.

Kendric's companions moved about from table to table laughing, making small bets or merely watching. But presently as half dollars were won and lost the insidious charm of hazard touched them. Monte stuck fast to the faro table for fifteen minutes, at the end of which time he rose with a sigh, tempted to go back to Kendric for a "real stake" and cut in for a man's play. But he thought better of it and strolled away, rolling a cigarette and watching the others. Jerry bought a ten dollar stack of chips and assayed his fortune with roulette, playing his usual luck and his usual system; with every hazard lost he lost his temper and doubled his bet. He was the first man to join Monte.

For upward of an hour of play Kendric was content with looking on and had not hazarded a cent beyond the money flung down on the table to be played by his friends. But now at last he looked about the room eagerly, his head up, his eyes blazing with the up-surge of the spirit riding him. About his middle was a money belt, safely brought back across the border; in his wild heart was the imperative desire to play. Play high and quick and hard. It was then that for the first time he noted Ruiz Rios. Evidently the Mexican had just now entered from the rear. At the far end of the room where the kerosene lamp light was none too good Rios was standing with a solitary slim-bodied companion. The companion, to call for all due consideration later, barely caught Jim's roving eye now; he saw Rios and he told himself that the gamblers' goddess had whisked him in at the magic moment. For in one essential, as in no others, was Ruiz Rios a man after Jim Kendric's own heart: the Mexican was a man to play for any stake and do no moralizing over the result.

"Ortega," cried Kendric, looking all the time challengingly at Rios, "there is only one game worth the playing. King of games? The emperor of games! Have you a man here to shake dice with me?"

Ortega understood and made no answer, Rios, small and sinister and handsome, his air one of eternal well-bred insolence, kept his own counsel. There came a quick tug at his sleeve; his companion whispered in his ear. Thus it was that for the first time Kendric really looked at this companion. And at the first keen glance, in spite of the male attire, the loose coat and hat pulled low, the scarf worn high about the neck, he knew that it was a woman who had entered with Ruiz Rios and now whispered to him.

"His wife," thought Kendric. "Telling him not to play. She's got her nerve coming in here."

The question of her relationship to the Mexican was open to speculation; the matter of her nerve was not. That was definitely settled by the carriage of her body which was at once defiant and imperious; by the tilt of the chin, barely glimpsed; by the way she stood her ground as one after another pair of eyes turned upon her until every man in the room stared openly. It was as useless for her to seek to disguise her sex thus as it would be for the moon to mask as a candle. And she knew it and did not care. Kendric understood that on the moment.

"Between us there has been at times trouble, senor," said Rios lightly. "I do not know if you care to play? If so, I will be most pleased for a little game."

"I'd shake dice with the devil himself, friend Ruiz," answered Jim heartily.

"I must have some money from Ortega here," said Rios carelessly. "Unless my check will satisfy?"

"Better get the money," returned Kendric pleasantly.

As Rios turned away with the proprietor Kendric was impelled to look again toward the woman. She had moved a little to one side so that now she stood in the shadow cast by an angle of the wall. He could not see her eyes, so low had she drawn her wide *sombrero*, nor could he make out much of her face. He had an impression of an oval line curving softly into the folds of her scarf; of masses of black hair. But one thing he knew: she was looking steadily at him. It did not matter that he could not see her eyes; he could feel them. Under that hidden gaze there was a moment during which he was oddly stirred, vaguely agitated. It was as though she, some strange woman, were striving to subject his mind to the spell of her own will; as though across the room she were seeking not only to read his thought but to mold it to the shape of her own thought. He had the uncanny sensation that her mind was rifling his, that it would be hard to hide from those probing mental fingers any slightest desire or intention. Kendric shook himself savagely, angered that even for an instant he should have submitted to such sickish fancies. But even so, and while he strode to the nearby table for the dice cup, he could not free himself from the impression which she had laid upon him.

She beckoned Rios as he came back with Ortega. He went to her side and she whispered to him.

"We will play here, at this end of the room, senor," Rios said to Kendric.

As Kendric looked quite naturally from the one who spoke to the one from whom so obviously the order had come, he saw for the first time the gleam of the woman's eyes. A very little she had lifted the brim of her hat so that from beneath she could watch what went forward. They held his gaze riveted; they seemed to glow in the shadows as though with some inner light. He could not judge their color; they were mere luminous pools. He started with an odd fancy; he caught himself wondering if those eyes could see in the dark?

Again he shrugged as though to shake physically from him these strange fancies. He snatched up the little table and brought it to where Ruiz Rios waited, putting it down not three feet from the Mexican's silent companion. And all the time, though now he refused to turn his head toward her, he was conscious of the strangely disturbing certainty that those luminous eyes were regarding him with unshifting intensity.

Kendric abruptly spilled the dice out of the cup so that they rolled on the table top.

"One die, one throw, ace high?" he asked curtly of Rios.

The Mexican nodded.

It was in the air that there would be big play, and men crowded around. Briefly, the unusual presence of a woman, here at Fat Ortega's, was forgotten.

"Select the lucky cube," Kendric invited Rios. The Mexican's slim brown fingers drew one of the dice toward him, choosing at random.

Kendric opened vest and shirt and after a moment of fumbling drew forth and slammed down on the table a money belt that bulged and struck like a leaden bar.

"Gold and U. S. bank notes," he announced. "Keep your eye on me, Senor Don Ruiz Rios de Mexico, while I count 'em."

Unbuttoning the pocket flaps, he began pouring forth the treasure which he had brought back with him after two years in Old Mexico. Boyish and gleeful, he enjoyed the expressions that came upon the faces about him as he counted aloud and Rios watched with narrow, suspicious eyes. He sorted the gold, arranging in piles of twenties and tens, all American minted; he smoothed out the bank notes and stacked them. And at the end, looking up smilingly, he announced:

"An even ten thousand dollars, senor."

"You damn fool!" cried out Twisty Barlow hysterically. "Why, man, with that pile me an' you could sail back into San Diego like kings! Now that dago will pick you clean an' you know it."

No one paid any attention to Barlow and he, after that one involuntary outburst, recognized himself for the fool and kept his mouth shut, though with difficulty.

Ruiz Rios's dark face was almost Oriental in its immobility.

He did not even look interested. He merely considered after a dreamy, abstracted fashion.

Again a quick eager hand was laid on his arm, again his companion whispered in his ear. Rios nodded curtly and turned to Ortega.

"Have you the money in the house?" he demanded.

"*Seguro*," said the gambling house owner. "I expected Senor Kendric."

"You do me proud," laughed Jim. "Let's see the color of it in American money."

With most men the winning or losing of ten thousand dollars, though they played heavily, was a matter of hours and might run on into days if luck varied tantalizingly. All of the zest of those battling hours Jim Kendric meant to crowd into one moment. There was much of love in the heart of Headlong Jim Kendric, but it was a love which had never poured itself through the common channels, never identified itself with those two passions which sway most men: he had never known love for a woman and in him there was no money-greed. For him women did not come even upon the rim of his most distant horizon; as for money, when he had none of it he sallied forth joyously in its quest holding that there was plenty of it in this good old world and that it was as rare fun running it down as hunting any other big game. When he had plenty of it he had no thought of other matters until he had spent it or given it away or watched it go its merry way across a table with a green top like a fleet of golden argosies on a fair emerald sea voyaging in search of a port of adventure. His love was reserved for his friends and for his adventurings, for clear dawns in solitary mountains, for spring-times in thick woods, for sweeps of desert, for what he would have called "Life."

"Ready?" Ruiz Rios was asking coldly. Ortega had returned with a drawer from his safe clasped in his fat hands; the money was counted and piled.

"Let her roll," cried Kendric heartily.

Never had there been a game like this at Ortega's. Men packed closer and closer, pushing and crowding. The Mexican slowly rattled the single die in the cup. Then, with a quick jerk of the wrist, he turned it out on the table. It rolled, poised, settled. The result amply satisfied Rios and to the line of the lips under his small black mustache came the hint of a smile; he had turned up a six.

"The ace is high!" cried Jim. He caught up die and box, lifting the cupped cube high above his head. His eyes were bright with excitement, his cheeks were flushed, his voice rang out eagerly.

"Out of six numbers there is only one ace," smiled Ruiz Rios.

"One's all I want, senor," laughed Jim. And made his throw.

When large ventures are made, in money or otherwise, it would seem that the goddess of chance is no myth but a potent spirit and that she takes a firm deciding hand. At a time like this, when two men seek to put at naught her many methods of prolonging suspense, she in turn seeks stubbornly to put at naught their endeavors to defeat her aims. Had Jim Kendric thrown the ace then he would have won and the thing would have been ended; had he shaken anything less than a six the spoils would have been the Mexican's. That which happened was that out of the gambler's cup Kendric turned another six.

Ruiz Rios's impassive face masked all emotion; Kendric's displayed frankly his sheer delight. He was playing his game; he was getting his fun.

"A tie, by thunder!" he cried out in huge enjoyment. "We're getting a run for our money, Mexico. Shall I shake next?"

"Follow your hand," said Ruiz Rios briefly.

That which followed next would have appeared unbelievable to any who have not over and over watched the inexplicable happenings of a gaming table. Kendric made his second throw and lifted his eyebrows quizzically at the result. He had turned out the deuce, the lowest number possible. A little eagerly, while men began to mutter in their excitement, Rios snatched up cup and die and threw. Once already he had counted ten thousand as good as won; now he made the same mistake. For the incredible happened and he, too, showed a deuce, making a second tie.

Ruiz cursed his disgust and hurled the box down. Kendric burst into booming laughter.

"A game for men to talk about, friend Rios!" he said. And at the moment he came near feeling a kindly feeling for a man whom he hated most cordially and with high reason. "Follow your hand."

Rios received the box from a hand offering it and made his third throw swiftly. The six again.

"Where we began, senor," he said, grown again impassive.

Kendric was all impatient eagerness to make his throw, looking like a boy chafing at a moment's restraint against his antici-pated pleasures.

"A six to beat," he said.

And beat it he did, with the odds all against him. He turned up the ace and won ten thousand dollars.

In the brief hush which came before the shouts and jabberings of many voices, Ruiz Rios's companion pulled him sharply by the arm, whispering quickly. But this time Rios shook his head.

"I am through," he said bluntly. "Another time, maybe."

But the fever, to which he had so eagerly surrendered, was just gripping Kendric. That he was playing for big stakes was the thing that counted. That he had won meant less to him than it would have meant to any other man in the room or any other man who had ever been in the room or any other man who would ever come into the room. He saw that Ruiz was through. But, as his dancing eyes sped around among other faces, he marked the twinkling lights of covetousness in Fat Ortega's rat eyes and he knew that, long ago, Ortega himself had played for any stake. Beside Ortega there was another man present who might be inclined to accept a hazard, Tony Munoz, who conducted the rival gambling house across the street and who was Ortega's much despised son-in-law. Long ago Ortega and Tony had quarreled and when Tony had run away with Eloisa, Ortega's pretty daughter, men said it was as much to spite the old man as for love of the girl's snapping eyes. Tony might play, if Ortega refused.

"One throw for the whole thing, Ortega?" challenged Kendric. "You and me."

"Have I twenty thousand *pesos* in my pocket?" jeered Ortega. "You make me the big gringo bluff."

"Bluff? Call it then, man. That's what a bluff is for. And you don't need the money in the pocket. This house is yours; your cellars are always full of expensive liquors; there is money in your till and something in your safe yet, I'll bet my hat. Put up the whole thing against my wad and I'll shake you for it."

Plainly Ortega was tempted. And why not? There lay on the green table, winking up alluringly at him, twenty thousand dollars. His, if simply a little cube with numbers on it turned in proper fashion. Twenty thousand dollars! He licked his fat pendulous lips. And, to further tempt him, he estimated that his entire holding here, bar fixtures, tables, wines and cash, were worth not above fifteen thousand. But then, this was all that he had in the world and though he craved further gains until the craving was acute like a pain, still he clung avidly to the power and the prestige and the luxury that were his as owner of la Casa Grande. In brief, he was too much the moral coward to be such a gambler as Kendric called for.

"No," he snapped angrily.

"Look," said Kendric, smiling. He shook the die and threw it, inverting the cup over it so that it was hidden. "I do not know what I have thrown, Ortega, and you do not know. I will bet you five thousand dollars even money that it is a six or better."

Here were odds and Ortega jerked up his head. Five thousand to bet—

"No," he said again. "No. I don't play. You have devil's luck."

With a flourish Jim lifted the cup to see what he had thrown. Again his utterly mirthful laughter boomed out. It was the deuce, the low throw. Ortega strained forward, saw and flushed. Had he but been man enough to say "Yes!" to the odds offered him he would have been five thousand dollars richer this instant! Five thousand dollars! He ran a flabby hand across a moist brow.

"Where's the luck in that throw?" demanded Kendric, fully enjoying the play of expression on Ortega's face.

"The luck," grumbled Ortega, "was that I did not bet you. If I had bet it would have been a six, no less."

"Tony Munoz," called Kendric, turning. "Will it be you?"

"No!" shouted Ortega, already angered in his grasping soul, ready to spew forth his wrath in any direction, always more than ready to rail at his son-in-law. "Munoz has no business in my house. Who is boss here? It is me!"

Kendric seeing that Tony Munoz was contenting himself with sneering and certainly would not play, began gathering up the money on the table. It was then that for the first time he heard the voice of Ruiz Rios's companion.

"I will play Senor Kendric."

The voice ran through the quiet of the room musically. The utterance was low, gentle, the accent was the soft, tender accent of Old Spain with some subtle flavor of other alien races. No man in the room had ever heard such sweet, soothing music as was made by her slow words. After the sound died away a hush remained and through men's memories the cadences repeated themselves like lingering echoes. Kendric himself stared at her wonderingly, not knowing why her hidden look stirred him so, not knowing why there should be a spell worked by five quiet words. Nor did he find the spell entirely pleasant; as her look had done, so now her speech vaguely disturbed him. His emotion, though not outright irritation, was akin to it. He was opening his lips to say curtly, "I do not play dice with women, senora," when Ortega's sudden outburst forestalled him.

Kendric had barely had the time to register the faint impression of the odd sensation which this companion of Ruiz Rios awoke in him, when he was set to puzzle over Ortega's explosion. Why should the gaming-house keeper raise so violent an objection to any sort of a game played in his place? Perhaps Ortega himself could not have explained clearly since it is doubtful if he felt clearly; it is likely that a childishly blind anger had spurted up venomously in his heart when Kendric had exposed the deuce and men had laughed and Ortega felt as though he had lost five thousand dollars. In such a case a man's wrath explodes readily, combustion breaking forth spontaneously like an oily rag in the sun. At any rate, his fat face grown hectic, he lifted hand and voice, shouting:

"I will have no women gambling here. This is my place, a place for men. You," and he leveled his forefinger at the slim figure, "go!"

She ignored him. Stepping forward quickly, she whipped off her left glove and in the bare white fingers, blazing with red and green stones set in golden circlets, she caught up the dice cup. Even now little was seen of her face for the other hand had drawn lower the wide hat, higher the scarf about the throat.

"One die, one throw for it all, Senor Kendric?" she asked.

"I tell you, No!" shouted Ortega. "And No again!"

Then, when she stood unmoved, her air of insolence like Ruiz Rios's, but even more marked, Ortega burst forward between the men standing in his way, shoving them to right and left with the powerful sweep of his thick arms. His uplifted hand came down on her shoulder, thrusting her backward. Her ungloved hand, the left as Kendric marked while he watched interestedly, flashed to her bosom, and leaped out again, a thin-bladed knife in the grip of the bejewelled fingers. Ortega saw and feared and, grown nimble, sprang back from her. Quickly enough to save the life in him, not so quickly as entirely to avoid the sweep of the knife. His sleeve fell apart, slit from shoulder to wrist, and in the opening the man's flesh showed with a thin red line marking it.

There was tumult and confusion for a little while, hardly more than a moment it seemed to Kendric. He only knew that at the end of it Ortega had gone grumbling away, led by a couple of friends who no doubt would bandage his wounded arm, and that the woman, having put her knife away, appeared not in the least disturbed. He knew then that while men talked and shouted about him he had not once withdrawn his eyes from her.

"One throw?" she was asking again, the voice as tender, as vaguely disquieting to his senses, as full of low music as before. He shook himself as though rousing from a trance.

"I do not play at dice with ladies, Senora," he said bluntly.

"Did you bluff, after all?" she asked curiously. She seemed sincere in her question; he fancied a note of disappointment in her tone. It was as though she had said before, "Here is a man who is not afraid of big stakes," and as though now she were revising her estimate of him. "Men will call you Big Mouth," she added. "And I, I will laugh in your face."

"Where is the money you would wager against mine?" demanded Jim, thinking he saw the short easy way out.

Already she was prepared for the question. In her gloved hand was a little hand bag, a trifle in black leather the size of a man's purse. She opened it and spilled the contents on the table. Poured out into the mellow lamp light a long glorious string of pearls appeared, each separate lustrous gem glowing with its silvery sheen, satiny and tremulous with its shining loveliness.

"Holy God!" gasped Twisty Barlow.

"There is the worth of your money many times over," came the quiet assurance in the low voice like liquid music.

"If they are real pearls," muttered Kendric. "And not just imitations."

She made no reply. He felt that from the shelter of the broad hat brim a pair of inscrutable eyes were smiling scornfully.

"Can't I tell real pearls like them, when I see 'em?" cried Twisty Barlow excitedly. He leaned forward and caught the great necklace up in his eager hands. "What would I be wantin' that steamer in San Diego Bay for if I didn't know?" He held them up to the lamp light; he fingered them one after the other; he put them down at the end reverently and with a great sigh. "The worth of them, Headlong, my boy," he said shakily, "would make your pile look sick."

"And yet I'd bet a thousand they're phony," burst from Kendric. Then he caught himself up short. Suppose they were or were not? A woman was offering to play him and he was holding back; he was making excuses, the second already; in his own ears his words, sensible though they were, began to ring like the petty talk of a hedger. "Turn out the die, Senora," he said abruptly. "As you say, one throw and ace high."

With her left hand she quietly shook the box, setting the white cube dancing therein. "You lose, Jim," said Monte at his elbow before the cast was made. "Look out for left-handers." Then she made her throw and turned up an ace.

Kendric caught up box and die and threw. And again he had turned the deuce, the lowest number on the die. He heard her laugh as she drew money and jewels toward her. All low music, ruining a man's blood, thrilling him after that strange perturbing fashion.

CHAPTER II

IN WHICH A SPELL IS WORKED AND AN
EXPEDITION IS BEGUN

For a moment she and Jim Kendric stood facing each other with only the little table and its cargo of treasure separating them, engulfed in a great silence. He saw her eyes; they were like pools of lambent phosphorescence in the black shadow of her hair. He glimpsed in them an eloquence which mystified him; it was as though through her eyes her heart or her mind or her soul were reaching out toward his but speaking a tongue foreign to his understanding. Her gaze was steady and penetrating and held him motionless. Nor, though he did not at the time notice, did any man in the room stir until she, turning swiftly, at last broke the charm. She went out through the rear door, Ruiz Rios at her heels.

When the door closed after them Kendric chanced to note Twisty Barlow at his elbow. A queer expression was stamped on the rigid features of the sailorman. Plainly Barlow, intrigued into a profound abstraction, was alike unconscious of his whereabouts or of the attention which he was drawing. His eyes stared and strained after the vanished Mexican and his companion; he, too, had been fascinated; he was like a man in a trance. Now he started and brushed his hand across his eyes and, moving jerkily, hurried to the door and went out. Kendric followed him and laid a restraining hand upon his shoulder.

"Easy, old boy," he said quietly. Barlow started at the touch of his hand and stood frowning and fingering his forelock. "I know what's burning hot in your fancies. Remember they may be paste, after all. And anyway they're not treasure trove."

"You mean those pearls might be fake?" Barlow laughed strangely. "And you think I might be slittin' throats for them? Don't be an ass, Headlong; I'm sober."

"Where away, then, in such a hurry?" demanded Kendric, still aware of something amiss in Barlow's bearing.

"About my business," retorted the sailor. "And suppose you mind yours?"

Kendric shrugged and went back to his friends. But at the door he turned and saw Barlow hastening along the dim street in the wake of the disappearing forms of Ruiz Rios and the woman.

Inside there were some few who sought to console Kendric, thinking that to any man the loss of ten thousand dollars must be a considerable blow. His answer was a clap on the back and a laughing demand to know what they were driving at and what they took him for, anyway? Those who knew him best squandered no sympathy where they knew none was needed. To the discerning, though they had never known another man who won or lost with equal gusto in the game, who when he met fortune or misfortune "treated those two impostors just the same," Jim Kendric was exactly what he appeared to be, a devil-may-care sort of fellow who had infinite faith in his tomorrow and who had never learned to love money.

Kendric was relieved when, half an hour later, Twisty Barlow came back. Kendric's mood was boisterous from the sheer joy of being among friends and once more as good as on home soil. He went up and down among them with his pockets turned wrong-side out and hanging eloquently, swapping yarns, inviting recitals of wild doings, making a man here and there join him in one of the old songs, singing mightily himself. He had just given a brief sketch of the manner in which he had acquired his latest stake; how down in Mexico he had done business with a man whom he did not trust. Hence Kendric had insisted on having the whole thing in good old U. S. money and then had ridden like the devil beating tan bark to keep ahead of the half-dozen ragged cut-throats who, he was sure, had been started on his trail.

"And now that I'm rid of it," he said, "I can get a good night's sleep! Who wants to be a millionaire anyway?"

He saw that though Barlow had once more command of his features, there was still a feverish gleam in his eyes. And, further, that with rising impatience Barlow was waiting for him.

"Come alive, Twisty, old mate," Kendric called to him. "Limber up and give us a good old deep-sea chantey!"

Twisty stood where he was, eyeing him curiously.

"I want to talk to you, Jim," he said. His voice like his look told of excitement repressed.

"It's early," retorted Kendric, "and talk will keep. A night like this was meant for other things than for two old fools like you and me to sit in a corner with long faces. Strike up the chantey."

"You're busted," said Barlow sharply; "You've had your fling and you've shot your wad. Come along with me. You know what shore I'm headin' to. You know I've got my hooks in that old tub down to San Diego—"

    "There's a craft in San Diego,"

improvised Kendric lightly.

"With no cargo in her hold,
And old Twisty Barlow's leased her
For to fill her up with Gold.
And he'd go a buccaneerin', privateerin', wildly steerin'
For the beaches where the sun shines on whole banks of
blazin' pearls—"

But his rhythm was getting away from him and his rhymes
petered out and he stopped, laughing while around him men
clamored for more.

"Oh, there'll be a tale to tell when Twisty sails back," he
conceded. "But until he's under way there's no tale to tell and
so what's the use of talk? A song's better; walk her up, Twisty,
old mate."

Barlow's impatience flared out into irritation.

"What's the sense of this monkey business?" he demanded.
"I'm off to San Diego by moon-rise. If you ain't with me, you
ain't. Just say so, can't you?"

"A song first, Twisty?" countered Kendric.

"Will you come listen to me then?" asked Barlow. "Word of
honor?"

It was plain that he was in dead earnest and Kendric cried,
"Yes," quite heartily. Then Barlow, putting up with Kendric's
mood since there was no other way that one might do for a
wilful, spoiled child over which he had no authority of the rod,
allowed himself to be dragged to the middle of the room and
there, standing side by side, the two men lifted their voices to
the swing and pulse of "The Flying Fish Catcher," through all
but interminable verses, while the men about them kept
enthusiastic time by tramping heavily with their thick boots.
At the end Kendric put his arm about the shoulders of his
shorter companion, and in lock step they went out. The party
was over.

"What's on your mind, Seafarer?" asked Kendric when they were outside.

"Loot, mostly," said Barlow. "But first, while I think of it, Ruiz Rios's wife wants a word with you."

"What about?" Kendric opened his eyes. And, before Barlow answered, "You saw her then?"

"I went up to the hotel. Tried to get a room. She saw me and sent for you. She didn't say what for."

"Well, I'll not go," Kendric told him. "Now spin your yarn about your loot."

He leaned against a lamp post while Twisty Barlow, upright and eager, said his say. A colorful tale it was in which the reciter was lavish with pearls and ancient gold. It appeared that one had but to sail down the coast of Lower California, up into the gulf and get ashore upon a certain strip of sandy beach in the shadows of the cliffs.

"And I tell you I've already got the hull off San Diego that will take us there," maintained Barlow. "All I'm short of is you to stand your share of the hell we'll raise and to chip in with what coin you can scrape. If you hadn't been a damn fool with that ten thousand," he added bitterly.

"Spilled milk. Forget it. It came out of Mexico and it goes back where it belongs. But if you're counting on me for any such amount as that, you're up a tree. I'm flat."

"We'll go just the same if you can't raise a bean," said Barlow positively. "But if you can dig anything, for God's sake scrape lively. We want to get there before somebody else does. And I was hopin' you'd come across for grub and some guns and odds and ends."

"I've got a few oil shares," said Kendric. "If they're roosting around par they're good for twenty-five hundred."

Barlow brightened.

"We'll knock 'em down in San Diego if we only get two fifty!" he announced, considering the sale as good as made. "And we'll do the best we can on what we get."

Not yet had Kendric agreed to go adventuring with Twisty Barlow. But in his soul he knew that he would go, and so did Barlow. There was nothing to hold him here; from elsewhere the voice which seldom grew quiet was singing in his ears. He knew something of the gulf into which Barlow meant to lead him, and of that defiant, legend-infested strip of little-known land which lay in a seven hundred mile strip along its edge; he knew that if a man found nothing else he would stand his chance of finding life running large. It was the last frontier and as such it had the singing voice.

"You'll go?" said Barlow.

But first Kendric asked his few questions. When he had answers to the last of them his own eyes were shining. His truant fancies at last had been snared; he was going headlong into the thing, he had already come to believe that at the end of it he would again have filled his pockets the while he would have drunk deep of the life that satisfied. It was long since he had smelled the sea, had known ocean sunrise and sunset, had gone to sleep with his bunk swaying and the water lapping. So when again Barlow said, "You'll come?" Kendric's hand shot out to be gripped by way of signing a contract, and his voice rang out joyously, "Put her there, old mate! I'm with you, blow high, blow low."

For a few minutes they planned. Then Barlow hurried off to make what few arrangements were necessary before they could be in the saddle and riding toward a railroad. Kendric meant to get two or three hours' sleep since he realized that even his hard body could not continue indefinitely as he had been driving it here of late. There was nothing to be done just now that Barlow could not do; before the saddled horses could be brought for him he could have time for what rest he needed.

The thought of bed was pleasant as he walked on for he realized that he was tired in every muscle of his body. The street was deserted saving the figure of a boy he saw coming toward him. As he was turning a corner the boy's voice accosted him.

"Senor Kendric," came the call. "*Un momenta.*"

Kendric waited. The boy, a half-breed in ragged clothes, came close and peered into his face. Then, having made sure, he whipped out a small parcel from under his torn coat.

"*Para usted,*" he announced.

Kendric took it, wondering.

"What is it?" he asked. "Who sent it?"

But the boy was slouching on down the street. Kendric called sharply; the boy hastened his pace. And when Kendric started after him the ragamuffin broke into a run and disappeared down an alley way. Kendric gave him up and came back to the street, tearing off the outer wrap of the package under a street lamp. In his hand was a sheaf of bank notes which he readily recognized as the very ones he had just now lost at dice, together with a slip of note paper on which were a few finely penned lines. He held them up to the light in an amazement which sought an explanation. The words were in Spanish and said briefly:

"To Senor Jim Kendric because under his laugh he looked sad when he lost. From one who does not play at any game with faint hearts."

His face flushed hot as he read; angrily his big hand crumpled message and bank notes together. He glanced down the empty street; then forgetful of bed and rest, his anger rising, he strode swiftly off toward the hotel, muttering under his breath. The hotel-keeper he found alone in the little room which served him as office and bed chamber.

"I want to see Mrs. Rios," said Kendric curtly.

"You'd be meaning the Mexican lady? Name of Castelmar." He drew his soiled, inky guest book toward him. "Zoraida Castelmar."

"I suppose so," answered Kendric. "Where is she?"

"Your name would be Kendric?" persisted the hotel-keeper. And at Kendric's short "Yes," he pointed down the hall. "Third door, left side. She's expecting you."

Had Kendric paused to speculate over the implication of the man's words he would inevitably have understood the trick Ruiz Rios's companion had played on him. But he was never given to stopping for reflection when he had started for a definite goal and furthermore just now his wrath was consuming him. He went furiously down the hall and struck at the door as though it were a man who had stirred his anger by standing in his path. "Come in," invited a woman's voice in Spanish, the inflection distinctly that of old Mexico. In he went.

Before him stood an old woman, her face a tangle of deep wrinkles, her hair spotted with white, her eyes small and black and keen. He looked at her in surprise. Somehow he had counted on finding Zoraida Castelmar young; just why he was not certain. But the surprise was an emotion of no duration, since a hotter emotion overrode it and crowded it out.

"Look here," he began angrily, his hand lifted, the bills tight clenched.

But she interrupted.

"You are Senor Kendric, *no*? She awaits you. There."

She indicated still another door and would have gone to open it for him. But he brushed by her and threw it back himself and crossed the threshold impatiently. And again his emotion surging uppermost briefly was one of surprise. The room was empty; it was the unexpected and incongruous trappings which astonished him. On all hands the walls, from ceiling to floor, were hidden by rich silken curtains, hanging in deep purple folds, displaying a profusion of bright hued woven patterns, both splendid and barbaric. The floor was carpeted by a soft thick rug, as brilliant as the wall drapes. The two chairs were hidden under similar drapes, the small square table covered by a mantle of deep blue and gold which fell to the floor. Beyond all of this the solitary bit of furnishing was the object on the table whose oddity caught and held his eye; a thin column of crystal like a ten-inch needle, based in a red disc and supporting a hollow cap, the size of an acorn cup, in which was a single stone or bead of glass, he knew not which. He only knew that the thing was alive with the fire in it and blazed red, and he fancied it was a ruby.

He glanced hurriedly about the room, making sure that it was empty. Again his eyes came back to the glowing jewel supported by the thin crystal stem. Now he was conscious of a sweet heavy perfume filling the room, a fragrance new to him and subtly exotic. Everything about him was fantastic, extravagant, absurd, he told himself bluntly, as was everything connected with an absurd woman who did mad things. He looked at the bank notes in his hand. What more insane act than to send an amount of money of this size to a stranger?

The familiarly disturbing feeling that eyes, her eyes, were upon him, came again. He turned short about. She stood just across the room, her back to the motionless curtains. Whence she had come and how, he did not know. She was smiling at him and for the first time he saw her eyes clearly and her dark passionate face and scarlet mouth. He did not know if she were fifteen or twenty-five. The oval face, the curving lips were those of a young maiden; her tall, slender figure was obscured by the loose folds of a snow white garment which fell to the floor about her; her eyes were just now of any age or ageless, unfathomable, and, though they smiled, filled with a sort of mockery which baffled him, confused him, angered him. Upon one point alone there could be no shadow of doubt; from the top of her proudly lifted head with its abundance of black hair wherein a jewel gleamed, to the tips of her exquisite fingers where gleamed many jewels, she was almost unhumanly lovely. She looked foreign, but he could not guess what land had cradled her. Mexico? Why Mexico more than another land? It struck him that she would have seemed alien to any land under the sun. She might have sprung from some race of beings upon another star.

She had marked the look on his face and in her eyes the laughter deepened and the mockery stood higher. He frowned and stepped to the table, tossing down the pad of bank notes.

"That is yours," he told her briefly. "I don't want it and I won't take it."

Then she, too, came forward to the table. Her left hand took up the money swiftly, eagerly, it struck him, and thrust it out of sight somewhere among the folds of her gown. Then finally her laughter parted her lips and the low music of it filled the room. He knew in a flash now that she had never meant to allow her winnings to escape her; that there had been craft in the wording of the message she had sent him; that all along she counted on his coming to her as he had come. She sank into the chair nearest her and indicated the other to him.

"If Senor Kendric will be seated," she said lightly, "I should like to speak with him."

In blazing anger had Kendric come here. Now, seeing clearly just how she had played with him the blood grew hotter in his face and hammered at his temples.

"*Senora*," he said crisply, "there need be no talk between you and me since we have no business together."

"*Senorita*," she corrected him curiously. "I am not married."

"Nor is that a matter for us to discuss." He meant, as he desired, to be rude to her. "Since it does not interest me."

"It has interested many men," she laughed at him lightly, but still with that intense probing look filling the black depths of her eyes. "With them it has been a vital matter."

Before he had marked something peculiar about the eyes; now he saw just what it was. They were Oriental, slanting upward slightly toward the white temples. No wonder she had impressed him as foreign. He wondered if she were Persian or Arabian; if in her blood was a strain of Chinese, even?

He gave no sign of having heard her but groped for the door through which he had come. It now, like the rest of the walls, was hidden under the silken hangings which no doubt had fallen into place when the door had closed behind him. He did not remember having shut it; perhaps the old woman in the outer room had done so. And locked it. For when at last his hand found the knob the door would not open.

"What's all this nonsense about?" he demanded. "I want to go."

It was her turn to pretend not to have heard. She sat back idly, looking at him fixedly, smiling at him after her strange fashion.

"I have heard of you," she said at last. "A great deal. I have even seen you once before tonight. I know the sort of man you are. I know how you made your money in Mexico; how you rode with it across the border. I have never known another man like you, Senor Jim Kendric."

"Will you have the door unlocked?" he said. "Or shall I smash it off its hinges?"

"A man with your look and your reputation," she said calmly, "was worth a woman's looking up. When that woman had need for a man." Her eyes were glittering now; she leaned forward, suddenly rigid and tense and breathing hard. "When I have found a man who stakes ten thousand, twenty thousand on one throw and is not moved; who returns ten thousand in rage because a word of pity goes with it, am I to let him go?"

"I don't like the company you keep," said Kendric. "And I don't like your ways of doing business. I guess you'll have to let me go."

"You mean Ruiz Rios?" Her eyes flashed and her two hands clenched. Then she sank back again, laughing. "When you learn to hate him as I do, senor, then will you know what hate means!"

He pressed a knee against the door, near the lock. The hangings getting in his way, he tore them aside. Zoraida Castelmar watched him half in amusement, half in mockery.

"There is a heavy oak bar on the other side," she told him carelessly.

"I have a notion," he flung at her, "to take that white throat of yours in my two hands and choke you!"

The words startled her, seemed to astound, bewilder.

"You think that you—that any man—could do that?" It was hardly more than a whisper full of incredulity.

"Well, I don't suppose that I would, anyway," he admitted. "But look here: I've got some riding ahead of me and I'm dog tired and want a wink of sleep. Suppose we get this foolishness over with. What do you want?"

"I want you. To go with me to my place where there are dangers to me; yes, even to me. I know the man you are and in what I could trust you and in what I could not. I would make your fortune for you." Again she looked curiously at him. "Under the hand of Zoraida Castelmar you could rise high, Senor Kendric."

He shook his head impatiently before she had done and again at the end.

"I am no woman's man," he told her steadily, "and I want no place as any woman's watchdog. Offer me what you please, a thousand dollars a day, and I'll say no."

From its place under his left arm pit he brought out a heavy caliber revolver, toying with it while he spoke. Her look ran from the black metal barrel to his face.

"Do you think you can frighten me?" she demanded.

"I don't mean to try. I'll shoot off the lock and the hinges and if the door still stands up I'll keep on shooting until the hotel man comes and lets me out." He put the muzzle of the gun at the lock.

"Wait!" She sprang to her feet. "I will open for you." She brushed by him and rapped with her knuckles on the door. Beyond was a sound of a bolt being slipped, of a bar grinding in its sockets. "One thing only and you can go: When you come before me again it may be you who begs for favors! And it will be I who grant or withhold as it may appear wise to me."

"Witch, are you?" he jeered. "A professional reader of fortunes? God knows you've got the place fixed up like it!"

"Maybe," she returned serenely, "I am more than witch. Maybe I do read that which is hidden. *Quien sabe*, Senor Kendric, scorner of ladies? At least," and again her laughter tantalized him, "I knew where to find you tonight; I knew you would win from Ruiz Rios; I knew I would win from you; I knew you would refuse to come to me and then would come. All this I knew when you took your ten thousand from the bank down in Mexico and rode toward the border. Further," and he was baffled to know whether she meant what her words implied or whether she was merely making fun of him, "I have put a charm and a spell over your life from which you are never going to be free. Put as many miles as it pleases you between you and Zoraida Castelmar; she will bring you back to her side at a time no more distant than the end of this same month."

He gave her a contemptuous and angry silence for answer. In the street he looked up at the stars and filled his lungs with an expanding sigh of relief. This companion of Ruiz Rios who paid passionate claim to an intense hatred of the man whom she allowed to escort her here and there, impressed him as no natural woman at all but as something of strange influences, a malign, powerful, implacable spirit incased in the fair body of a slender girl. He told himself fervently that he was glad to be beyond the reach of the black oblique eyes.

Two hours later he was in the saddle, riding knee to knee with Twisty Barlow, headed for San Diego Bay and a man's adventure. "In which, praise be," he muttered under his breath, "there is no room for women." And yet, since strong emotions, like the restless sea, leave their high water marks when they subside, the image of the girl Zoraida held its place in his fancies, to return stubbornly when he banished it, even her words and her laughter echoing in his memory.

"I have put a spell and a charm over your life," she had told him.

"Clap-trap of a charlatan," he growled under his breath. And when Barlow asked what he had said he cried out eagerly:

"We can't get into your old tub and out to sea any too soon for me, old mate."

Whereupon Barlow laughed contentedly.

CHAPTER III

OF THE NEW MOON,
A TALE OF AZTEC TREASURE AND A MYSTERY

On board the schooner *New Moon* standing crazily out to sea, with first port of call a nameless, cliff-sheltered sand beach which in his heart he christened from afar Port Adventure, Jim Kendric was richly content. With huge satisfaction he looked upon the sparkling sea, the little vessel which *scooned* across it, his traveling mate, the big negro and the half-wit Philippine cabin boy. If anything desirable lacked Kendric could not put the name to it.

Few days had been lost getting under way. He had gone straight up to Los Angeles where he had sold his oil shares. They brought him twenty-three hundred dollars and he knocked them down merrily. Now with every step forward his lively interest increased. He bought the rifles and ammunition, shipping them down to Barlow in San Diego. And upon him fell the duty and delight of provisioning for the cruise. As Barlow had put it, the Lord alone knew how long they would be gone, and Jim Kendric meant to take no unnecessary chances. No doubt they could get fish and some game in that land toward which their imaginings already had set full sail, but ham by the stack and bacon by the yard and countless tins of fruit and vegetables made a fair ballast. Kendric spent lavishly and at the end was highly satisfied with the result.

As the *New Moon* staggered out to sea under an offshore blow, he and Twisty Barlow foregathered in the cabin over the solitary luckily smuggled bottle of champagne.

"The day is auspicious," said Kendric, his rumpled hair on end, his eyes as bright as the dancing water slapping against their hull. "With a hold full of the best in the land, treasure ahead of our bow, humdrum lost in our wake and a seven-foot nigger hanging on to the wheel, what more could a man ask?"

"It's a cinch," agreed Barlow. But, drinking more slowly, he was altogether more thoughtful. "If we get there on time," was his one worry. "If we'd had that ten thousand of yours we'd never have sailed in this antedeluvian raft with a list to starboard like the tower of Pisa."

"Don't growl at the hand that feeds you or the bottom that floats you," grinned Kendric. "It's bad luck."

Nor was Barlow the man to find fault, regret fleetingly though he did. He was in luck to get his hands on any craft and he knew it. The *New Moon* was an unlovely affair with a bad name among seamen who knew her and no speed or up-to-date engines to brag about; but Barlow himself had leased her and had no doubts of her seaworthiness. She was one of those floating relics of another epoch in shipbuilding which had lingered on until today, undergoing infrequent alterations under many hands. While once she had depended entirely for her headway on her two poles, fore sail set flying, now she lurched ahead answering to the drive of her antiquated internal combustion motor. An essential part of her were Nigger Ben and Philippine Charlie; they knew her and her freakish ways; they were as much a portion of her lop-sided anatomy as were propeller and wheel.

Barlow chuckled as he explained the unwritten terms of his lease.

"Hank Sparley owns her," he said, "and the day Hank paid real money for her is the first day the other man ever got up earlier than Hank, you can gamble on it. Now Hank gets busy gettin' square and he's somehow got her insured for more'n she'll bring in the open market in many a day. Hank figures this deal either of two ways; either I run her nose into the San Diego slip again with a fat fee for him; or else it's Davy Jones for the *New Moon* and Hank quits with the insurance money."

"Know what barratry is, don't you?" demanded Kendric.

"Sure I know; if I didn't Hank would have told me." Barlow sipped his champagne pleasantly. "But we'll bring her home, never you fret, Headlong. And we'll pay the fee and live like lords on top of it. Hank ain't frettin'. I spun him the yarn, seein' I had to, and he'd of come along himself if he hadn't been sick. Which would have meant a three way split and I'm just as glad he didn't."

Kendric went out on deck and leaned against the wind and watched the water slip away as the schooner rose and settled and fought ahead. Then he strolled to the stern and took a turn at the wheel, joying in the grip of it after a long separation from the old life which it brought surging back into his memory. And while he reaccustomed himself to the work Nigger Ben stood by, watching him jealously and at first with obvious suspicion.

Nigger Ben, as Kendric had intimated, was a man to be proud of on a cruise like this one. If not seven feet tall, at least he had passed the half-way mark between that and six, a hulking, full-blooded African with monster shoulders and half-naked chest and a skull showing under his close-cropped kinks like a gorilla's. He was an anomaly, all taken: he had a voice as high and sweet-toned as a woman singer's; he had an air of extreme brutality and with the animals on board, a ship cat and a canary belonging to Philippine Charlie he was all gentleness; he had by all odds the largest, flattest feet that Kendric had ever seen attached to a man and yet on them he moved quickly and lightly and not without grace; he held the *New Moon* in a sort of ghostly fear, his eyes all whites when he vowed she was "ha'nted," and yet he loved her with all of the heart in his big black body.

"Sho', she's ha'nted!" he proclaimed vigorously after a while during which he had come to have confidence in the new steersman's knowledge and had been intrigued into conversation. "Don't I know? Black folks knows sooner'n white folks about ha'nts, Cap'n. Ain't I heered all the happenin's dat's done been an' gone an' transcribed on dis here deck? Ain't I *seen* nothin'? Ain't I *felt* nothin'? Ain't I spectated when the ha'r on Jezebel's back haz riz straight up an' when she's hunched her back up an' spit when mos' folks wouldn't of saw nothin' a-tall? Sho', she's ha'nted; mos' ships is. But dem ha'nts ain' goin' bodder me so long's I don't bodder dem. Dat's gospel, Cap'n Jim; sho' gospel."

"It's a hand-picked crew, Twisty," conceded Kendric mirthfully when Nigger Ben was again at the wheel and the two adventurers paced forward. "The kind to have at hand on a pirate cruise!"

For Nigger Ben offered both amusement during long hours and skilful service and no end of muscular strength, while, in his own way, Charlie was a jewel. A king of cooks and a man to keep his mouth shut. When left to himself Charlie muttered incessantly under his breath, his mutterings senseless jargon. When addressed his invariable reply was, "Aw," properly inflected to suit the occasion. Thus, with a shake of the head, it meant no; with a nod, yes; with his beaming smile, anything duly enthusiastic. He was not the one to be looked to for treasons, stratagems and spoils. His favorite diversion was whistling sacred tunes to his canary in the galley.

As the *New Moon* made her brief arc to clear the coast and sagged south through tranquil southern days and starry nights, Kendric and Barlow did much planning and voiced countless surmises, all having to do with what they might or might not find. Barlow got out his maps and indicated as closely as he could the point where they would land, the other point some miles inland where the treasure was.

"Wild land," he said. "Wild, Jim, every foot of it. I've seen what lies north of it and I've seen what lies south of it, and it's the devil's own. And ours, if Escobar's fingers haven't crooked to the feel of it. And if they have, why, then," and he looked fleetingly to the rifles on the cabin wall, "it belongs to the man who is man enough to walk away with it!"

More in detail than at any time before Twisty Barlow told all that he knew of the rumor which they were running down. Escobar was one of the lawless captains of a revolutionary faction who, like his general, had been keeping to the mountainous out-of-the-way places of Mexico for two years. In Lower California, together with half a dozen of his bandit following, he had been taking care of his own skin and at the same time lining his own pockets. It was a time of outlawry and Fernando Escobar was a product of his time. He was never above cutting throats for small recompense, if he glimpsed safety to follow the deed, and knew all of the tricks of holding wealthy citizens of his own or another country for ransoms. Upon one of his recent excursions the bandit captain had raided an old mission church for its candlesticks. With one companion, a lieutenant named Juarez, he had made so thorough a job of tearing things to pieces that the two had discovered a secret which had lain hidden from the passing eyes of worshipful padres for a matter of centuries. It was a secret vault in the adobe wall, masked by a canvas of the Virgin. And in the small compartment were not only a few minor articles which Escobar knew how to turn into money, but some papers. And whenever a bandit, of any land under the sun, stumbles upon papers secretly immured, it is inevitable that he should hastily make himself master of the contents, stirred by a hope of treasure.

"And right enough, he'd found it," said Barlow holding a forgotten match over his pipe. "If there's any truth in it three priests, way back in the fifteen hundreds, stumbled onto enough pagan swag to make a man cry to think about it. Held it accursed, I guess. And didn't need it just then in their business, any way. Just what is it? I don't know. Juarez himself didn't know; Captain Escobar let him get just so far and decided to hog the whole thing and slipped six inches of knife into him. How the poor devil lived to morning, I don't know and I don't care to think about it. But live he did and spilled me the yarn, praying to God every other gasp that I'd beat Fernando Escobar to it. He said he had seen names there to set any man dreaming; the name of Montezuma and Guatomotzin; of Cortes and others. He figured that there was Aztec gold in it; that the three old priests had somehow tumbled on to the hiding place; that they three planned to keep the knowledge among themselves and, when they devoutly judged the time was right, to pass the news on to the Church in Spain.

"I wish Juarez had had time to read the whole works," meditated Barlow. "Anyway he read enough and guessed enough on top of it for me to guess most of the rest while I've been millin' around, getting goin'. Two of the three priests died in a hurry at about the same time, leavin' the other priest the one man in on the know. There was some sort of a plague got 'em; he was scared it was gettin' him, too. So he starts in makin' a long report to the home church, which if he had finished would have been as long as your arm and would of been packed off to Spain and that would of been the last you and me ever heard of it. But it looks like, when he'd written as far as he got, he maybe felt rotten and put it away, intendin' to finish the job the next day. And the plague, smallpox or whatever it was, finished him first."

"Fishy enough, by the sound of it, isn't it?" mused Kendric.

"Fishy, your hat! There's folks would say fishy to a man that stampeded in sayin' he'd found a gold mine. Me, while they guyed him, I'd go take a look-see. And it didn't read fishy to Juarez and it didn't to Fernando Escobar, else why the six inches of knife?"

"Well," said Kendric, "we'll know soon enough. If you can find your way to the place all right?"

"Juarez had a noodle on him," grunted Barlow. "And he was as full of hate as a tick of dog's blood. From the steer he gave me I can find the place all right."

Days and nights went by monotonously, routine merely varying to give place to pipe-in-mouth idleness. But the third night out came an occurrence to break the placidity of the voyage for Kendric, and both to startle him and set him puzzling. He was out on deck in a steamer chair which he had had the lazy forethought to bring, his feet cocked up on the rail, his eyes on the vague expanse about him. There was no moon; the sky was starlit. Barlow had said "Good night" half an hour before; Philippine Charlie was muttering over the wheel; Nigger Ben's voice was crooning from the galley where he was making a friendly call on the canary. The water slipped and slapped and splashed alongside, making pleasant music in the ears of a man who gave free rein to his fancies and let them soar across a handful of centuries, back into the golden day of the last of the Aztec Emperors. The Montezumas *had* had vast hoards of gold in nuggets and dust and hammered ornaments and vessels; history vouched for that. And it stood to reason that the princes and nobles, fearing the ultimate result of the might of the Spaniards, would have taken steps to secrete some of their treasure before the end came. Why not somewhere in Lower California, hurried away by caravan and canoe to a stronghold far from doomed Mexico City?

He was conscious now of no step upon the deck, no sound to mar the present serene fitness of things. But out of his dreamings he was drawn back abruptly to the swaying, swinging deck of a crazy schooner by the odd, vague feeling that he was not alone.

"Barlow," he called quietly. "That you?"

There was no answer and yet, stronger than before, was the

certainty that someone was near at hand, that a pair of eyes were regarding him through the obscurity of the night. So strong was the emotion, and so strongly did it recall the emotion of a few nights ago when he had felt the influence of a strange woman's eyes, that he leaped to his feet. On the instant he half expected to see Zoraida Castelmar standing at his elbow.

What he saw, or thought that he saw, was a vague figure standing against the rail across the deck from him, beyond the corner of the cabin wall. A luminous pair of eyes, glowing through the dark. Kendric was across the deck in a flash. No one was there. He raced sternward, whisked around the pile of freight cluttered about the mast, tripped over a coil of rope and ran forward again. When he still found no one, so strong was the impression made on him that someone had been standing looking at him, he made a stubborn search from prow to stern. Barlow was in bed and looked to be asleep; the Philippine was muttering over the wheel and when Kendric demanded to know if he had seen anything said, "Aw," negatively; Nigger Ben had given over singing and was feeding the canary and freshening its water supply.

Afterwards Kendric realized that all the time while he was racing madly up and down, peering into cabin and galley and nook and corner, there had been a clear image standing uppermost in his mind; the picture of Zoraida Castelmar as she had stood and looked at him when she had said, "I have put a charm and a spell over your life." Now he simply knew that he had the mad thought that she was somewhere on board and that, hide as she would, he would find her. But when he gave up and went sullenly back to his toppled chair, he knew that all he had succeeded in was in making both Nigger Ben and Philippine Charlie marvel. Nigger Ben, he thought sullenly, had come close enough to understanding something of what was in his mind. For the giant African rolled his eyes whitely and said:

"Ha'nts, Cap'n Jim? You been seein' ha'nts, too?"

"What makes you say that, Ben?" demanded Kendric. "Did you see anything?"

Nigger Ben looked fairly inflated with mysterious wisdom. But, thought Kendric, what negro who ever lived would have denied having seen something ghostly? Kendric had searched thoroughly high and low; he had turned over big crates below deck, he had peered up the masts. Now, before settling himself back in his chair, he looked in on Barlow again. Twisty was turning over; his eyes were open.

"I don't want any funny business," said Kendric sternly. "Did you smuggle Zoraida Castelmar on board?"

Barlow blinked at him.

"Who the blazes is Zoraida Castelmar?" he countered. "The cat or the canary?"

Kendric grunted and went out, plumping himself down in his chair. He supposed that he had imagined the whole thing. He had not seen anything definitely; he had merely felt that eyes were watching him; what had seemed a figure across deck might have been the oil coat hanging on a peg or a curtain blowing out of a window. The more he thought over the matter the more assured was he that he had allowed his imaginings to make a fool of him. And by the time the sun flooded the decks next morning he was ready to forget the episode.

They rounded San Lucas one morning, turned north into the gulf and steered into La Paz where Barlow said he hoped to get a line on Escobar and where they allowed custom officials an opportunity to assure themselves that no contraband in the way of much dreaded rifles and ammunition were being carried into restive Sonora. "Loco Gringoes out after burro deer," was how the officials were led to judge them. Barlow, gone several hours, reported that Escobar had not turned up at the waterfront dives to which, according to the murdered

Juarez, he reported now and then to keep in touch with his outlaw commander. Steering out again through the fishing craft and harbor boats, they pounded the *New Moon* on toward Port Adventure.

Then came at last the night when Barlow, looking hard mouthed and eager, announced that in a few hours they would drop anchor and go ashore to see what they would see. Nigger Ben and Philippine Charlie were instructed gravely. They were to remain on board and were to maintain a suspicious reserve toward all strangers, denying them foothold on deck.

"The gents who'd be apt to make you a call," Barlow told them impressively, "would cut your throats for a side of bacon. You boys keep watches day and night. When we get back into San Diego Bay, if you do your duties, you both get fifty dollars on top of your wages."

It was shortly before they hoisted the anchor overboard to wait for dawn that for the second time Kendric felt again that oddly disturbing sense of hidden eyes spying at him. Again he was alone, standing forward, peering into the darkness, trying to make some sort of detail out of the black wall ahead which Barlow had told him was a long line of cliff. As before Charlie was at the wheel while Nigger Ben was listening to instructions from Barlow aft of the cabin. The voices came faint against the gulf wind to Kendric. The words he did not hear since all of his mental force was bent to determine what it was that gave him that uncanny feeling of eyes, the eyes of Zoraida Castelmar, in the dark.

This time he was guarded in his actions. He stood still a moment, his jaw set, only his eyes turning to right and left. As he had asked himself countless times already so now did he put the question again: "How could a man feel a thing like that?" At his age was he developing nerves and insane fancies? At any rate the sensation was strong, compelling. Making no sound, he turned and stared into the darkness on all sides. He saw no one.

Suddenly, startling him so that his taut muscles jumped involuntarily, came an excited shout from Nigger Ben.

"Ha'nts, Cap'n Barlow! Oh, my Gawd, save me now! Looky dar! Looky dar! It's a lady g-g-ghost! Oh, my Gawd, save me now!"

Kendric ran back. Nigger Ben was clutching wildly at Barlow's arm.

"You superstitious old fool," growled Barlow. "It's only that piece of torn sail flappin' that Charlie was goin' to sew. Can't you see? I thought you weren't afraid of the *New Moon's* ha'nts, any way."

Nigger Ben shifted his big feet uneasily and little by little crept forward to look at the flapping bit of sail cloth. Slowly his courage returned to him. He hadn't been afraid at all, he declared, but just sort of shook up, seeing the thing all of a sudden that way. Kendric passed on as though nothing had happened, as he reasoned perhaps nothing had. But just the same he made his second quiet search, in the end finding nothing. But as he went back to his place up deck he turned the matter over and over in mind stubbornly. Coincidences were all right enough, but reasonable explanations lay back of them. If a man could only see just where the explanation lay.

He sought to reason logically; if in truth someone had been standing looking at him, if Nigger Ben had seen something other than the flapping canvas, then that someone or something had gone aboard the *New Moon* at San Diego and had made the entire cruise with them. That could hardly have been done without Barlow's knowledge. Two points struck him then. First, Barlow had demanded who Zoraida Castelmar was; had not Barlow even learned the name of the girl of the pearls? Second, it recurred to him that Barlow had followed her to the hotel in the border town, had even had word with her, since he had brought Kendric a message. Why had Barlow gone to the hotel at all? His explanation at the time had been reasonable enough; he had said that he had gone to get a room. But now Kendric remembered how Barlow, on that same night, had expressed his determination to be riding by moonrise! What would he have done with a hotel room?

But slowly the dawn was coming, the ragged shore was revealing itself, Barlow was calling for help with the small boat. Kendric shrugged his shoulders and kept his mouth shut.

CHAPTER IV

INDICATING THAT THAT WHICH APPEARS THE
EARTHLY PARADISE MAY PROVE QUITE ANOTHER
SORT OF PLACE

A strip of white beach three hundred feet long, a score of paces across at its widest, with black barren cliffs guarding it and the faint pink dawn slowly growing a deeper rose over it, such was the port of adventure into which nosed the row boat bringing Jim Kendric and Twisty Barlow treasure seeking. In the stern crouched Nigger Ben, come ashore in order to row the boat back to the *New Moon*, his eyes bulging with wonderment that men should come all the way from San Diego to disembark upon so solitary a spot. The dingey shoved its nose into the sand, Kendric and Barlow carrying their small packs and rifles sprang out, Nigger Ben shook his head and pushed off again.

"Up the cliffs the easiest way," cried Barlow, his eyes shining with excitement. "Up there I'll get my bearin's and we'll steer a straight-string line for what's ahead, Headlong, old mate! Step lively is the word now while it's cool. And by noon, if we're in luck—"

He left the rest to any man's imagination and hastened across the sand and to the rock wall. But more forbidding than ever rose the cliffs against the path of men who did not know their every crevice, and it was full day and the sun was up before they came panting to the top. Down went packs, with two heaving-chested, bright-eyed men atop of them, while Barlow, compass in hand, got his bearings.

The devil's own he had named this country from afar; the devil's own it extended itself, naked and dry and desolate before their questing eyes, a weary land, sun-smitten, broken, looking deserted of God and man. As far as they could see there were no trees, little growth of any kind, no birds, no grazing beasts. Just swell after swell of arid lands, here and there cut by ancient gorges, tumbled over by heaps of black rocks, swept clean of dust on the high places by racing winds, piled high with sand and small stones in the depressions. Where growing things thrust up their heads, they were the harsh, fanged and envenomed growth of desert places. The place had an air of unholiness in the light of the new day. A thorn, as Barlow turned carelessly, tore the skin on the back of his hand painfully. The parent stem had an evil look and he cursed it as though it had been a conscious malign agent, and struck at it with his clubbed rifle. From the place where the branch was wrenched away exuded a slow red sticky ooze like coagulating blood.

"There's our course," announced Barlow, pointing, "with half a dozen hours of damned unpleasant walking, according to poor old Juarez. See those three peaks, standing up together? We bear a little off to the south for a spell and then straight toward 'em. And never a spring until we get there! Look out you don't poke a hole in your canteen."

"Ready," said Jim. "Let's go."

They went on. Now that a new phase had come into their quest, with the days of distant speculation giving place to action on the ground, a certain difference of character was manifest in the two men. A growing taciturnity, accompanied by deep frowning thoughtfulness, locked Barlow's lips, while Kendric, to whom any such experience was always primarily a lark, expanded and mounted steadily to fresh stages of light-heartedness. It mattered less to him than to his companion what might lie at the end of their journey; the journey itself was with Jim Kendric the golden thing. He felt alive, jubilant, keenly in sympathy with the lure and zest of the expedition. He felt like singing, would no doubt have sung out in some wild border ballad or bit of deep sea melody with a piratical swing to it, had he not been half the time fairly breathless from the pace they maintained over the broken country.

In a couple of hours they left behind them the worst of the gorges and canons, flinty peaks and ridges, and dropped down into a long crooked valley floored with dry sand ankle deep and grown over with a gray shrub plainly akin to California sage brush. Here was some scant evidence of animal life, a dusty jack rabbit, a circling buzzard, a thin spotted snake, a wild pony with up-flung head staring at them from the further ridge, gone whisking away as they drew on. And they came to trees whose shade was grateful, oaks and, later, a few dusty straggling pinons. Wisps of dry grass, an occasional patch of flowering weeds or taller plants, a flock of bewildered-looking birds that had the appearance of having strayed hitherward by mistake. No water, no sign of water; no man-owned herds, no sign of man. The open valley under the high, hot sun was a drearier place than the mountain slopes.

Then came the up-hill climb as they passed out of the western edge of the sandy flats, a steep spur of the Cordillera, a region silent and saturnine and unthinkably hot. Three times, though they guarded against profligacy with their water, they unstoppered their canteens and rested in the shade on the way up. At last they came to the crest of the barrier of the blistering hills, having been on foot for a full five hours. And now, for the first time, looking forward, down the steep slopes and across the miles, they saw the Valley of Las Flores, the place of flowers. At first it was hard for them to believe that their eyes, which the desert lands befool so often and so readily, had not tricked them. It was as though in a twinkling the world had changed about them.

The long wide valley below was one sweep of green: fresh, colorful, cool green. Across it wandered many cows and horses and donkeys, browsing where the herbiage was lushest, dozing in the shade of the wide-spread oaks, standing indolent in the golden sunshine. A bright stream of water cut the emerald sward in two, coming from the bordering mountains at one end, gone flashing into the mountain-guarded pass at the other. From a distance Kendric heard a bird singing away like mad and saw the sweep and flutter of a butterfly's wing.

"The earthly paradise!" he cried admiringly.

But already Barlow's fixed eyes were upon the mountainous country across the valley.

"Come on," he said, slipping his pack-straps over his shoulders and swinging up his rifle. "It would be three to five miles, easy going, and we're there! There are our three peaks, straight across."

Only when they were fairly down on the floor of the valley did they see the ranch houses. There were several, a big, rambling adobe with white-washed walls, barns and smaller outbuildings, all making a sizeable group. They stood in an oak grove at the opposite side of the valley, close to the common bases of Barlow's peaks. The two men stopped and looked, reflecting.

"Neighbors," said Kendric. "They'll be wanting to know what we're about, pottering around on the rim of their holding."

"It's anybody's land over there," growled Barlow. "They'd best keep out of it."

They pushed on across the fields, noting casually how they were all leveled and ditched for irrigation, and came at last to the creek where they rested under an oak and drank deeply and smoked. As they rose to go on they saw four horsemen bearing down upon them from the direction of the ranch houses.

"*Vacqueros*," said Barlow. "They'll be wantin' to know if we're lost."

"They look more like brigands than cow men," grunted Kendric. "Every man jack of them wears a rifle. And they're in a rush, Twisty, old mate. What will you bet they don't herd us back where we came from?"

"Let 'em try it on," Barlow shot back at him, his eyes narrowing on the oncoming riders. "I'm goin' to roll up in my blanket under those three peaks tonight if the whole Mexican army shows up."

The two Americans stopped and stood ready to ease their shoulders out of their packs and start pumping lead if the newcomers turned out to be half the desperadoes they appeared. "The way to argue with these sort of gents," said Barlow contemptuously, "is shoot their eyes out first and talk next." But as the foremost of the little cavalcade drew up in front of them, with his three followers curbing their horses a few paces in his rear, the fellow's greeting was amazingly hospitable.

"*Buenas dias, amigos,*" he called to them. But, though he hailed them in the name of friendship, his eyes were sullen and gave the lie to his speech. "You would be fatigued with walking across the cursed desert; you would be parched with thirst. Yonder," and he pointed toward the distant white walls, "is coolness and pleasant welcome awaiting you."

His followers were out-and-out ragamuffins, wild-looking fellows with their unshaven cheeks and tangled hair and fierce eyes. Their spokesman stood apart in appearance as well as in position, being somewhat extravagantly dressed, showing much ornamentation both on his own person and that of his mount in the way of silver buckles and spangles. He was the youngest of the crowd, not over twenty-two or three from the look of him, with a nicely groomed black mustache. The horse under him was a superb creature, a great savage fiery-eyed sorrel stallion.

"Thanks," returned Barlow. "But my friend and I are on our

way over there." He pointed. "We are students of entymology and are studyin' certain new butterflies." All along, until the very moment, he had fully intended explaining by saying they were on a hunting trip. But as he spoke it struck him that the slopes about his three peaks would not harbor a jack rabbit, and furthermore on the instant a big golden butterfly went flapping by him, putting the idea into his head.

The young Mexican nodded but insisted.

"There will be time for butterfly catching tomorrow," he said carelessly. "Today you will honor us by riding back to the Hacienda Montezuma. You are expected, senores; everything is prepared for you. *Oyez*, Pedro, Juanito," turning in his saddle and addressing two of his men. "Rope two horses and let *los Americanos* have yours." And when both Pedro and Juanito frowned and hesitated, his eyes flashed and he cried out angrily at them: "*Pronto*! It is commanded!"

They rode away toward a herd of horses half a mile down the valley, their riatas soon in their hands and widening and swinging into great loops. Presently they were back, leading two captured ponies. Dismounting, they made impromptu hackamores of their ropes and mounted bareback, leaving their own saddles empty for Kendric and Barlow.

"Look here, *amigo*," said Kendric then. "We're much obliged for the kind invitation. But you've got the wrong guests. If your outfit was expecting newcomers it was someone else."

The Mexican lifted his fine black brows.

"Then are you not Senores Kendric and Barlow?" he asked impudently.

They stared wonderingly at him, then at each other.

"You're some little guesser, stranger," grunted Barlow. "Who told you all you know?"

"Go easy, Twisty," laughed Kendric, his interest caught. Affably, to the Mexican, he said: "You're right, senor. And, to complete the introductions, would you mind telling us who you are?"

"I?" He touched up his mustache and again his eyes flashed; involuntarily, as he spoke his name, he laid his hand on the grip of the revolver bumping at his hip, giving the perfectly correct impression that the man who wore that name must ever stand ready to defend himself: "I am Fernando Escobar, at your service for what you please, senor!"

Never a muscle of either Kendric's face or Barlow's twitched at the information though inwardly each man started. Before now, many times in the flood of their tumultous lives, they had lived through moments when the thing to do was control all outward expression of emotion and think fast.

"I'd say, Twisty," said Kendric lightly, "that it is downright kind of Senor Escobar to extend so hearty an invitation. It would be the pleasant thing to rest up in the shade during the afternoon. Tomorrow, perhaps, it could be arranged that he would let us have a couple of horses to make our little trip into the hills butterfly-catching?"

But Barlow, fingering his forelock, looked anything but pleased. His eyes went swiftly to the three peaks across the valley, then frowning up the valley to the ranch houses. Obviously, he meant to go straight about his business, all the more eager to come to grips with the naked situation since Escobar was on the ground and had made himself known. He opened his lips to speak. On the instant Kendric saw a swift, subtle change in his eyes, a look of surprise and of uncertainty. And then, abruptly, Barlow said:

"Oh, all right. I'm tired hoofin' it, anyway," and swung up into the saddle on the nearest horse, pack and all.

Escobar wheeled his horse, as though glad to have his errand done, and rode back toward the upper end of the valley, his ragged following close at his heels, Kendric and Barlow bringing up the rear.

"What was it, Twisty?" demanded Kendric softly. "What did you see? What made you change your mind all of a sudden."

"Look at the cordillera just back of the ranch house, Jim," answered Barlow, guardedly.

Kendric looked and in a moment understood Barlow's perplexity. There again were three upstanding peaks, much in general outline and height like those across the valley. For the life of him Barlow did not know which was the group toward which he had been directed by Juarez to steer his course. Doubtless Escobar did know. And if Escobar were going up valley, it would be just as well to go with him.

As they drew near the big adobe house both men were interested. The building had once upon a time, perhaps two or three hundreds of years ago, been a Spanish mission; so much was told eloquently by the lines of high adobe walls ringing the buildings and by the architecture of the main building itself. There were columns, arches, corridors after the old mission style. But it had all been made over, added to, so that it was now a residence of a score or more of rooms. It spread out covering the entire top of a knoll whereon were many large oaks. At the back, rising sharply, was the barren slope of the mountain.

Their gaze was drawn suddenly from the house itself to a rider darting out through the high arched gateway in the adobe wall. A beautiful horse, snowy, glistening white, groomed to the last hair, an animal of fine thin racing forelegs proudly lifted and high-flung head, shot out of the shadows like a shaft of sunlight. On its back what at first appeared an elegantly dressed young man, a youth even fastidiously and fancifully accoutered, with riding boots that shone and a flaunting white plume and red lined cape floating wildly. Only when the approaching rider came close and threw up a gauntleted hand to the wide black hat, saluting laughingly, did they recognize this for the same youth who had come with Ruiz Rios to Ortega's gambling house.

"Zoraida Castelmar!" gasped Kendric.

Turning in his amazement to his companion he caught a strange look in Barlow's eyes, a strange flush in Barlow's cheeks. Then he saw only the girl's dark, passionate face and scarlet lips and burning eyes as she called softly:

"Welcome to the Hacienda Montezuma! The gods have willed that you come. The gods and I!"

And into Kendric's bewildered face, ignoring Barlow, she laughed triumphantly.

CHAPTER V

HOW ONE NOT ACCUSTOMED TO TAKING ANOTHER MAN'S ORDERS RECEIVES THE COMMAND OF THE QUEEN LADY

Had horse and rider been only a painting, immovable upon hung canvas, they would have drawn to themselves the enrapt eyes of mute, admiring artists. Endowed with the glorious attribute of pulsating life, they fascinated. Kendric saw the white mare's neck arch, marked how the satiny skin rippled, how the dainty ears tipped forward, how the large intelligent eyes bespoke the proud spirit. He could fancy the mare prancing forth from the stables of an Eastern prince, the finest pure bred Arabian of his stud, the royal favorite, the white queen-rose of his costly gardens. From the mare he looked to the rider, not so much as a man may regard a woman but as he must pay tribute to animal perfection. He told himself that as a woman Zoraida Castelmar displeased him; that there was no place in his fancies for the bold eyes of an adventuress. But he deemed a man might look upon her as impersonally as upon the white mare, giving credit where credit was due. It struck him then that all that was wrong with Zoraida Castelmar was that she was an anachronism; that had he lived a thousand years ago and had she then, a barbaric queen, stepped before him, he would have seen the superb beauty of her and would have gone no further. Before now he had felt that she was "foreign." That was on the border. Here, deep in Old Mexico, she still remained foreign. Rightly she belonged to another age, if not to another star.

Jackson Gregory

For the moment she sat smiling at him, her eyes dancing and yet masking her ultimate thought. Triumph he had glimpsed and, as always, a shadowy hint of mockery. Suddenly she turned from him and put out her gauntleted hand to Barlow, flashing him another sort of smile, one that made Barlow's eyes brighten and brought a hotter flush to his tanned cheeks.

"You have kept your promise with me," she said softly. "I shall not forget and you will not regret!" Even while she spoke her eyes drifted back to Kendric, laughing at him, taunting him.

He looked sharply at Barlow. But he said nothing and Barlow, intent upon the girl, did not note his turned head.

Zoraida turned imperiously upon Fernando Escobar. "These men are my guests," she said sharply, her tone filled with defiant warning. "Remember that, *Senor el Capitan*. You will escort them to the house where my cousin will receive them. Until we meet at table, senores all."

From her neck hung a tiny whistle from a thin gold chain; she lifted it to her lips, blew a long clear note and with a last sidelong look at Kendric touched her dainty spurs to her mare's sides and shot away.

"You will follow me," said Escobar stiffly. "This way, *caballeros.*"

He pressed by them, dismissing his following with a glance, and rode through the wide arched gateway. Barlow turned in after him but hesitated when Kendric called coolly:

"I have small hankering to accept the lady's hospitality, Barlow. Why should we establish ourselves here instead of going on about our business? By the lord, her invitation smacks to me too damned much of outright command!"

"No use startin' anything, Jim," said Barlow. "Come ahead."

At them both Escobar smiled contemptuously.

"Look," he said, pointing toward the adobe. "Judge if it be wise to hesitate when *la senorita reina* says enter."

They saw graveled driveways and flower bordered walks under the oaks; blossoming, fragrant shrubs welcoming countless birds; an expanse of velvet lawn with a marble-rimmed pool and fountain. A beautiful garden, empty one instant, then slowly filling as from about a far corner of the house came a line of men. Young men, every one of them, fine-looking, dark-skinned fellows dressed after the extravagant fashion of the land which mothered them, with tall conical hats and slashed trousers, broad sashes and glistening boots. They came on like military squads, silent, erect, eyes full ahead. Out in the driveway they halted, fifty of them. And like one man, they saluted.

"Will you enter as a guest?" jeered Escobar.

Kendric's anger flared up.

"I'll tell you one thing, my fine friend Fernando Escobar," he said hotly, "I don't like the cut of your sunny disposition. You and I are not going to mix well, and you may as well know it from the start. As for this 'guest' business, just what do you mean?"

Escobar shrugged elaborately and half veiled his insolent eyes with the long lashes.

"You mean," went on Kendric stubbornly, "your 'Queen Lady' as you call her, has instructed her rabble to bring us in, willy-nilly?"

"Ai!" cried Escobar in mock surprise. "*El Americano* reads the secret thought!"

"Come ahead, Jim," urged Barlow anxiously. "Don't I tell you there is no sense startin' a rumpus? Suppose you weeded out half of 'em, the other half would get you right. And haven't we got enough ahead of us without goin' out of our way, lookin' for a row?"

For answer Kendric gave his horse the spur and dashed through the gate. If a man had to tie into fifty of a hard-looking lot of devils like those saturnine henchmen of Zoraida, it would at least be a scrimmage worth a man's going down in; but Barlow was right and there was no doubt enough trouble coming without wandering afield for it.

So, close behind Escobar, they rode under the oaks and to the house. Here was a quadrangle, flanked about with white columns; through numerous arches one saw oaken doors set into the thick walls of the shaded building. The three men dismounted; three of the men in the driveway took the horses. Escobar stepped to the broad double door directly in front of them. As his spurred boot rang on the stone floor the door opened and Ruiz Rios opened to them. He bowed deeply, courteously, his manner cordial, his eyes inscrutable.

At his invitation they entered. He led them through a great, low-ceiled room where dim light hovered over luxurious appointments, across Oriental rugs and hardwood floors to a wide hallway. Down this for a long way, past a dozen doors at each hand and finally into a suite looking out into the gardens from a corner of the building. As they went in, two Mexican girls, young and pretty, with quick black eyes and in white caps and aprons, came out. The girls dropped their eyes, curtsied and passed on, as silent as little ghosts.

"Your rooms, senores," said Rios, standing aside for them. "When you are ready you will ring and a servant will show you to the *patio*, where I will be waiting for you. If there is anything forgotten, you have but to ring and ask."

He left them and hurried away, obviously glad to be done with them. They went in and closed the door and looked about them. Here were big leather chairs, a mahogany table, cigars, smoking trays, cigarets, a bottle of brandy and one of fine red wine standing forth hospitably. Through one door they saw an artistically and comfortably furnished bedroom; through another a tiled, glisteningly white bath; beyond the bath the second bedroom.

All this they marked at a glance. Then Kendric turned soberly to his companion.

"I've known you a good many years off and on, Twisty," he said bluntly, "for the sort of man to name pardner and friend. For half a dozen years, however, I've seen little of you. What have those half-dozen years done to you?"

"What do you mean?" asked Barlow.

"I mean that for a mate on a crazy expedition like this I want a man I can tie to. That means a man that turns off every card from the top, straight as they come. A man that doesn't bury the ace. I haven't held out anything on you. What have you held out on me?"

Barlow looked troubled. He uncorked the brandy bottle and helped himself, sipping slowly.

"You've got in mind what she said outside?" he asked.

"Yes. That and other things."

"If I had told you at the beginnin'," said Barlow, "that you and me were comin' to a place, lookin' for treasure, that was right next door to where Zoraida Castelmar lived, would you of come?"

"No. I don't think I would."

"Well, that's why I didn't tell you."

"And you promised her—just what?"

"That I'd be showin' up down this way. And that you'd be comin' along with me." He finished off his brandy and set his glass down hard.

Kendric took a cigaret and wandered across the room, looking out into the gardens. The string of men who had appeared at Zoraida's whistle, were filing off around the house again, going toward the nearby outbuildings.

"I'm not going to pump questions at you, Barlow," he said without turning. "What you do is up to you. Only, if you can't play the game straight with me, our trails fork for good and all. Now, let's get a bath and see the dance through."

Five minutes later Jim Kendric, splashing mightily in a roomy tub, began to sing under his breath. After all, matters were well enough. Life was not dull but infinitely profligate of promise. He fancied that Ruiz Rios was boiling inwardly with rage; the thought delighted him. His old zest flooded back full tide into his veins. His voice rose higher, his lively tune quickened. Barlow's face brightened at the sound and his lungs filled to a sigh of relief.

Within half an hour a servant ushered them into the *patio*. There, under a grape arbor, their chairs drawn close up to the little fountain, were Rios and Escobar, talking quietly. Both men rose as they appeared, offering chairs. Both were all that was courteous and yet it needed no guessing to understand that their courtesy was but like so much thin silken sheathing over steel; they were affable only because of a command. And that command, Zoraida's.

"As far as they are concerned," mused Kendric, "she is absolutely the Queen Lady. Wonder how she works it? Wouldn't judge either one of them an easy gent to handle."

The conversation was markedly impersonal. They spoke of

stock raising, of the best breeds of beef cattle, of what had been done with irrigation and of what Rios planned for another year. It became clear that Zoraida was the sole owner of several thousand fair acres here and that Ruiz Rios stood in the position of general manager to his cousin. That he envied her her possessions, that it galled him to be her underling over these acres, was a fact which lay naked on top of many mere surmises. Once, with simulated carelessness, Escobar said:

"The rancho would have been yours, had there been no will, is it not so, amigo Rios?" And Ruiz flashed an angry look at him, knowing that the man taunted him.

"It is called the Rancho Montezuma, isn't it?" put in Kendric. "Why that name, Rios?"

"It is the old name," said Rios lightly. "That is all I know."

When a servant announced dinner they went to an immense dining-room wherein a prince might have taken his state meals. But Zoraida did not join them, sending word by one of the little Mexican maids that she would not appear. It was significant that no reason was offered; from the instant that they had set foot down at the hacienda it was to be known that here Zoraida did as she pleased and accounted to none. Two tall fellows, looking pure-bred Yaqui Indians, served perfectly, soft voiced, softer footed, stony eyed. During the meal Kendric fell into the way of chatting with young Escobar, seeking to draw him out and failing, while Barlow and Rios talked together, Rios regarding Barlow intently. When they rose from table Barlow accepted an invitation from Rios to look over the stables, while Kendric was led by Escobar back to the *patio*. Even then Kendric had the suspicion that the intention was to separate him from his friend, but he saw nothing to be done. He hardly looked for any sort of violence, and were such intended there was scant need to waste time over such trifles as separating two men who would have to stand against two score.

"If you will pardon me a moment, senor?" said Escobar briefly.

He left Kendric standing by the little fountain and disappeared. On the instant one of the little maids stole softly forward.

"This way, senor," she said, looking at him curiously.

"Where?" he demanded. "And why?"

She smiled and shook her head.

"It is commanded," she replied. "Will *el senor Americano* be so kind as to follow?"

He had asked why and got no answer. Now he demanded of himself, "Why not?" He was playing the other fellow's game and might as well play straight on until he saw what was what.

"Lead on," he said. "I'm with you."

CHAPTER VI

CONCERNING THAT WHICH LAY IN
THE EYES OF ZORAIDA

Jim Kendric guessed, before the last door was thrown open for him, that he was being led before Zoraida Castelmar. The serving maid flitted on ahead, out through a deep, shadow-filled doorway into the dusk, down a long corridor and into the house again at an end which Kendric judged must be close to the flank of the mountain. Down a second hallway, to a heavy, nail-studded door which opened only when the little maid had knocked and called. This room was lighted by a swinging lamp and its rays showed its scanty but rich furnishings, and the one who had opened, a tall, evil-looking Yaqui who wore in his sash a long-barreled revolver on one side and a longer, curved knife at the other. The girl sidled about the doorkeeper and, safe behind his back made a grimace of distaste at him, then hurried on. Again she knocked at a locked door; again it was swung open only when she had added her voice to her rapping. Who opened this door Kendric did not know; for it was pitch dark as soon as the door was shut after them and they stood in a room either windowless or darkened by thick curtains. But the girl hastened on before him and he followed the patter of her soft moccasins, albeit with a hand under his left arm pit; all of this locking and unlocking of doors and the attendant mystery struck him as clap-trap and he set it down as further play for effect by the mistress of the place, but none the less he was ready to strike back if a wary arm struck at him through the dark.

The girl had stopped before another door, Kendric close behind her. This time she neither knocked nor called. He heard her fingers groping along the wall; then the silvery tinkle of a bell faintly heard through the thick oak panels.

"You will wait," she whispered. And he knew that she was gone.

He was not forced to wait long. Suddenly the door was opened; he heard it move on its hinges and made out a pale rectangle of light. A softly modulated voice said: "*Entra, senor.*" He stepped across the threshhold and into the presence of another serving girl, taller than the other two maidens, finer bred, a calm-eyed, serene girl of twenty dressed in a plain white gown girdled with a smooth gold band.

They were in a little anteroom; the curtains between them and the main apartment had made the light dim, for just beyond he could make out the blurred glowing of many lamps.

The girl's great calm eyes looked at him frankly an instant, vague shadows drifting across them. Then, abruptly, she put her lips quite close to his ear, and whispered: "Do not anger her, senor!" Then, stepping quickly to the curtain, she threw it back and he entered.

A vain, headstrong girl, deemed Kendric, given the opportunity and very great wealth, might be looked to for absurdities of this kind. But was all of this nothing more, nothing worse, than absurdity? Suppose Zoraida were sincere in all that she had said to him, in all the things she did? He had heard a rumor concerning Ruiz Rios, long ago, half forgotten. Certain wild deeds laid to the Mexican's door had brought forth the insinuation that he was a little mad. Zoraida had claimed kinship with him.

At any rate, to Kendric's matter-of-fact way of thinking, here was further clap-trap that might well have been the result of a mad mind working extravagantly. The room was empty. All four walls, from ceiling to floor, were draped in gorgeously rich hangings, oriental silks, he imagined, deep purples and yellows and greens and reds cunningly arranged so that their glowing colors and the ornamental designs worked upon them made no discordant clash of color. The chamber in which he had met Zoraida at the hotel was mild hued, colorless compared to this one. There were no chairs but a couch against each wall, each a bright spot with its high heaped cushions. In the middle of the room was a small square ebony stand; upon it, glowing like red fire upon its frail crystal stem, the familiar stone.

He had stepped a couple of paces into the room, his boots sinking without sound into the deep carpet. In no mood for a girl's whims, mad or sane, he waited, impatient and irritated. He regretted having come; he should have sat tight in the *patio* and let her come to him. No doubt she was spying on him now from behind the hangings somewhere. There was no comfort in the thought, no joy in imagining that while he stood forth in the clear light of the hanging lamps she and her maidens and attendants might all be watching him. He vastly preferred solid walls and thick doors to silken drapes.

While he waited, two distinct impressions slowly forced themselves upon him. One was that of a faint perfume, coming from whence he had no way of knowing, the unforgettable, almost sickeningly sweet fragrance he remembered. One instant he was hardly conscious of it, it was but a suspicion of a fragrance. And then it filled the room, strongly sweet, strangely pleasant, a near opiate in its soothing effect.

The other impression was no true sensation in that it was registered by none of the five senses; a true sensation only if in truth there is in man a subtle sixth sense, uncatalogued but vital. It was the old uncanny certainty that at last eyes, the eyes of none other than Zoraida Castelmar, were bent searchingly on him. So strong was the feeling on him that he turned about and fixed his own eyes on a particular corner where the silken folds hung graceful and loose. He felt that she was there, exactly at that spot.

Jackson Gregory

He strode across the room and laid a sudden hand on the fabric. It parted readily and just behind it, her eyes more brilliant, more triumphant than he had ever seen them, stood Zoraida.

"Can you say now, Senor Americano," she cried out, the music of her voice rising and vibrating, "that I have not set the spell of my spirit upon your spirit, the influence of my mind upon your mind? You stood here and the chamber was empty about you. I came, but so that you might not hear with your ears and might not see with your eyes. And yet, looking at you through a pin hole in a drawn curtain, I made you conscious of me and called voicelessly to you to come and you came!"

There was laughter in her oblique eyes and upon her scarlet lips, and Kendric knew that it was not merely light mirth but the deeper laughter of a conqueror, a high rejoicing, the winged joy of victory.

"I am no student of mental forces," said Kendric. "But to my knowledge there is nothing unusual in one's feeling the presence of another. As for any power which your mind can exert over mine, I don't admit it. It's absurd."

Contempt hardened the line of her mouth and the laughter died in her eyes.

"Man is an animal of little wisdom," she murmured as she passed by him into the room, "because he has not learned to believe the simple truth."

"If there is anything either simple or true in your establish- ment," he blurted out, "I haven't found it."

She went to the table before she turned. A flowing garment of deep blue fell about her; on her black hair like a coronet was a crest of many colored, tiny feathers, feathers of humming birds, he learned later; throat and arms were bare save for many blazing red and green stones, feet bare save for exquisitely wrought sandals which were held in place by little golden straps which ended in plain gold bands about the round white ankles.

Slowly she turned and faced him. But not yet did she speak. She clapped her hands together and the curtains at her right bellied out, parted and a man stepped before her, bending deeply in genuflection. No Yaqui, this time; no Mexican as Kendric knew Mexicans. The man was short, but a few inches over five feet, and remarkably heavy-muscled, the greater part of the body showing since his simple cotton tunic was wide open across the deep chest, and left arms and legs bare. The forehead was atavistically low, the cheek bones very prominent, the nose wide and flat, the lips loose and thick. The man looked brutish, cruel and ugly as he stood face to face with the noble beauty of Zoraida. And yet Kendric, glancing swiftly from one to the other, saw a peculiar resemblance. It was the eyes. This squat animal's eyes were like Zoraida's in shape though they lacked the fire of spirit and intellect; long eyes that sloped outward and upward toward the temples.

Zoraida spoke briefly, imperiously. Kendric did not understand the words though he readily recognized the tongue for one of the native Nahua dialects. Old Aztec it might have been, or Toltec.

The man saluted, bowed and was gone. But in a moment he returned, another man with him who might have been his twin brother, so strongly pronounced in each were the racial physiognomic characteristics. Between them they bore a heavy chair of black polished wood the feet of which were eagles' talons gripping and resting on crystal balls. They placed it and stood waiting for orders or dismissal. She gave both, the first in a few low words in the same ancient tongue, the latter with a gesture. They bowed and disappeared. Zoraida, one hand resting upon the stand near the jewel glowing upon the transparent stem, sank gracefully into the seat.

"All very imposing," muttered Kendric. "But if you have

anything to say to me I am waiting."

From somewhere in the room a parrot which he had not seen until now and which had no doubt been released by one of her low-browed henchmen behind the curtains, flew by Kendric's head and perched balancing upon an arm of her chair. Idly she put out her hand, stroking the bright feathers. From somewhere else, startling the man when he saw it gliding by him on its soft pads, a big puma, ran forward, threw up its head, snarling, its tail jerking back and forth restlessly. Zoraida spoke quietly; the monster cat crept close to her chair and lay down before her, stretched out to five feet of graceful length. Zoraida set one foot lightly upon the tawny back. The big cat lay motionless, its eyes steady and unwinking upon Kendric.

He felt himself strangely impressed though he sought to argue with himself that here was but more absurdity from an empty-headed girl who had the money and the power to unleash her extravagant desires. But since everything about him was stamped with the barbaric, even to the oblique-eyed woman staring boldly at him; since everything in the exotic atmosphere was in keeping, even to the parrot at her elbow and the heavy, honey-sweet perfume filling the room, he was unable to shake off, as he wished to, the impression made upon him.

"In your heart," said Zoraida gravely, "you censure me for empty by-play, you accuse me of vain trifling. You are wrong, Senor Americano! And soon you will know you are wrong. There is no woman throughout the wide sweep of my country or yours who has the work to do that I have to do; the destiny to fulfil; or the power to wrest from the gods that which she would have. And will have!"

Steadfast conviction, fearlessly voiced, rang through her speech. What she said she meant with all of the fiery ardor of her being. Her words spoke her thought. Whatever the fate which she judged was hers to fulfil, she accepted it with a fervor not unlike some ecstatic religious devotion. Of all this he was confident on the instant; she might surround herself with colorful accessories but her purpose was none the less serious.

"Symbols, if you like," she said carelessly—she had been staring at him profoundly and well might have glimpsed something of his train of thought—"as are statues and pictures symbols in the Roman church. My bright colored bird is older now than you will be, or I, when we die. Age, bright feathers and chatter! My puma means much to me that you would not understand, being of another race. Further, did you or another lift a hand against his mistress he would tear out your throat."

"You have had me brought here for some purpose?" said Kendric.

She sat forward, straight in her chair, her two hands gripping the carved arms.

"Did I not tell you when first we spoke together that I had use for you? Since then have I not sent myself into your thoughts many times? Did I not come to you, that you should remember, on the boat that brought you here?"

"I am no man for mysteries," he said. "Tell me: Did you somehow get aboard the *New Moon* at San Diego? Or did my fancy play me a trick?"

"You ask me questions!" she mocked. "When you would believe what pleased you, no matter what word I spoke! If I said that across the miles, over mountain and desert and water I sent my spirit to you—would you believe?"

"No. Not when there are other readier explanations."

She raised a quick hand and pointed to the parrot.

"Chatter! Questions put when you do not expect an answer. A hundred years of words and only a red and yellow bundle of feathers at the end. It is deeds we want, Senor Americano, you and I!"

He returned her look steadily.

"Then tell me what you want of me," he said. "And in one word I'll give you yes or no."

"That is man talk!" she cried. "And yet, Senor Jim Kendric, there come times even in a man's life when the yes or no is spoken for him." She paused for him to drink in all that her statement meant. Then, when he remained silent, his eyes hostile upon hers, she went on, her speech quick and passionate. "There are great happenings on foot, American. There will be war and death; there will be tearing down and building up. And it is I who will direct and it is you who will take my orders and make them law. And in the end I shall be a Zoraida whom the world shall know and you shall be a mighty man, *the* man of Mexico."

"Fine words!" It was his time to mock, his time to glance at the ancient bird.

"Yes, Jim Kendric. Fine words and more since they are great truths. Lest you think Zoraida Castelmar a girl of mad fancies, I will speak freely with you. Since all depends on me and it is in my mind that much will depend on you. And why on you? Why have I put my hand out upon you, a foreigner? Because you are such a man as I would make were I God; a man strong and fearless and masterful; a man trustworthy to the death when his word is given and his honor is at stake. No, I do not judge you alone by what happened at Ortega's gambling house. But that fitted in with all I knew of you. Where else can I find a man to lose ten thousand, twenty thousand dollars, all that he has and think no more of the matter than of a cigaret paper that the wind has blown from his hands? I have heard of you, Jim Kendric, and I have said to myself: 'Is there such a man? I know none like him!' Then I went for myself, saw for myself, judged for myself. And now I offer you what I offer no other man and what no other mortal can offer you."

"You give me a pretty clean bill of health," he said quietly. "Now what follows?"

"This: There will be war in Mexico—"

"No new thing," he cut in. "There is always war in Mexico."

"And I will direct that war," she went on serenely, "from this chair in this room and from elsewhere. Lower California will raise its own standard and it will be my standard. Already has word stirred Sonora into restlessness and a beginning of activity; already is Chihuahua armed and eager. Already have the thousands of Yaquis listened and agreed; already have I made them large promises of ancient tribal lands restored and money. A Yaqui guards my door yonder. But you did not know that he was the son of Chief Pima, nor that in ten days the son will be Chief after having served in the household of Zoraida! And Sonora and Chihuahua and the Yaqui tribes are pledged to one thing: To an independent Lower California over which I shall rule."

"Wild schemes," muttered Kendric. "Foredoomed, like other mad schemes in Mexico. And if your great plannings are feasible, which I very much doubt, has your feathered companion failed to remind you that talk with a stranger is rash?"

"You are no stranger," she said coolly. "Nor have I spoken a word to you that is not known already to all about me. My cousin, Ruiz Rios, whom I distrust and detest; the Captain Escobar who is a small man and a murderer, the other men whom I have gathered about me, they all know, for in this, if in nothing else, I can trust them all."

"But if I went away," he asked, "and talked?"

"You are not going away."

He lifted his brows quickly at that.

"I go where I please," he reminded her. "When I please. I am my own man, Senorita Castelmar."

"Large words." She smiled at him curiously.

"You mean that my going would be interfered with?"

"I mean that you may make yourself free of the house; that you may walk in the gardens; that, if you sought to pass the outer wall, you would be detained. You remain my prisoner, Senor Kendric, until you become my trusted captain!"

"You're a devilish hospitable hostess," he remarked. She was watching him shrewdly, interested to see just how he would accept her ultimatum. He returned her look with clear, untroubled eyes.

"You will think of what I have told you," she said slowly. "My wealth is very great; the fertile lands which I have inherited and those which I have purchased, embrace hundreds of thousands of acres; the barren lands which are mine, desert and mountain, stretch mile after mile. There is no power like mine in all Mexico, though until now it has lain hidden, giving no sign. It is in my heart to make you a rich man and, what you like more, Jim Kendric, a man to play the biggest of all games and for the biggest of all stakes. And further—further—"

"Further?" He laughed. "What comes after all that, Queen Zoraida?"

"Look into my eyes," she said softly. "Look deep."

He looked and though to him were women unread books, at last a slow flush crept up into his cheeks. For now neither he nor any other man could have failed to understand the silent speech of Zoraida's eyes. It was as though she invited him not so much to look into her eyes as through them and on, deep into her heart; as though these were gates, open to him, through which he might glimpse paradise. Zoraida, her look clinging to his passionately, was seeking to offer the final argument. The case would have not been plainer had she whispered with her lips: "I, even I, Zoraida, love you! You shall be my master; I your willing slave. What you will, I will also. My beauty shall be yours; my wealth, my estate, my ambitions, my power, all those shall be my lord's. Of a kingdom which shall be built you shall be king. You shall go far, you shall climb high. All because I, Zoraida, love you!"

She stood there watching him, her eyes burning into his. In her own mind were pictures made, pictures of pride and power and, as a mirror reflects the scene before it, so for a little did Jim Kendric's mind hold an image of the thing in Zoraida's. He felt her influence upon him; he felt that odd stirring of the blood; he stared back into her eyes like a man bewildered as pictures rose and swept magnificently by. He saw the red of her parted lips and heard her soft breathing; for a certain length of time—long or short he had little conception—he was motionless and speechless under her spell.

He stirred restlessly. Those visions conjured up within him, either by Zoraida's previous words and what had gone before or by the subtle workings of her mind now, were not unbroken. He thought of Twisty Barlow. Barlow had gone to her at the border town hotel; from his own experiences with her Kendric thought that he could imagine how she stood before the sailor, how she talked with him and looked at him, how in the first small point she won over him. He thought of an ancient tale of Circe and the swine. Was he a free man, a man's man or was he a woman's plaything? . . . It flashed over him again that it might be that Zoraida was mad. Even now, that he seemed to be reading her inmost soul, was she but playing the siren to his imaginings? Was this some barbaric whim of hers or was she, for the once, sincere? While appearing to be all yielding softness, was she but playing a game? Would she, at one instant swaying toward a man's arms, the next whip back from him, laughing at him?

Confused thoughts winging through his chaos of uncertainty

held him where he was, his eyes staring at hers. Zoraida might read some of his mind but surely not all. What she realized was that she had offered much, everything, and that he stood, seemingly unmoved and frowned at her. Quick in all her emotions, now suddenly her cheeks flamed and the light in her eyes altered swiftly to blazing anger.

"Go!" she cried, pointing. She leaped to her feet, her eyes flaming. "By the long vanished Huitzil, I swear that I am of a mind to let those dogs, Rios and Escobar, have their way with you! What! am I Zoraida Castelmar, of a race of kings, daughter of the Montezumas, to have a man stand up before me weighing me in the balance of his two eyes? Go!"

He turned to go, eager to be out in the open air. But as he moved she called out to him:

"Wait! At least I will say my say. You and that fool Barlow came here, into my land, seeking gold. Escobar comes slinking in like a desert wolf on the same errand. Oh, I know something of it as I know something of all that goes forward from end to end of a land that will one day all be mine. Juarez died from Escobar's knife but his last gasp was for one of my agent's ears. When you or Barlow or Escobar lay hand on the treasure of the Montezumas, it will be to step aside for the last Montezuma. It will be mine!"

Fury filled her eyes. The hands at her sides clenched until the knuckles shone white through the blaze of her rings. The great cat rose and yawned, showing its glistening teeth and red throat. Its eyes were no more merciless and cruel than its mistress's. Kendric felt queerly as though he were looking back across dead centuries into ancient Mexico and upon the angry princess of the most cruel of all peoples, the blood-lusting Aztecs.

"Go!" she panted.

With one after another of the doors thrown open before him Kendric hurried away.

CHAPTER VII

OF A GIRL HELD FOR RANSOM
AND OF A TOAST DRUNK BY ONE INFATUATED

Jim Kendric returned straightway to the rooms allotted to him and Barlow, hoping to find his companion there. They must talk together, they must understand each the other; they must know, and know without delay, just in what and to what lengths friend could count on friend. To the uttermost, Kendric would have said a week ago. Now he only pondered the matter, recalling that in some ways Barlow did not seem quite the old mate.

He found the rooms empty and threw himself into one of the big chairs to wait. As he regarded the situation it had little enough to recommend itself to a man of his stamp. He had not the least desire to meddle in any way with Mexican revolutionary politics; upheavals would come and come again, no doubt, for thus would a great country in due time work out its own salvation. But it was no affair of his. This fomenting nucleus into which he and Barlow had come was, he estimated, foredoomed to failure and worse; one fine day Ruiz Rios and Fernando Escobar and their outlaw followings would find themselves with their backs to an adobe wall and their faces set toward a line of rifles. And Zoraida Castelmar had best think upon that, too. For turbulent times had borne women along with men to a quick undoing.

All this was clear to him. But here clarity gave way to groping

Jackson Gregory

uncertainty. Less than anything else did he have a stomach for being bottled up in any house in the world, Zoraida's house least of all, and denied the freedom of the open. It looked as though he, who had never done another man's command, must now do a girl's. At call she had fifty, perhaps a hundred retainers, ugly-looking devils all and no lovers of Americans who came unbidden into their country.

"There's always a way out of a mess like this," he told himself, determined to find it. "But right now I don't see it."

There was also the lodestone toward which he and Barlow had steered and which had drawn Fernando Escobar. And that amazing creature who coolly laid claim to the royal blood of the Montezumas, laid claim as well to their treasure trove. Just how any of them could make a move toward it without her knowledge baffled him. And hence, more than ever before, did his desire mount to get his own hands on it.

When presently Barlow entered, Kendric looked up at him thoughtfully. Barlow bore along with him a subdued air of excitement.

"You've just left Rios?" asked Kendric.

"Yes." Barlow came in and closed the door, looking quickly and questioningly at his friend. He appeared to hesitate, then said hurriedly: "There are big things ahead, old Headlong! Big!"

"Shoot," answered Kendric sharply. "What's the play, man?"

Again Barlow hesitated, plainly in doubt just how far Kendric might be in sympathy with him.

"It wouldn't make you mad to fill your pockets, Headlong, would it?" he asked. "Bulgin' full? And you wouldn't mind a scrap or two and a blow or two in the job, would you?"

"Watch your step, Twisty, old timer," said Kendric. "Rios has been talking revolution to you, has he? Sometimes an uprising down here is a nasty mess that it's easier to get into than out of again. And, if we get our hooks on the loot that brought us down here, why should we want to mix it with the federal government?"

Barlow began tugging at his forelock.

"I'm up a tree, Jim," he muttered at last. "Clean up a tree."

"Then look out you light on your feet instead of on your head when you decide to come down. It would be easy to make a mistake right now."

"Yes, easy; dead easy.—Old Headlong counseling caution!" Barlow laughed but with little genuine mirth.

"I want a straight talk with you, Twisty," said Kendric soberly. "I for one don't like the lay-out here and I'm going to break for the open. You and I have fallen among a pack of damned thieves, to draw it mild. It strikes me we'd better understand each other."

"Right!" cried Barlow eagerly. "Let's talk straight from the shoulder."

But events, or rather Zoraida Castelmar who sought to usurp destiny's prerogatives here, ruled otherwise. There came a quiet rap at the door, then the voice of one of the housemaids, saying:

"La Senorita Zoraida desires immediately to speak with Senor Barlow."

Barlow, just easing himself into a chair, jumped up.

"Coming," he called.

Kendric, too, sprang up, his hand locking hard upon Barlow's arm.

"Twisty," he said, "hold on a minute. The house isn't on fire."

"Well?" Barlow's impatience glared out of his eyes. "What is it?"

"I've got a very large, life-sized suspicion that it would be just as well if you sent back word you couldn't come. At least, not until we've had our talk."

"She said immediately," said Barlow. And then, "You don't want me to see her? Why?"

"Because, it you want to know, she isn't good for you. She'll seek to draw you in on this fool scheme of hers, and if you don't look out you'll do just what she says do. There never was a mere woman like her. She's uncanny, man! She will give you the same line of mad talk she gave me, she will make you the same sorts of offers—"

"You've seen her then? Tonight? While I was out with Rios you were with her?"

"Yes. And not because I found any pleasure in her company, either."

Barlow jerked free, laughing his disbelief, his look at once unpleasant and suspicious.

"Tell that to the marines," he jeered. He threw the door open and went out. In the hall Kendric could hear his steps sounding quick and eager. Kendric returned to his chair, perplexed. Then again he sprang up, throwing out his hands, shaking his shoulders as though to rid them of a troublesome weight.

"Too much thinking isn't good for a man," he told himself

lightly. "The game's made; let her roll!"

He took a cigar from the table, lighted it and passed through the bath and adjoining room. A door opened to the outer corridor. He stepped out upon the flagstones and strolled down the aisle flanked on one side by the adobe wall of the house, on the other by the white columns and arches. The night was fine, clear and starlit; the fragrance of a thousand flowers lay heavy upon the-air; the babble of the outdoor fountain made merry music. He left the stone floor for the graveled driveway and put his head back to send a little puff of smoke upward toward the flash of stars.

"It's a good old land, at that," he mused. "Big and clean and wide open."

He strolled on, looking to right and left. Before him the gardens appeared deserted. But there were patches of inpenetrable blackness under the wider flung trees, and it seemed likely, from what Zoraida had said, that some of her rabble were watching him. If so, he deemed it as well to know for certain. So he kept straight on toward the whitewashed wall glimpsed through the foliage. He came to it and stopped; it was little higher than his head and would be no obstacle in itself. He shot out his hands, gripped the top and went up.

And still no one to dispute his right to do as he pleased. He sat for a moment atop the wall, looking about him curiously. He marked that at each of the corners of the enclosure to be seen from where he sat, was a little square tower rising a dozen feet higher than the wall. In each tower a lamp burned. From the nearest one came the voices of two men. Tied near this tower and outside the wall were two horses; he saw them vaguely and heard the clink of bridle chains. Saddled horses. There would be saddled horses at each of the four towers; night and day, if Zoraida's talk were not mere boasting. The temptation to know just how strict was the guard kept moved him to drop to the ground, on the outside of the wall. He moved quickly, but his feet had not struck the grass when a sharp whistle cut through the still night. The whistle came from somewhere in the shadows within the enclosure.

Kendric stood stone still. But had he been ready for flight he knew now that he could not have gone twenty paces before they stopped him. Where he had heard the voices of two men he now heard an overturned chair, jingle of spur and thud of boots, a sharp command. He saw two figures run out on the wall and leap down into the saddles just below. And he knew that in the other towers there had been like readiness and like action. For already he saw four mounted men and needed no telling that each man carried a rifle.

He climbed back on the wall, his curiosity for the moment satisfied. And there he sat until one of the riders galloped to him. The man came close and said gruffly:

"It is not permitted to cross the wall. It would be best if Senor Americano remembered. And went back to the house."

"Right-o!" agreed Kendric cheerily. "I just wanted to be sure, *compadre*," and he turned and dropped back into the garden. "She holds the cards, ace, face and trump!" he conceded sweepingly. "But the game's to play." And, as again he strolled along the driveway, his thoughts were not unpleasant. For what had he come adventuring into Lower California if he weren't ready for what the day might bring? The situation had its zest. He wondered how many men were hidden about the garden, like the fellow who had watched him and whistled? How many were watching him now? He reflected as he walked on, but his conjectures were not so deep as to make him oblivious of his cigar. On the whole, for the night, he was content.

Just as he turned the corner of the house a rider, coming from the double front gate, raced down the driveway and flung himself to the ground. A figure stepped out from the shadowy corridor and Kendric was near enough to recognize the second figure as that of Captain Escobar, even before he heard his sharp:

"Is that you, Ramorez? What luck?"

"Si, Senor Capitan. It is Ramorez. And the luck is fine!"

"You have her?" Escobar's tone was exultant.

"Just outside. Sancho is bringing her. I am here for orders. Where shall we take her?"

"Here. Into the house. Senorita Castelmar knows everything and is with us."

Ramorez swung back up into the saddle and spurred away, gone into the darkness under the trees toward the gate. Kendric stood where he was, receptive for any bit of understanding which might be vouchsafed him. He was satisfied with his position in the shadows; glad when Escobar stepped out so that the lamp light from within streamed across his face. Actually the man's hard eyes gloated.

It was only a moment until Ramorez returned, another man riding knee and knee with him, a led horse following them. It was this animal and its rider that held Kendric's eyes. In the saddle was what appeared a weary little figure, drooping forward, clutching miserably at the horn of the saddle with both hands. As she came nearer and there was more light he saw the bowed head, made out that it was hatless, even saw how the hair was all tumbled and ready to fall about her shoulders.

"You will get down, senorita." It was Escobar's voice, gloating like his eyes.

The listless figure in the saddle made no reply, seemed bereft of any volition of its own. As Ramorez put up his hands to help her, she came down stiffly and stood stiffly, looking about her. Kendric, to see better, came on emerging from the shadows and stood, leaning against the wall, drawing slowly at his cigar and awaiting the end of the scene. So now, for the first time, he saw the girl's face as she lifted it to look despairingly around.

"Oh," she cried suddenly, a catch in her voice, throwing out her two arms toward Escobar. "Please, please let me go!"

The hair was falling about her face; she shook it back, still standing with her arms outflung imploringly. Kendric frowned. The girl was too fair for a Mexican; her hair in the lamp light was less dark than black and might well be brown; her speech was the speech of one of his own country.

"An American girl!" he marveled. "These dirty devils have laid their hands on an American girl! And just a kid, at that."

With her hair down, with a trembling "Please" upon her lips, she did not look sixteen.

"I am so tired," she begged; "I am so frightened. Won't you let me go? Please?"

Kendric fully expected her to break into tears, so heartbroken was her attitude, so halting were her few supplicating words. A spurt of anger flared up in his heart; to be harsh with her was like hurting a child. And yet he held resolutely back from interference. As yet no rude hand was being laid on her and it would be better if she went into the house quietly than if he should raise a flurry of wild hope in her frightened breast and evoke an outpouring of terrified pleadings, all to no avail. What he would have to say were best said to Escobar alone.

Slowly her arms dropped to her sides. Her look went from face to face, resting longest on Jim Kendric's. He kept his lips tight about his cigar, shutting back any word to raise false hope just yet. The result was that the girl turned from him with a little shudder, seeing in him but another oppressor. She sighed wearily and, walking stiffly, passed to the door flung open by

Ramorez and into the house. Escobar was following her when Kendric called to him. The bandit captain muttered but came back into the yard.

"Well, senor?" he demanded impudently. "What have you to say to me?"

"Who is that girl?" asked Kendric. "And what are you doing with her?"

Escobar laughed his open insolence.

"So you are interested? Pretty, like a flower, *no*? Well, she is not for you, Senor Americano, though she is of your own country. She is the daughter of a rich gentleman named Gordon, if you would know. Her papa calls her Betty and is very fond of her. Him I have let go back to the United States. That he may send me twenty-five thousand dollars for Senorita Betty. Are there other questions, senor?"

"You've got a cursed high hand, Captain Escobar," muttered Kendric. "But let me tell you something: If you touch a hair of that poor little kid's head I'll shoot six holes square through your dirty heart." And he passed by Escobar and went into the house.

He meant to tell the daughter of Gordon that he, too, was an American; that Barlow, another American, was on the job; that, somehow, they would see her through. But he was given only a fleeting glimpse of her as she passed out through a door across the room, escorted by the grave-eyed young woman who an hour ago had warned him not to anger Zoraida. He saw Betty Gordon's face distinctly now; she was fair, her hair was brown, he thought her eyes were gray. But before he could call to her she was gone, clinging to the arm of Zoraida's maid.

"Poor little kid," muttered Kendric, staring after her. "I'd give my hat to have her on a horse, scooting for the *New Moon*. All alone among these pirates, with her dad the Lord knows where trying to dig up twenty-five thousand dollars for her!"

At least she was no doubt well enough off for the night. She looked too tired to lie awake long, no matter what her distress. He returned to his rooms and sat down to wait again for Barlow.

 When at last Barlow came Kendric knew on the instant what success Zoraida had had with him. Twisty's eyes were shining; his head was up; he walked briskly like a man with his plans made and his heart in them.

"You poor boob," muttered Kendric disgustedly. "Once you let a woman get her knife in your heart you're done for."

Barlow swept up the brandy bottle and filled a glass brim full.

"To Zoraida, Queen of Lower California!" he cried ringingly. He drank and smashed the glass upon the floor.

Kendric sighed and shook his head hopelessly. And thanked God that he had never been the man to go mad over a pretty face.

CHAPTER VIII

HOW A MAN MAY CARRY A MESSAGE AND NOT KNOW HIMSELF TO BE A MESSENGER

"There's no call for bad blood between you and me, Jim," said Barlow, plainly ill at his ease. "We've always been friends; let's stay friends. If we can't pull together in the deal that's comin', why, let's just split our trail two ways and let it go at that."

"Fair enough," cried Kendric heartily. His companion thrust out a hand; Kendric took it warmly. Barlow looked relieved.

"And," continued the sailor, "there's no sense forgettin' what we ran into this port for in the first place. There's the loot; no matter how or when we come at it, both together or single, we split it even?"

"Fair again. The old-time Barlow talking."

"All I've held out on you, Jim, is the exact location, so far as I know it. I'll spill that to you now, best I can. Then you can play out your string your way and I can play it out my way. As Juarez tipped me off, you've got three peaks to sail by; whether it's the three we saw first or the ones right off here, back of the house, I don't know any more than you do. But it ought to be easy tellin' when a man's on the spot. The middle peak ought to be a good fifty feet higher than the others and flat lookin' on top. In a ravine, between the tall boy and the one at the left, Juarez said there was a lot of scrub trees and brush. He said plow through the brush, keepin' to the up edge when you can get to it, until you come to about the middle of the patch. There a man would find a lot of loose rock, boulders that looked like they'd slid off the mountain. This rock, and the Lord knows how much of it there is, covers the hole that the old priest's writin' said that loot was in. And that's the yarn, every damn' word of it."

"If it's the place back of the house," said Kendric, "it'll be a night job, all of it. It's not a half mile off and plain sight from here. Now, what's the likelihood of Escobar having been there ahead of us?"

"Escobar's out of the runnin'." Barlow's eyes glinted with his satisfaction. "He's corked up here tighter'n a fly in a bottle. He isn't allowed to stick nose outside the walls after dark; and he isn't allowed to ride out of sight in the daytime. Those are little Escobar's orders. And, by cracky, I'll bet he minds 'em."

"Who told you all that?"

"She did."

"What's she close-herding him for?"

"Doesn't trust him; can you blame her? She's takin' her chances, and she knows it, plannin' the big things ahead. And she's not missin' a bet."

"And more," remarked Kendric drily, "she hankers for the loot herself?"

"She wouldn't know a thing about it," protested Barlow. "Escobar would keep his mouth shut; he's wise hog enough for that."

"But she does know, Twisty. She knows that Escobar knifed Juarez; she knows why; she knows pretty nearly as much about the thing as we know."

"She knows a lot of things," mused Barlow. But he shook his head: "She's shootin' high, Headlong; no penny-ante game for her! Not that what we're lookin' for sounds little; but it ain't in her path and she's not turnin' aside for anything. And she's the richest lady in Mexico right now. Those pearls of hers, man, are worth over a hundred thousand dollars, or I'm a fool. I saw them again tonight; she let me have them in my hands. And that ruby; did you see it? Why, kings can't sport stones like that in their best Sunday crowns."

"She contends that she is a descendent of the old Mexican kings," offered Kendric coolly. "And any treasure, left by the Montezumas, she claims by right of inheritance!"

"She couldn't get across with a claim like that, could she? Not in any law court, Jim?"

"Not unless the jurors were all men and she could get them off alone, one at a time, and whisper in their ears," grunted Kendric.

Barlow laughed and they dropped the subject. Kendric told Barlow what he had learned during the evening; how the walls were sentinelled and how at the present moment under the same roof with them was an American girl, held for ransom.

"And, according to Escobar," he concluded, watching his old friend's face, "the trick is put over with the connivance of Miss Castelmar. This would seem to be one of the headquarters of the great national game!"

"Well?" snapped the sailor. "What of it? If you can get away with a game like that it pays big and fast. And who the devil sent you and me down this way to preach righteousness? It's their business—but, cut-throat cur that that little bandit hop o' my thumb is, I don't believe a word he says."

"And if you did believe, it would be just the same?" There was a queer note in his voice. "Well, Twisty, old mate, I guess you've said it. Our trail forks. Good night."

"Good night," growled Barlow. Each went into his own bedroom; the doors closed after them.

For a couple of hours Kendric sat in the dark by his window, staring out into the gardens, pondering. Of two things he was certain: He was not going to remain shut up in the Hacienda Montezuma if there was a way to break for the open; and he was not going to leave Lower California without his share of the buried treasure or at least without knowing that the tale was a lie. And, little by little, a third consideration forced itself in with its place with these matters; he could not get out of his mind the picture of the "poor little kid of a girl" in Escobar's hands. Like any other strong man, Kendric had a quick sympathy and pity for the weak and abused. Never, he thought, had he seen an individual less equipped to contend with such forces than was the little American girl.

"What I'd like," he thought longingly, "would be to make a break for the border; to round up about twenty of the boys and to swoop down on this place like a gale out of hell! Clean 'em for fair, pick the little Gordon girl up and race back to the border with her. If it wasn't so blamed far—"

But he realized, even while he let his angry fancies run, that he was dreaming impossibilities. He knew, also, that to take up the matter through the regular diplomatic channels would be a process too infinitely slow to suit the situation. It was either a single-handed job for Jim Kendric, or else it was up to the girl's father to pay down the twenty-five thousand dollars.

"I'd give a good deal for a talk with old Bruce West," he told himself. "His outfit lies close in to these diggings; wonder if he has any American boys working for him? Why, a dozen of us, or a half dozen, would stand this place on end! Yes; I'd like to see Bruce."

A score of reasons flocked to him why it was desirable to see young West. The boy was a friend, and it would be a joy just to grip him by the hand again after three years; Bruce had written to him to come and now that events had led him so near, he should grant the request; Bruce was having his own troubles, no doubt against the lawlessness of Escobar, Rios and the rest. And finally, he and Bruce might work things together so that both should derive benefit. Bruce might be in a position to befriend Gordon's little daughter.

So much did Kendric dwell on the subject that night that it claimed his first thoughts when he woke in the early dawn. And therefore, when Zoraida's message was handed to him at the breakfast table, he stared at it with puzzled eyes asking himself if the amazing creature had read his thoughts through thick walls of adobe.

The message was typewritten, even to the signature. It said:

"No doubt Senor Kendric would like to see his old friend Senor West. If he will only set his signature below what follows he will be given a horse, permission to ride and instructions as to direction. Zoraida."

And below were the words, with date and a dotted line for him to sign:

"I pledge my word, as a gentleman, to Zoraida Castelmar, that I will return to her at Hacienda Montezuma not later than daybreak twenty-four hours from now. . . ."

"A take or leave proposition, clean cut," he comprehended promptly. And as promptly he decided to take it. The maid who had brought him the paper was offering pen and ink. He accepted and wrote swiftly: "Jim Kendric."

"Has Barlow breakfasted yet?" he asked, returning to his coffee.

"An hour ago, Senor. He has gone out."

Jackson Gregory

"Alone?"

"No, senor. With La Senorita Zoraida."

"Hm," said Kendric. "And Rios? And Escobar?"

"Senor Rios went to bed late; it is his custom, senor." The girl looked as though she could tell him more but, with a quick glance over her shoulder, contented herself with saying only: "Senor Escobar is with the men outside."

"And the American girl? Miss Gordon?"

"Asleep still, senor."

"Has Escobar been near her?"

"No, senor. She has been alone except for me and Rosita. *La pobrecita,*" she added, almost in a whisper. "She is so frightened."

"Be kind to her," said Kendric. He, too, looked over his shoulder. In his pocket were the few fifty-dollar bills left to him from his oil shares. "What is your name?"

"Juanita," she told him.

"All right, Juanita; take this." He slipped a bill along the tablecloth toward her. "Give Rosita half, you keep half. And be kind to Miss Gordon."

"Oh, senor!" she cried, as in protest. But she took the bank note. Kendric felt better for the transaction; he finished his breakfast with rare appetite.

"Now," he cried, jumping up, "for the horse. Is it ready?"

Juanita, the folded paper in her hands, went with him to the door.

"The horse is ready, Senor Americano," she told him. "It remains only for me to tell the boy that you have promised to return."

Sure enough, pawing the gravel in front of the house, half jerking off his feet the *mestizo* holding it, was a tall, rangy sorrel horse looking as fine an animal as any man in a hurry could wish.

"Senor Kendric will ride, Pedro," called Juanita. "Give him the horse."

Pedro gave the reins over to Kendric and turned away toward the stables. Kendric swung up into the saddle and for a moment curbed the big sorrel's dash toward the gates, to say meditatively to Juanita:

"If I took that paper away from you and made a run for it, what then?"

A look of fear leaped into the girl's dark eyes and she drew hastily back, clutching the paper to her breast.

"Senor!" she cried, breathless and aghast. "You would not! She—she would kill me!"

"She would *what?*" he scowled.

"She would give me to her cat, her terrible, terrible cat, to play with!" Juanita shivered, and drew still further back. "With my life I must guard this paper until it goes from my hand into her hand."

He laughed his disbelief and gave his horse his head at last. They shot away through the shrubbery; the horse slid to a standstill before the closed gate. Of the man smoking a cigaret before it Kendric said curtly:

"You are to let me through. And direct me to Bruce

West's ranch."

"Si, senor." The man opened the gate. "It is yonder; up the valley. The trail will carry you up over the mountain; there are piled stones to mark the way to the pass. In an hour, from the other side of the ridge, you will see houses. Ten miles from there."

Kendric rode through and as he did so his figure straightened in the saddle, his shoulders squared, he put up his head. Free and in the open, if only for twenty-four hours. And with a horse, a real horse, between his knees. He looked off to the left to Barlow's three peaks; the sun was gilding the top of the tallest and it was unquestionable that it was flat-topped. But he did not dwell long upon buried gold nor yet on the query which suggested itself: "Where were Barlow and Zoraida riding so early?" The immediate present and the immediate surroundings were all that he cared to interest himself in on a day like this.

The man at the gate had said it was ten miles from the far side of the ridge to the Bruce West ranch house; the entire distance, therefore, from the Hacienda Montezuma would be about double that distance. The trail, once he reached the hills, was a dilatory, leisurely affair, thoroughly Mexican; it sought out the gentlest slope always and appeared in no haste to arrive anywhere. Well, his mood could be made to suit the trail's; he was in no hurry, having all day for his talk with young West.

The higher he rose above the floor of Zoraida's grassy valley the steeper did his trail become, flanked with cliffs, at times looking too sheer ahead for a horse. But always the path twisted between the boulders and found the possible way up. So he came into a splendid solitude, a region of naked rocks, of a few windblown trees, of little open level spaces grown up with dry brush and wiry grass; of defiles through stone-bound ways that were so narrow two men could not have ridden through them abreast, so crooked that a man often could not see ten steps ahead or ten steps behind, so deep that he must throw his head far back to see the barren cliff tops above him. Strips of sky, seen thus, were deep, deep blue.

It was not at all strange, he told himself during one of his meditative moments while his horse climbed valiantly, that Zoraida should know of his friendship with Bruce West, nor that she should understand his natural desire to ride where he was going this morning. Everyone in the border town had known of his letter at the postoffice; further, it was not in the least unlikely that Senorita Castelmar would know of the letter when it was dropped into the slot at the Mexican postoffice. What did strike him as odd, however, was that she should consent to his leaving the ranch, realizing that he knew much of her own plans and would doubtless speak freely of them and of the American girl held in her house for ransom.

"Not only was she willing for me to see Bruce," he decided; "she wanted me to. Why?"

His trail led him into the last narrow defile to be encountered before reaching the summit. So closely did the rocks press in on each side that often his tapaderos brushed the sheer wall. He made a turn, none too wide for the body of his horse and drew sudden rein, looking into two rifle barrels. The men covering him lay a dozen feet above his head upon a bare, flat rock. He could see only the hands upon their guns, the heads under their tall hats, the shoulders. But he was near enough to mark a business-like look in the hard black eyes.

"You've got the drop on me, *companeros*," he said lightly. "What's the game?"

A third man appeared on foot in the trail before him, stepping out from behind a shoulder of rock. He came on until he could have put out a hand to the sorrel's reins.

"Where do you ride so early?" asked the man on foot, his voice quiet but vaguely hostile. "On what errand?"

"What business is it of yours, my friend?" returned Kendric.

"I know the horse," called one of the figures above. "It is El Rey, from the stables of La Senorita."

"Then the rider must have a message. Or a sign. Or he has stolen the horse, which would go bad with him!"

"Curse you and your signs and messages," cried Kendric hotly. "It's a free country and I ride where I please."

The man before him only smiled.

"Let me look at your saddle strings," he said.

Kendric stared wonderingly; was the fellow insane? What in the name of folly did he mean by a thing like this? Surely not just the opportunity to draw close enough to strike with a knife; the rifles above made such strategy useless.

So he sat still and contented himself with watching. The man came a step closer, twisted El Rey's head aside, pressed close and looked at the rawhide strings on one side of the saddle. Then he moved to the other side and repeated the process. Immediately he drew back, lifting his hat widely.

"Pass on, senor," he said courteously. "*Viva La Senorita!*"

Kendric spurred by him and rode on, passing abruptly out of a wilderness of tumbled boulders into a grassy flat. He turned in the saddle; nowhere was there sign of another than himself upon the mountain. Curiously he looked at his saddle strings; in one of them a slit had been made through which the end of the string had been passed; a double knot had been tied just below the slit. In no other particular was any one of the strings in the least noteworthy.

"As good a way to carry a message as any," he grunted. "With not even the messenger aware of the tidings he brings!"

The incident impressed him deeply. Zoraida, at the game she played, was in deadly earnest. Her commands went far and through many channels and were obeyed. The passes through the mountains were in her hands. The sunlight fell warm and golden about him; the full morning was serene; a stillness as of ineffable peace lay across the solitudes. And yet he felt that the placid promise was a lie; that the laughing loveliness of the day was but a mask covering much strife. In the full light he moved on not unlike a man groping in absolute darkness, uncertain of the path he trod, suspicious of pitfalls, knowing only that his direction was in hands other than his own. Hands that looked soft and that were relentless; hands that blazed with barbaric jewels. There had been a knot in a rawhide string, and a bandit in the mountains had lifted his hat and had said simply: "Long live *La Senorita*!"

CHAPTER IX

WHICH BEGINS WITH A LITTLE SONG AND ENDS
WITH TROUBLE BETWEEN FRIENDS

Speculation at this stage was profitless and the day was perfect. Kendric told himself critically that he was growing fanciful; he had been cooped up too much. First on board the schooner *New Moon*, then in four walls of a house. What he needed was day after day, stood on end, like this. If he didn't look out he'd be growing nerves next. He grinned widely at the remote possibility, pushed his hat far back and rode on. And by the time his horse had carried him to the far edge of the level land and to the first slope of the downward pitch, he was singing contentedly to himself and his horse and all the world that cared to listen.

Far below, far ahead, he caught his first glimpse of the ranch houses marking the Bruce West holdings. From the heights his eye ran down into valley lands that stretched wide and far away, rolling, grassy, with occasional clumps of trees where there were water holes. A valley by no means so prodigally watered as Zoraida's, but none the less an estate to put a sparkle into a man's eyes. It was large, it was sufficiently level and fertile; above aught else it was remote. It gave the impression of a great, calm aloofness from the outside world of traffic and congestion; it lay, mile after mile, sufficient unto itself, a place for a lover of the outdoors to make his home. No wonder that young West had gone wild over it. Hills and mountains shut it in, rising to the sky lines like walls actually sustaining the blue cloudless void. As Jim Kendric rode on and down his old song, his own song, found its way to his lips.

"Where skies are blue
And the earth is wide
And it's only you
And the mountainside!"

"Twenty miles between shacks," he considered approvingly. "And never a line fence to cut your way through. It's near paradise, this land, wherever it isn't just fair hell. No half way business; no maudlin make-believe." But all of a sudden his face darkened. "Poor little kid," he said. "If Bruce could only loan me half a dozen ready-mixed, rough and ready, border cowboys; Californians, Arizonans and Texans!"

His hopes of this were not large at any time; when he came upon the first of Bruce West's riders they vanished entirely. An Indian, or half breed at the best, ragged as to black stringy hair, hard visaged, stony eyed. Kendric called to him and the rider turned in his saddle and waited. And for answer to the question: "Where's the Old Man? Bruce West?" the answer was a hand lifted lazily to point up valley and silence.

"*Gracias, amigo*," laughed Kendric and rode on.

There was not a more amazed man in all Lower California when Jim Kendric rode up to him. Bruce West was out with two of his men driving a herd of young, wild-looking horses down toward the corrals beyond the house. For an instant his blue eyes stared incredulously; then they filled with shining joy. He swept off his broad hat to wave it wildly about his head; he came swooping down on Kendric as though he had a suspicion that his visitor had it in his head to whirl and make a bolt for the mountains; he whooped gleefully.

"Old Jim Kendric!" he shouted. "Old Headlong Jim! Old r'arin', tearin', ramblin', rovin', hell-for-leather Kendric! Oh, mama! Man, I'm glad to see you!"

Only a youngster, was Bruce West, but manly for all that, who wore his heart on his sleeve, his honesty in his eyes and who would rather frolic than fight but would rather fight than do nothing. When last Kendric had seen him, Bruce was nursing his first mustache and glorying in the triumphant fact that soon he would be old enough to vote; now, barely past twenty-three, he looked a trifle thinner than his former hundred and ninety pounds but never a second older. He was a boy with blue eyes and yellow hair and a profound adoration for all that Jim Kendric stood for in his eager eyes.

"Why all the war paint, Baby Blue-eyes?" Kendric asked as they shook hands. For under Bruce's knee was strapped a rifle and a big army revolver rode at his saddle horn.

Bruce laughed, his mood having no place for frowns.

"Not just for ornament, old joy-bringer," he retorted. "Using 'em every now and then. I'm in deep here, Jim, with every cent I've got and every hope of big things. Times, a man has to shoot his way out into the clear or go to the wall. Hey, Gaucho!" he called, turning in his saddle. "You and Tony haze the ponies in to the corrals. And tell Castro we've got the King of Spain with us for grub and to put on the best on the ranch; we'll blow in about noon. Come ahead, Jim; I'll show you the finest lay-out of a cow outfit you ever trailed your eye across."

They rode, saw everything, both acreage and water and stock, and talked; for the most part Bruce did the talking, speaking with quick enthusiasm of what he had, what he had done, what he meant to accomplish yet in spite of obstacles. He had bought outright some six thousand acres, expending for them and what low-bred stock they fed all of his inherited capital. From the nearest bank, at El Ojo, he had borrowed heavily, mortgaging his outfit. With the proceeds he had leased adjoining lands so that now his stock grazed over ten thousand acres; he had also bought and imported a finer strain of cattle. With the market what it was he was bound to make his fortune, hand over fist—

"If they'd only leave me alone!" he exclaimed hotly.

"They?" queried Kendric.

"Of course the country is unsettled," explained the boy. "Ever since I came into it there has been one sort or another of unrest. When it isn't outright revolution it's politics and that's pretty near the same thing. There are prowling bands of outlaws, calling themselves soldiers, that the authorities can't reach. Look at those mountains over there! What government that has to give half its time or more to watching its own step, can manage to ferret out every nest of highwaymen in every canon? Those boys are my big trouble, Jim! A raid from them is always on the books and there are times when I'm pretty near ready to throw up the sponge and drift. But it's a great land; a great land. And now you're with me!" His eyes shone. "I'll make you any sort of a proposition you call for, Jim, and together we'll make history. Not to mention barrels of money."

Kendric's ever-ready imagination was snared. But he was in no position to forget that he had other fish to fry.

"What do you know of your neighbors?" he asked.

"Not much," admitted Bruce. "And yet enough to *sabe* what you're driving at. The nearest are twenty miles away, at the Montezuma ranch. The boss of the outfit is your old friend Ruiz Rios. I told you that in my letter. I haven't the dead wood on him but it's open and shut that he'd as soon chip in on a cattle-stealing deal as anything else."

"He doesn't own the Montezuma," said Kendric.

"It's the same thing. The owner is a woman, his cousin, I believe. But she's away most of the time, and Rios does as he pleases."

"You don't know the lady, then?"

"Never saw her. Don't want to, since she's got Rios blood in her."

"Let's get down and roll a smoke and talk," offered Kendric. They were on a grassy knoll; there were oaks and shade and grass for the horses. Bruce looked at him sharply, catching the sober note. But he said nothing until they were lying stretched out under the oaks, holding the tie ropes at the ends of which their horses browsed.

"Cut her loose, Jim," he said then. "What's the story?"

Kendric told him: Of his quest with Twisty Barlow; of Zoraida Castlemar and her ambitions; of his own situation in the household, a prisoner with today granted him only in exchange for his word to return by dawn; and finally of Betty Gordon.

"Good God," gasped Bruce. "They're going it that strong? Out in the open, too! And laying their paws on an American girl. Whew!"

Kendric added briefly an account of his being stopped in the pass.

"It's a fair bet," he concluded, "that your raiders get their word straight from the Montezuma ranch. Which means, straight from the lips of Zoraida Castlemar."

Bruce fell to plucking at the dry grass, frowning.

"Funny thing, it strikes me, Jim, that if you're right she should give you the chance to tip me off. How do you figure that out?"

"I haven't figured it out. Here's what we do know: When I was a dozen miles from her place and naturally would suppose that, if I chose, I was free to play out my own hand, up popped those three men; a reminder, as plain as your hat, that through their eyes I was still under the eyes of Zoraida Castlemar.

Further, as innocent as a fool, I carried a message to them in a cut and tied saddle string. A message that was a passport for me; what other significance it carried, *quien sabe*? There's a red tassel on my horse's bridle; that might be another sign, as far as you and I know. The quirt at my saddle horn, the chains in my bridle, the saddle itself or the folds of the saddle blanket— how do we know they don't all carry her word? An easy matter, if only the signal is prearranged."

"The fine craft of the Latin mind," muttered Bruce.

"Rather the subtlety of the old Aztecs," suggested Kendric.

"But all this could have been done as well, and taking no chances, by one of the Montezuma riders."

"Of course. Hence, the one thing clear is that it was desired that I should see you. Since it was obvious that I'd tell you what I knew, that's the odd part of it."

"Why, it's madness, man! It gives us the chance, if no other, to get word back home about the little Gordon girl."

"I'd thought of that. Just how would we do it? A letter in the nearest postoffice?"

"You mean that the postmaster would be on the watch for it? And would play into her hands? Well, suppose we took the trouble to send a cowboy to some other, further postoffice? Or, by golly, to send him all the way to the border? Or, if I should go with the word myself?"

"Answer: If you sent an Indian, how much would you bet that he did not circle back to the Montezuma ranch with the letter? If you went yourself, how far do you suppose you'd ever get?"

Bruce's eyes widened.

"Do you suppose they're going that strong, Jim?"

"I don't know, Bruce. But tell me: if it seemed the wise thing to do, could you drop everything here and make a try to get through with the word?"

Bruce looked worried.

"It's my hunch," he answered, "that it would be a cheaper play for me to pay the twenty-five thousand dollar ransom and be done with it! You don't know how bad things are here, Jim; if I went and came back it would be to find that I'd been cleaned. No, I'm not exaggerating. And with the mortgage on the place, the next thing I would know was that it was foreclosed and in the end I'd lose everything I've got."

"From which I gather you don't put a whole lot of confidence in your cowboys?"

"That's the plain hell of it! Not only have I got to sleep with one eye on my stock; I've got to keep the other peeled on the men that are taking my pay. I never know what other man's pay they're taking at the same time."

"Or what woman's. Well, I imagine Miss Castlemar knows conditions as well as we do, if not a good deal better. So it looks as though she were taking no chances in letting me ride over to see you; and it remains possible that by so doing I am furthering her purpose. Though just how, is another thing I don't know."

"She must be some corker of a female," muttered Bruce. "What does she look like, Jim?"

"Tall. Young and not bad looking. Vain as a peacock and high and mighty."

"That kind of a girl makes me sick," was young Bruce's quick decision. "Let's ride back, Jim; it'll be time to eat."

As they rode slowly down toward the ranch house Bruce

pointed out how, living in constant expectation of the operations of cattle and horse thieves, he took what precautions he could. The pick of his saddle horses, a dozen of them, were grazed during the day in the fields near the house and at night were brought in and stabled. A number of the finest cattle, including a thoroughbred Hereford bull and forty beautiful Hereford cows, recently purchased, were driven each evening into the nearest fields where from dark to daylight they were herded by a night rider.

"I've got to take it for granted," explained West, "that at least some of my vacqueros are on the level. I pick my best men for jobs like this. And I've always got night riders out, making their rounds from one end of the valley to the other. On top of all that I've got my dogs; look, here they come to meet us."

There were ten of them, big tan and white collies, vying with one another to come first to their master. Splendid animals all of them, but at the fore ran the most splendid of them all, the father and patriarch of his flock. It was his keen nostril and eye that was wont first to know who came; his superb strength and speed carried him well in the lead and he guarded his supremacy jealously. His sharp teeth snapped viciously when a hardy son ran close at his side and the youngster, though he snarled and bristled, swerved widely and thus fell back. They barked as they swept on, the sharp, stacatto bark of their breed.

"They're something I can trust," said Bruce proudly. "No hand but mine feeds them; if I catch a man carressing one of them he draws his pay and quits. And I go to sleep of nights reasonably sure that their din will wake me if an outsider sets foot near the home corrals. Hi! Monarch! Jump for it."

From his pocket he brought out a bit of dried beef, the "jerky" of the southwest. He held it out arm's length, sending his horse racing forward with a sudden touch of his spur. The big dog barked eagerly and launched his sinewy body into the air; the sunlight flashed back a moment from the bared sharp teeth; Monarch dropped softly back to earth with the dried beef already bolted. Bruce laughed.

At the house, like Zoraida's in the matters of age and thick, cool walls, but much smaller, they found an excellent meal awaiting them. They ate under a leafy grape arbor on the shady side of the house, half a dozen of Bruce's men sitting at table with them. Kendric regarded the men with interest, feeling that their scrutiny of him was no less painstaking. They were swarthy Indians and half-breeds and little else did he make of them. Their eyes met his, steady and unwinking, but gave no clue to what thoughts might lie back of them.

"I'll bet Bruce sleeps with a gun under his pillow," was Kendric's thought at the end of the meal.

By the well, under some shade trees in the yard, the two friends sat and smoked, watching the men laze away to the stables. Thereafter they spoke quietly of the captive in the Hacienda Montezuma.

"It's not to be thought of," said Bruce, "that a scared little kid like her is to be held that way and we sit like two bumps on a log. Looks like her troubles were up to you and me, Jim."

In the end they agreed that at least it was unthinkable that Betty Gordon would suffer any bodily injury in the same house with Zoraida and her girls; further, that the greatest access of terror had no doubt passed. One grew accustomed to pretty nearly everything. Kendric, bound by his parole to return, would seek the girl out and extend to her what comfort he could; just to know that she was not altogether friendless would bring hope and its own sort of gladness. Tonight, as soon as the men came in and it was dark, they would send Manuel, Bruce's most trustworthy man, to a forty-mile distant postoffice. He would carry with him two letters: one would be addressed to the governor of Lower California and one to friends in San Diego.

"It's about the best we can do on short notice," admitted

Kendric, though he was dissatisfied. "I'm not figuring, though, that it's in the cards for me to stick overlong under the same roof with Rios and his crowd. There's the schooner down in the gulf and there's you for us to count on. Never fret, old Baby Blue-eyes; we'll have her out of that yet."

The letters were written; a little after dusk Manuel set forth, promised a double month's pay if he succeeded and in return promising by all the saints he could call to tongue that he would guard the letters with his life. From their chairs on the porch Kendric and Bruce saw the man depart. When his figure had dimned and blurred into the gathering night they still sat on, silent, watching the stars come out. Bruce had brought out cigars and the red embers glowed companionably. Presently Bruce sighed.

"It's a great little old land," he said, and the inflection of the quietly spoken words was that of affection. "A man could ask for no better, Jim. Conditions right now are damnable; you've got to scrap all along the line for what's yours. But what do you know that is worth the having that isn't worth the fighting for? And one of these fine days when Mexico settles down to business, sort of grows up and gets past the schoolboy stage, we'll have the one combination now lacking—law and order."

Kendric, who had been reflecting upon other matters, made no immediate reply. Bruce had the answer to his suggestion of a new order of things but it came from the darkness beyond his barns. There was a sudden sharp bark from one of his dogs, then a rising clamor as the whole pack broke into excited barking. From so far away that the sound barely reached them came a man's voice, exclaiming angrily. Then a rifle shot, a long, shrill whistle, shouts and the sudden thud of many racing hoofs.

Bruce West toppled over his chair and plunged through the nearest door. It was dark in the house and Kendric heard him strike against a second chair, send it crashing to the floor and dash on. In a moment Bruce was back on the porch, a rifle in each hand. One he thrust out to Kendric, muttering between his teeth,

"Raiders, or we're in luck. Damned rebel outlaws. Come on!"

He ran out into the yard, Kendric at his heels pumping a shell into the barrel. As they turned a corner of the house Bruce stopped dead in his track and Kendric bumped into him and stopped with him. Already the barns were on fire; two tall flames stabbed upward at the dark; the hissing of burning wood and fodder must have reached their ears in five minutes had the pack given no warning. In the rapidly growing light they saw the dogs where, bunched together, they snarled and snapped and broke into wilder baying.

Bruce began shouting, calling to his men, three or four of whom came running out of the house. Beyond the barns they made out vague forms, whether of cattle or horses or riders it was at first impossible to know. Again they ran forward; from somewhere in the direction of the corrals came several rifle reports. With the gun shots a confusion of shouts through the heavier notes of which rose one voice, as high pitched as a woman's.

In the barn lofts the flames were spreading in a thousand directions, each dry stalk serving as a duct of destruction. The fire shot upward and the roof blossomed in red flames. Bruce groaned and cursed and prayed wildly for a glimpse of one of the devils who had done this for him. Big clouds of smoke drifted upward across the stars, shot through with flying sparks. Swiftly the lurid light spread until the white walls of the house stood out distinctly and the forms near the corrals were no longer vague. They were running cattle, Bruce's choice forty cows; Kendric saw the fine bred Hereford bull's horns glint, heard the snort of fear and rage, made out the big bulk crushing a way to the fore among his terrified companions. There were horses, too, running wild, the animals from the stables and the near corral. And behind them, shouting and now and then firing into the air to hasten the laggards, were many horsemen. How many it was impossible to estimate, a dozen at the least, perhaps fifty.

As the black mass of frightened beasts gathered forward headway and shot through the area of light, Kendric saw one horseman clearly. On the instant he threw up his rifle. Already his finger was crooking to the trigger when, with a mutter of rage, he lowered his arm. There was no mistaking that great white horse and he thought that there was as little mistaking its rider, a slender, upright figure leading the rush of the raiders, calling out sharp orders in the clear ringing voice, sweeping on recklessly. He cursed her but he held back his fire. Of women he knew little enough and for women there had been no place reserved in his life; but, for all that and all that Zoraida Castlemar might be and might do, he had not learned to lift his hand against her sex.

But there was nothing in what Bruce saw to restrain him. He fired while his rifle was rising to his shoulder and again and again with the stock against his cheek.

"Damn the light!" he growled, and fired again.

Through the tumult Kendric heard her laughter. None other than Zoraida could laugh like that. Again the suspicion flashed into his quickened brain that the girl was mad. He heard several shots behind him; Bruce's men were taking a hand. Then, close behind the white mare came a second horseman and Kendric thanked God for a man for a target and fired at it. Luck if he hit it, he told himself, at that distance and running and in that flickering light. But he fired again, ran in closer and fired the third time. And just as the white mare passed on through the illumed area and was lost in the dark with its rider he saw his man pitch forward and plunge to the ground. Other forms swept by, other shots were fired both from the outlaws and toward them. The darkness accepted them all and no other man fell.

Shouts floated back to them above the hammering thud of the

fleeing cows and horses. Into the darkness after them Bruce and Kendric and Bruce's men sent many questing bullets while now and then an answering leaden pellet screamed over their heads. Swiftly the clamor of the receding hoof-beats lessened; no voices returned to them; no wild rider was to be seen. The night pulsed only to the barks of the dogs and the roar of the devastating flames.

Bruce was calling loudly to his men to get to horse and follow. But while he spoke he broke off hopelessly realizing that not a horse was left to him. Before he and his herders could get into saddle they must wait for daylight and must waste hours in driving in horses from the distant pastures, wild brutes for the most part that a man could never get near enough on foot to rope. He threw out his arms in a wide gesture of despair. Thereafter he stood, silent and moody, watching his hay-filled barns burn.

"If I could get my hands on the man that engineered this," he said, his voice broken, barely carrying to Kendric a few paces away. "That's all I ask."

Kendric, his rage scarcely less than Bruce's, called back to him:

"I could lead you as straight as a string. It's the handiwork of your neighbor."

"Rios?" cried Bruce eagerly.

"Zoraida Castelmar."

"Damn her!" cried the boy. In the firelight Kendric saw his steady eyes glisten and knew that they were filled with tears, the terrible tears of rage rising above anguish. "Damn her!"

After that he stood silent again looking at the burning buildings. When a new flame spurted skyward, when a section of roof fell, he twitched as though his muscles knew physical pain. At last he turned away and Kendric saw a face that it was hard to recognize as the boyish face of blue-eyed Bruce West.

"This beats me," said Bruce, quietly. "Best stock gone, new barns and hay turned to cinders. Ten thousand dollars wiped out in an hour. Yes; done for, Jim, old man. Clean."

Kendric found no word of answer. He turned away and went down to the broken corrals where the man behind Zoraida had fallen. If the man were not dead he might be induced to talk. And in any case, thief though he was, he was a man and not a dog. He found the huddled body lying still. Kneeling, he turned it over so that the wavering light shone on the face. He did not know whether the man was dead or not; he knew only that it was Twisty Barlow. He squatted there, looking from the white face to the sky full of stars. And his thought was less on the instant of Twisty Barlow than of Zoraida Castlemar.

"This is what she has done for two old friends," he said aloud.

Jackson Gregory

CHAPTER X

IN WHICH A MAN KEEPS HIS WORD AND
ZORAIDA DARES AND LAUGHS

Kendric called to Bruce. Together they carried the unconscious Barlow into the house. Kendric, once satisfied that his old friend's heart still beat, scarcely breathed until he lighted a lamp and found the wound. It was in the shoulder and not only did not appear dangerous, but failed to explain the man's condition of coma. There was a trickle of blood across the pale forehead; Kendric pushed back the hair and found a cut there, ragged and filled with dirt. Plainly the impact of the heavy bullet had sufficed to unseat the sailor who, pitching out of the saddle and striking on his head, had been stunned by the fall.

Kendric bathed and bandaged both wounds while Bruce went for a bottle of brandy.

"He's coming around," said Kendric as Barlow's throat received the stinging liquor. "I don't want to be on hand when he opens his eyes, Bruce; for ten years I've called Twisty by the name of friend. He's down and out for a little and what we two have to say to each other can wait a spell."

Bruce, stolidfaced now and morose, nodded. Kendric went outside and stood watching the flames work their will with Bruce's barns, his heart heavy within him. One friend down, a bullet hole in his shoulder, shot as a raiding cattle thief; another friend looking to have lost his boyish nature with the loss of his hope. And both rendered what they were through the wickedness of a woman. Woman? As he brooded over the devastation she had wrought he began to think of her as an evil spirit. He recalled with a shiver the feel of her burning eyes, hidden but potent; he thought of the nights at sea when he had felt her presence. For the first time he allowed himself to wonder in all seriousness if she had powers above a mere woman's as she had a character set apart.

And, after all that happened, he must return to her! He, Jim Kendric, must leave Twisty Barlow, wounded, and Bruce West, ruined, and return to Zoraida Castlemar who had set her brand upon both them. His twenty-four-hour leave would expire at daybreak. He had meant to spend the evening with Bruce and then to ride back during the night. Now, for the first time, he realized that the raiders had set him on foot. The twenty miles to the Montezuma ranch would have to be walked.

"And I'd better be on my way," he decided promptly. It did not enter his head that he had an excuse to offer for making a tardy appearance. He had pledged his word, and, while it was humanly possible, he would keep it. Even were it impossible it would have been Jim Kendric's way to try. And now he was not sorry for an excuse for leaving early. He could do nothing for Bruce; what must be said between him and Twisty Barlow could come later.

It was then, while he was returning to the house that he saw a steady light shining out in the fields. He stopped, at first fearing that a fresh fire was breaking out.

"Not thieves but cursed marauders," he named the crowd to which Bruce had already lost so heavily. "They've fired the dry grass."

But while he watched it the light did not alter, neither flaring up nor dying down, burning steadily like a lamp. When after two or three minutes he observed this he left the house and walked out into the field, keeping to the shadows when he could, watchful and suspicious. Thus presently he came to see what it was: a lantern tied from a low limb of a tree. Below the lantern he saw a dark object; it moved and he heard the clink of a bridle chain. Again he went forward, puzzled and curious. He made out that the saddle was empty; he could see no one near. A man might be hiding behind the bole of the oak or might even be above in the branches. Inwardly Kendric prayed that he was. He was ready for a meeting with any loiterer of Zoraida's following. His pulses stirred as he thought that it might even be Rios or Escobar.

But though he circled the tree and peered long into the shadows among the branches, he still saw no one. At last he came close to the tethered horse. It was his own, the sorrel El Rey he had ridden here this morning, saddled and bridled, spurs slung to the horn. The lantern shed its rays upon the saddle and Kendric saw something else at the horn; a bunch of little blue field flowers, held in place by a bit of white ribbon.

He snatched the flowers down angrily, trampled on them, ground them under foot. They seemed to him a bit of Zoraida herself; they taunted him, they bore the message she sent. They were her summons to come back to her. He jerked free the tie rope and swung up into the saddle, eager and anxious to go back to her the swiftest way in order that the time might come the more swiftly when he could fulfil his word and be free to leave her. He'd get a rifle from Bruce; with that and his revolver he'd take his chance, let all of her infernal rabble bar the way.

From the rear of the house he called to Bruce.

"I've found my horse; they left him behind," he said as Bruce came out. "I've got to go back, so back I go the quickest I know how. Take decent care of Barlow; he was a real man once and may be again, if he can shake that damned woman off. Lend me a rifle if you can spare it. I'll see you again as soon as the Lord lets me. So long."

"So long, Jim," returned Bruce drearily. He brought out a rifle, holding it out wordlessly. And Kendric rode away into the night.

In the mountains, though in another narrow pass, he was stopped as he had been this morning. A lantern was flashed in his face and over his horse. Then he was allowed to go on while from the darkness a voice cried after him:

"*Viva La Senorita!*"

From afar he saw lights burning down in the valley and recognized them as the lamps in the four wall towers. The gates were closed but at his call a man appeared from the shadows and opened to him. He rode in; dismounting, he let the rifle slip into a hiding place in the shrubbery; another man at the front corridor took his horse. At about midnight he again entered the old adobe building. The main hall into which he stepped through the front door was still brightly lighted with its several lamps; through open doors he saw that nowhere in the house were lights out. Yet it was very quiet; he heard neither voice nor step.

He knew where Zoraida was; no doubt Rios and Escobar were with her. He had kept his word and returned to his prison like a good dog; what reason why he should not take advantage of what appeared an unusual opportunity and make his attempt at escape? Zoraida would not have counted on his returning so early; he carried a revolver under his arm pit and hidden in the garden was a rifle. To be sure there were risks to be run; but now, if ever, struck him as the time to run them.

If he could only find where Betty Gordon slept. He must give her a word of hope before he left her here among these devils; assuring her that he would return for her and bring the law with him. Or, if she had the nerve and the desire to attempt escape with him now, that was her right and he would go as far as a man could to bring her through to safety. Noiselessly he crossed the room. He would pass through the music room and down the hall toward the living quarters of the house. If luck were with him he would find her.

It was only when he was about to pass out of the music room door going to the hallway that he heard voices for the first time. They came from a distance, dulled and deadened by the oak doors, but he knew them for the voices of men, raised in anger. A louder word now and then brought him recognition of Ruiz Rios's voice; a sharp answer might have been from Escobar. He stopped and considered. If these men quarreled, how would it affect him? Quarrel they would, soon or late, he knew. For both were truculent and in the looks he had seen pass between them there was no friendship. Two rebellious spirits held in check by the will of Zoraida Castelmar. But now Zoraida was away.

Then for the moment he forgot them and his conjectures. He had heard a faint sound and turning quickly saw for the first time that he was not alone in the music room. In a dim corner beyond the piano was a cushioned seat and on it, her hands clasped in her lap, her eyes wide with the sleeplessness and anxiety of the night, crouched Betty Gordon. He took a quick step toward her. She drew back, pressed tight against the wall, her look one of terror. Terror of him!

But he came on until he stood over her, looking down into her raised face. He felt no end of pity for her, she looked so small and helpless and hopeless. Big gray eyes pleaded with him and he read and understood that she asked only that he go and leave her. An impulse which was utterly new to him surged over him now, the impulse to gather her up into his arms as one would a child and comfort her. Not that she was just a child. She had done her shining brown hair high up on her head; she fought wildly for an air of serene dignity; he judged her at the last of her teens. But she was none the less flower-like, all that a true woman should be according to the beliefs of certain men of the type of Jim Kendric, a true descendant of her sweet, old-fashioned grandmothers. Her little high-heeled slippers, her dainty blue dress, the flower which even in her distress she had tucked away in her hair, were quite as he would have had them.

"Betty Gordon," he said softly so that his words would not carry to other ears, "I want to help you if you will let me. Will you?"

Her clasped hands tightened; he saw the lips tremble before she could command her utterance.

"I—I don't know what to do," she faltered. Her eyes clung to his frankly, filled with shining eagerness to read the heart under the outer man. For the first time Jim was conscious of his several days' growth of beard; he supposed that it was rather more than an even chance that his face was grimy and perhaps still carried evidences of the fight at Bruce West's ranch. To assure her of his honorable intentions toward her he could have wished for a bath and a shave.

"You're in the hands of a rather bad crowd," he said when he saw that she had no further words but was waiting for him. "I thought that at least it would be a relief to know that you had one friend on the job. And an American at that," he concluded heartily.

"How am I to know who is a friend?" She shivered and pressed tight against the wall. "That terrible man named Escobar spoke to me of friendship, and he is the one who gave orders to bring me here! And the other man, Rios, he spoke words that did not go with the look in his eyes. And you—you—"

"Well? What about me?"

"You are one of them. I find you staying in their house. You are the lover of Senorita Castelmar and she is terrible! Oh, I don't know what to do."

"Who told you that?" he demanded sharply. "That I was Zoraida's lover?"

"One of the maids, Rosita. She told me that Zoraida is mad about you. And that you are a great adventurer and have killed many men and are a professional gambler."

"Rosita lied. I am just a prisoner here, like you."

Sheer disbelief shone in Betty's eyes.

"You rode away, alone, this morning," she said. "I saw you through my window. You come in alone tonight. You are not a prisoner."

"I was allowed to leave the house only when I promised to come back. Can't you tell when a man is speaking the truth? Good Lord, why should I want to lie to you?"

Betty hesitated a long time, her hands nervous, her eyes unfaltering on his. She looked at once drawn and repelled, fascinated like a little bird fluttering under the baleful eyes of a snake.

"What do you want me to do?" she asked finally.

"I, for one," he retorted, "refuse to squat here like a fool because I'm told. I'm going to make a break for it. You can take the chance with me or you may remain here and know that I'll do what can be done outside."

Betty shook her head, sighing.

"I don't know what to do," she said miserably.

Jim pondered and frowned. Then he shrugged his shoulders.

"It's up to you, Betty Gordon," he said. "You're old enough to think for yourself. I can't decide for you. But if you were mine, my sister for instance, I'd grab you up and make a bolt for it. A clean bullet is a damned sight more to my liking than the dirty paws of such as Rios and Escobar and their following. They've got a guard around the house which they seem to think sufficient" Again he shrugged. "I've got my notion we can slip through and make the mountains at the rear."

"If I only knew I could trust you," moaned Betty.

A glint of anger shone in Jim's eyes.

"Suit yourself," he told her curtly. "I can promise you it will be a lot easier for me in a scrimmage and a get-away without a woman to look out for."

Immediately he was ashamed of having been brusque with her. For she was only a little slip of a girl after all and obviously one who had never been thrown out into the current of life where it ran strongest. More than ever she made him think of the girl of olden times, the girl hard to find in our modern world. All of her life she had had others to turn to, men whom she loved to lean upon. Her father, her brothers would have done everything for her; she would have done her purely feminine part in making home homey. That was what she was born for, the lot of the sweet tender girl who is quite content to let other girls wear mannish clothing and do mannish work. Kendric knew instinctively that Betty Gordon could have made the daintiest thing imaginable in dresses, that she would tirelessly and cheerfully nurse a sick man, that she would fight every inch of the way for his life, that she would stand by a father driven to the wall, broken financially, that she would put hope into him and bear up bravely and with a tender smile under adversity—but that she would call to a man to kill a spider for her. God had not fashioned her to direct a military campaign. And thinking thus of her, he thought also of Zoraida. Betty Gordon, just as she was, was infinitely more to his liking.

"I can only give you my word of honor, my dear," he said gently, and again he felt as though he were addressing a poor little kid of a girl in short dresses, "that I wouldn't harm a hair of your head for all Mexico."

Betty, though this was her first rude experience with outlaws, was not without both discernment and intuition. Perhaps the maid Rosita had lied to her, carried away by a natural relish in telling all that she knew and more. A look of brightening hope surged up in Betty's gray eyes; her pretty lips were parting when a rude interruption made her forget to say the words which were just forming.

Fitfully voices had come to them from the *patio* where Ruiz Rios and the rebel captain were arguing, but Jim and Betty with their own problem occupying their minds had paid scant attention. Now a sudden exclamation arrested both words and thought, a sharp cry of bitter anger and more than anger; there was rage and menace in the intonation. And then came the shot, a revolver no doubt but sounding louder as it echoed through the rooms. Betty started up in terror, both hands grasping Kendric's arm. His own hand had gone its swift way to the gun slung under his coat.

They waited a moment, both tense. Then Jim patted her hand reassuringly, removed it from his sleeve and said quietly:

"Wait a second. I'll see which one it was."

But before he could cross the room the door was thrown open and Ruiz Rios stood looking in on them queerly.

"Senor Escobar has shot himself," he said. "Through the heart."

Betty fell back from him, step by step, her eyes staring, her face white. Then she looked pleadingly t to Kendric. When he went to her side, she whispered:

"Take me away! Let's try to go now. Now!"

Ruiz Rios's eyes glittered, his mouth hardened. He closed the door behind him, watching them keenly.

"It is in my mind to do you a kindness, Senor Kendric," he said, speaking evenly and emotionlessly.

"You are a murderous cur," rapped out Kendric. "I'd do a clean job if I shot you dead in your tracks."

Rios smiled.

"Let us speak business, *amigo*," he said. "Moralizing is nice when there is plenty of time and nothing else to be done. You are kept here against your will. It might not fit in ill with my plans to see you go."

"I will have a look at Escobar first," said Kendric. Rios stepped aside and again threw open the door. But he did not stir from the spot, awaiting Kendric's return. Nor did Kendric tarry long. Escobar was dead already, shot through the heart, as Rios had said. A revolver lay on the ground, close to his right hand.

"You ought to hang for that," said Kendric as he came back into the room. "But from the way you're going you won't last long enough for the law to get you. Now, what have you to say to me?"

"A part I have said," returned Ruiz Rios. "I can guess much that my fair cousin has said to you. I know her desires and—I know my own!" His eyes flashed. "More, you appear interested in the charming Miss Betty Gordon. If you would like to go yourself, if you would like to take her with you, I think I can arrange matters. At a price, of course."

"Naturally. And the price?"

"Escobar asked twenty-five thousand dollars. Surely she is worth that and more? Ah! Well, what you came to Lower California to find may be worth as much, may be worth nothing. The risk is mine. Tell me where the place is and I will arrange that you and Miss Betty have horses and an open trail."

"Rios," began Jim, speaking slowly.

But it was Betty who answered.

"No!" she cried. "No and no and no! You are a terrible man, Senor Rios, and some day God will bring you to a terrible end. Be sure I would be happy to see the last of you and your cousin and your kind. But the thing you ask is impossible. Why should Jim Kendric, to whom I am only a bothersome stranger, pay you a sum like that—for me? You are crazy!"

Jim himself was perplexed. He had no desire to put Ruiz Rios in the way of appropriating that which had brought both himself and Barlow here. More than that, the secret was not solely his to give away, were he so minded. Barlow had a claim to half and he knew there would be nothing left for Barlow once Rios scented it. Of these matters he thought and also of Betty. Her quick vehemence had surprised him. Until now he would have thought her eager to consent to anything to insure her immediate departure.

"Fine words, senorita," said Rios, his lips twitching so that the white teeth showed. "But you had best think. Many things might happen to a girl, a pretty girl like you, which are not pleasant for her to experience. You had better throw your arms about your countryman's neck and beg him to pay the price for you."

Betty shook her head violently, so violently that the white flower fell from her hair. Rios was going on angrily, when there came into the yard a clatter of hoofs.

"It is Zoraida," he said sharply. "Now be quick; is it yes or no!"

"No!" cried Betty.

"Little fool!" muttered Rios. Under his glare she drew back. "Before again such help is offered you you will wish you were dead!"

Outside they heard Zoraida's laughter, low and rich with its music. Then her voice as gay as though there were in all the world no such shadows as those cast by destruction and death. And then she entered, slender and graceful in her elaborate riding suit, her white plume nodding, her eyes dancing, her red mouth triumphant. Behind her came Bruce West.

Kendric stared at him in amazement. For Bruce came of his own free will and his own eyes were shining. There was no sign of his recent distress upon his face. Rather it looked more joyous, more boyish and glad than Kendric had seen it for years. The boy hardly noted anyone in the room but Zoraida. His eyes were for her alone and they were on fire with adoration.

CHAPTER XI

IN WHICH THERE IS MORE THAN ONE LIE TOLD AND THE TRUTH IS GLIMPSED

"You!" cried Kendric in amazement as his look went swiftly from Bruce's radiant face to Zoraida's and back to Bruce. "With her!"

Young Bruce West advanced eagerly.

"It's been a mistake, Jim," he said earnestly. "A cursed mistake all along the line. When I explain to you—"

"Boy," cut in Kendric sternly, "where's your head? Don't you know that she was one of the crowd raiding you? Have you forgotten all I told you?"

Zoraida, head held high, her cheeks flushed, stood eyeing him defiantly. The mockery of her look disturbed him; she appeared fully confident of herself, her destiny and her place in Bruce's estimation. Bruce himself frowned and shook his head.

"You've always been a fair man, Jim," he said. "Suspend judgment until we've talked."

While Kendric held his tongue and pondered angrily, Zoraida's eyes flashed about the room. Only for an instant did they tarry with Betty who, drawn away from her almost to the table against the wall, looked back at her with unhidden distrust. Longer did they hold to Ruiz Rios.

"My cousin," she said softly, "you have something to say to me. What is it?"

"Not here, senorita," urged Rios. "In another room."

Kendric, but not Bruce, saw the deeply significant regard she shot at Rios. Her answer puzzled Kendric for the moment, not so much the words as the tone. She spoke to Rios as one might speak to a dreaded master.

"I am ready," was all that she said. And when Rios threw open the door for her, it was to Bruce that she said gently, her eyes melting into his, "A moment only, if Senor Rios will permit that I return so soon." And she went out, Rios at her heels.

"Can't you see, Jim?" Bruce was all excitement and his hands were clenched at his side; his boyish eyes blazed. "It's that damned Ruiz Rios! He dictates to her; he has put the fear of death and worse into her heart. She is made to suffer for all of his crimes!"

"So that's the story?" Kendric grunted his disgust. "And you've let her stuff you hide-full of lies?"

"Go easy, Jim." Bruce appeared sincerely pained and troubled. "I've called you a fair man; won't you open your mind to the truth? She has been misrepresented, I know. Her enemies—" He clenched his hands. "She is a wonderful creature!" he burst out. "And she has honored me with her confidence and her friendship."

This very night Zoraida Castelmar had ruthlessly pillaged Bruce's ranch and from Bruce's mouth now gushed the words: "She has honored me with her confidence and her friendship!" Was there no end to the woman's audacity? Was there no end to the blind stupidity of mankind which permitted of lawlessness like tonight's being glossed over, which went to the insane extreme of worshiping when normally the logical emotion would be hatred? Was there finally, no end to the power of Zoraida?

What had happened between Bruce West and Zoraida? Kendric knew something of Zoraida's bravado, no little of her supreme assurance, much of her methods. Plainly she had gone straight to Bruce after the raid. He could see the picture of her coming out of the lurid night and into the experience of a boy all unnerved by his anger and grief. He could understand how she offered her softened beauty to the hard eyes; how her voice had caressed and distorted fact; how Zoraida had had the wit to tell her own story, make her own impression, before Bruce could have had time to steel himself against her. But what tale could she have told to convince a man like Bruce who, at the least, was not a fool?

Somehow, decided Kendric, she had lied out of the whole thing. Further, she had used every siren trick she knew to drug his better judgment. She had been tender and feminine and seductive. While with one hand she had robbed him, she had caressed him with the other. And not too boldly; she had not overdone it. She probably wept for him; she treated him to the flash of her eyes through spurious tears. She employed her beauty like a lure and had little trouble in putting the boy's suspicions to sleep. What chance would a simple, open-hearted fellow like Bruce have against the wiles which were Zoraida's stock in trade? Kendric recalled vividly that subtle influence which Zoraida had cast even upon him; which he had felt even when steeled against her, and asked himself again what chance Bruce could have with her in the hour of her boldest triumph? The very fact of her having come immediately on the heels of the catastrophe gave her a look of innocence. . . . Had Zoraida the trick of hypnosis over men? It began to look like it.

"Poor old Baby-blue-eyes," muttered Jim. He looked at the boy wonderingly. Then only did it occur to him that Bruce and Betty Gordon were strangers to each other and that Bruce, when his sanity should return to him, would make a desirable friend for Betty. So he said, turning toward the girl: "Miss Gordon, this is an old friend of mine; another American, too, Bruce West."

Betty looked her frank interest upon Bruce and her speculation was obvious: among so many men whom she feared and distrusted she wondered if here was one of whom any girl might be sure. She put out her hand, even smiled. But Bruce held stiffly back, his eyes full of accusing light.

"I have heard of Miss Gordon," he said coolly. "She is also known as Pansy Blossom, I believe, over in Sonora."

Kendric failed to understand and looked to Betty. Her eyes widened. Then her cheeks crimsoned.

"Oh!" she gasped. "Mr. West, what do you mean? I have heard of her, everyone has. She is the most terrible creature!" She shuddered. "What made you say that?"

Bruce laughed his disbelief of her words and attitude.

"Jim, here, doesn't seem to remember," he said brusquely. "If you'd been down in Sonora lately, Jim, you'd know all about Pansy Blossom. She sings rather well, I hear, and dances. It would seem that she has the makings of a highly successful actress," he concluded meaningly. Kendric stared at him.

"You mean that Betty Gordon here is some sort of an adventuress?" he demanded.

For answer Bruce shrugged elaborately and returned Kendric's stare. Jim looked to Betty again. Her face was stamped in the image of shocked amazement, she scarcely breathed through her slightly parted lips.

"You're talking nonsense, Bruce," Jim said emphatically. "Sheer rot. She's just Betty Gordon and in a peck of trouble. It's up to you and me, being countrymen of hers, to see her through instead of hurting her feelings."

Bruce regarded him somberly.

"Old Headlong," he said slowly, "you're just the man to mistake a woman. You've judged Zoraida Castelmar wrong; you're making a mistake with Miss Pansy Blossom."

"You fool!" cried Jim angrily. "Where the devil have your wits gone? You call this child an adventuress? Why, man alive, can't you see she's just baby?"

"Pansy Blossom's record—" began Bruce.

"Deuce take Pansy Blossom! We're talking about Betty Gordon, this poor little lost kid here. Who told you that she was the same as that dancing woman?" Bruce made no answer. "Was it Zoraida Castelmar?" demanded Kendric. "Tell me. Is that what Zoraida Castelmar had to say about her?"

"Well?" challenged Bruce. "Suppose it was?"

"What else did she tell you?" Jim had him by the arm now and his eyes were blazing. "Spit it out, boy. What other rot?"

"It's not rot, Jim. If you'll keep your eyes open and think a little you'll know as much as I know."

Kendric groaned. "There's a game on foot that has a bad look to it. Escobar is in it and Rios and—your young lady friend. If you'll give me a few minutes presently, I'll explain."

"Escobar and Betty Gordon! Why, there's nothing between them but fear and hatred. Or rather that's all there was; Escobar's lying dead out there now. Ruiz Rios plugged him square through the heart just now. And now he's taking *your* lady friend out to tell her about it! Betty is their captive, held for ransom, as I told you."

"Or appears to be?" Bruce jerked his arm away and began moving restlessly up and down, looking always toward the door through which Zoraida had gone. Kendric turned toward Betty. She had not stirred; her cheeks were still burning. Apparently she had heard a very great deal of unsavory report of the lady Bruce mistook her for. Only the expression in her eyes and about her lips had changed; now it was one of passionate anger. The look surprised him. He began to think of Betty in altered terms. She wasn't just the baby he had named her and she wasn't just the little kid of sixteen he had at first taken her to be. During the interview with Ruiz Rios he had learned that she had a mind of her own. To her other possessions he now saw added an American girl's fiery temper.

Then Zoraida and Rios returned. Before a word was spoken Kendric knew that he was to be treated to some more play-acting. Zoraida had elected to look frightened and uncertain; the glance she cast toward her cousin spoke of terror as well as loathing. Rios glared and looked important. Swiftly Zoraida crossed the room, her bejeweled fingers finding Bruce West's arm.

"My friend," she whispered so that they could all hear. "I don't know which way to turn. A man has killed himself—the Captain Escobar. Or so Ruiz Rios says. And I—" She broke off, shuddering. And then, bewildering Jim Kendric if no one else, two big tears gathered in her eyes and spilled down to her cheeks!

"Senores Kendric and West," announced Rios autocratically, "you will take all orders from me now. You will not leave the house, either of you, unless I give the word. Senorita Zoraida, you will go to your room and wait until I send for you. Senorita Pansy," and suddenly his teeth showed in his quick smile, "a word with you please in the *patio*?"

"My cousin," said Zoraida, all soft supplication now, her two hands held out toward Rios, "it is only a little thing I beg of you. May I have a few words with Senor West?"

"Go to your room," answered Rios shortly. "Senor West remains with us. You may see him later."

Zoraida looked lingeringly at Bruce, shook her head sorrow-fully as he appeared to be gathering himself to spring at the man who terrorized her, murmured gently, "Wait—for my sake, senor!" and went out of the room. Out of the corners of her oblique eyes, when her back was to Bruce, she mocked Jim Kendric.

Rios held the door open for Betty.

"Will you come to the *patio* with me, senorita?" he asked.

"No!" cried Betty. "You terrible man. No."

Rios, though not the actor Zoraida was, managed to appear startled that she should speak so. Then, as he looked from her to Jim and Bruce, he smiled as though in comprehension.

"There is no need to pretend further, Senorita Pansy," he said. "They know."

"There is a great deal we know, Ruiz Rios," broke out Bruce. "You hold the upper hand just now but there's a new deal coming!"

"Will you come, Senorita Pansy?" Rios grew truculent. "Or shall I call for a dozen men to escort you?"

"Rios," snapped Kendric, "I'm getting damned tired of this foolishness. Betty Gordon is a friend of mine and I'm going to see her through. She goes nowhere she does not want to. If you want to take me on, I'm ready for you. Ready and waiting!"

"No," said Betty again. "Mr. Kendric, I will go with him as far as the *patio*." She took a step forward, then whipped back at a sudden thought. "He is lying out there—dead!" she whispered.

"The unfortunate Captain Escobar," Rios told her equably, "has been removed to another part of the house. And, if you like, we will speak together in the dining-room."

Betty came to Jim Kendric then. She looked up into his eyes and said gently:

"I do trust you. You are the only one I trust. I can look to no one else. If I want you I will call. And you will come to me, won't you?"

"Come to you? Why, bless your heart, I'd come running!"

So Betty and Rios went out and for a little while Jim and Bruce were left alone.

"Bruce, old man," said Kendric, "let's come down to earth. Put your sentimental heart in your pocket and use your brains a while. You know me well enough to know that I won't lie to you. Will you listen to me?"

"Yes. But tell me only what you know, not what you surmise. What do you *know* against Zoraida Castelmar?"

"I know she is an adventuress, playing for big stakes, stakes so big that in the end they are bound to crush her."

"Speculation, old chap." Bruce smiled faintly. "Keep away from doping out the future and stick to facts."

"So you want facts? All right: She is planning a revolution; she has the mad idea that she can rip Lower California away from the government and make of it a separate empire, herself its queen!"

"Why not? Wilder things have been done. And where would you find a more likely queen?"

"When I first saw her she came, disguised as a man, into

Ortega's gaming hell, Rios with her. She played dice with me for twenty thousand dollars."

Bruce's eye brightened.

"She's wonderful!" he said eagerly.

"She's hand and fist with Rios and Escobar and a lot of other riff-raff I don't know. She is instrumental in Betty Gordon's being held for ransom—"

"How do you *know*? Or are you just guessing again? Betty Gordon! How do you *know* she isn't what I called her, the infamous dancing woman with an evil record a mile long?"

"Haven't I talked with her?" Kendric grew impatient. "Haven't I seen her terror? Haven't I looked into her eyes?"

"Haven't I talked with Zoraida?" countered Bruce. "Haven't I heard her explanations? Haven't I seen her terror of Rios? Haven't I looked into her eyes?"

"You were burned out tonight. Have you forgotten that? Your herds were raided. Even old Twisty Barlow, once a square man, followed Zoraida Castelmar into that! And Zoraida, herself, was one of the raiders!"

"How do you *know*?" demanded Bruce. And always he laid significant stress on the word of certainty.

"I saw the horse she rode. I heard the whistle which she wears on a chain about her throat. I even saw the white plume in her hat."

"Is there only one white horse in Mexico? And only one whistle? And only one white plume? These things, if it had been Zoraida, she would have left behind. In the dark you guessed. I am afraid you have guessed all along the line."

"Then tell me how the devil it came about that Zoraida showed up at your place? A pretty tall coincidence."

"Nothing of the kind. The whole thing was engineered by Rios. She overheard a little, guessed it all. Dangerous though the effort was, she tried to be in time to warn me. She came just too late."

Kendric stared at his friend incredulously. First Barlow, then young Bruce West drawn from his side and to Zoraida's. She required men, men of his stamp. And she seemed to have the way of drawing them to her. He felt utterly baffled; he could at the moment think of no argument which Bruce's infatuation would not thrust aside. Where he would depict a heartless, ambitious adventuress Bruce would see a glorified and heroic superwoman.

Rios came to the door.

"Senor West," he said as they turned expectantly toward him, "Senorita Zoraida implores so eloquently for word with you that I have consented. If you will step this way she will come to you."

Bruce required no second invitation. With Rios's words he forgot Kendric's arguments and Kendric's very presence. He went out, his step eager. Before Rios followed him Kendric called:

"Where is Miss Gordon?"

"Gone to her room, senor. If you will look at your watch you will note that it is time."

It was well after midnight and Kendric thought that for all the good he could do, he, too, might as well go to bed. But he was too stubborn a man to give up his friend so easily and he hoped that since Bruce was not a fool he would come in time to see the real Zoraida under the mask she had donned for his benefit. So he waited, walking up and down.

Zoraida entered so quietly that she was in the room and the door shut after her before he felt her presence.

"Bruce has gone out that way, looking for you," he said.

"I can see him presently," she answered lightly. "I think he will wait, don't you?"

"I fancy he will," he returned bitterly. "What do you want with the boy, Zoraida? What has he done to you that you should ruin him, first financially and then every other way? Aren't you afraid of what you are building up for yourself? Men like Barlow and Bruce West may let you sing their souls to sleep for a little; look out when they wake up!"

She laughed softly.

"I think that all along you have doubted my power," she said, her eyes steady on his. "Are you beginning to see that Zoraida Castelmar is a girl to reckon with? You have said that the great things I attempt are beyond me; have I failed in anything I have tried?"

"To infatuate a man is not the same thing as to build a state!"

"And yet infatuated men make obedient lieutenants."

They grew silent. In each there was much which was of its nature incomprehensible to the other and which, of necessity, must remain so. Slowly there came a different look upon the girl's face. Her eyes softened and were more wistful that he had ever thought they could be. Her breast rose and fell in a profound sigh. All of the triumph and mockery went out of her.

"Why are you so unlike other men?" she asked. And her voice, too, had softened and grown tender.

"What do you mean by that?" he asked.

"Escobar hated me but he would have followed me through fire had I beckoned. You have seen the look in your friend Barlow's eyes when he turns to me, and this after only a few days, a few smiles! You glimpsed just now the love that has sprung up in Bruce West's heart like a flower full blown. There have been many, many men, my friend, who have looked upon Zoraida Castelmar as they look. Until you came there has been no man who turned his head away." Again she sighed unhiddenly. Her eyes melted into his, yearning, promising, beseeching. "And to you I have offered what would have made any other man mad with joy."

He looked into her eyes and it seemed impossible that they could speak shameless lies. For the moment at least she had the appearance of a young girl without sophistication, without the skill to hide her thoughts. Her eyes seemed unusually large, wide open frankly, as innocent as spring violets. Was she always like this—was this the real, true Zoraida—He felt her influence upon him, pervading his senses like heavy perfume, and spoke hurriedly.

"You and I are different sorts of people," he answered. "Our ideas as well as our ideals are of different orders."

"And what if I altered?" whispered Zoraida, coming closer to him. "What it I discarded all of my ideas and ideals. Yes, and my ambitions with them! What then, Senor Jim Kendric?"

He shook his head and moved restlessly.

"I am no woman's man, you know that. And if I were, you know also that you are not my kind of woman."

And still no passionate outburst came from Zoraida denied! Rather she grew more deeply meditative. Almost she seemed saddened and weary.

"Your kind of woman," she mused. And then, in pure jest, "Like Escobar's captive?"

For some obscure reason after which he did not grope the half sneer of the words stung Kendric into a sharp retort.

"By heaven, yes!" he cried. "There's the sort of girl for any man to put his trust in, to give the best that is in him!"

Zoraida gasped. Utter amazement filled her eyes. Then came incredulity: she would not believe. But when she saw the seriousness of his eyes, her passion burst out upon him. Her two hands rose and clenched themselves on her panting breast, her eyes lost their shadow of amazement and grew brilliant with anger.

"That little baby-faced doll!" she cried. "She has dared make eyes at you. And you, blind fool that you are, have turned from *me* to *her!*" Her voice shook, her whole body trembled visibly, then stiffened. In a flash all girlish softness was gone; she looked as cold and cruel as steel. "I had thought to let her go when the ransom came. Now I shall have other plans for her."

Kendric stared.

"In the first place," he said with an assumption of carelessness, "you have overshot the mark: Betty Gordon hasn't made eyes at me at all and I'm not in love with her and have no intentions of being. Next, I fail to see what has happened that would alter your plans in her regard?"

Zoraida laughed her disbelief.

"Any girl in her place would make eyes at you," she retorted. "And as for my plans, perhaps you may be allowed to watch the working out of them! Would you enjoy," she taunted him, "the sight of Betty Gordon in a steel cage into which we allowed to enter a certain pet of mine?"

At first he did not understand. Then he stared at her speechlessly. Words of Juanita, spoken fearfully that morning, recurred to him: "She would give me to her cat, her terrible, terrible cat, to play with!" He opened his mouth to lift his voice in hot protest; then he bit back the words, savagely calling himself a fool for the mad thought. Even to Zoraida's lawlessness there must be a limit; even the cold cruelty looking out of her oblique eyes now could not carry her so far. And yet the laugh with which he answered her was a trifle shaky.

"We are talking nonsense," he said abruptly. "And Bruce is expecting you. When you finish distorting facts for his consumption I'd like a word with him."

Zoraida's face went white.

"It is in my heart," she said in a dry whisper, "to give orders that you will never see another sun rise!"

"Give your orders then," he snapped. "I'm sick of things as they are. Send in a gang of your cutthroats and I'll give you my word I'd rather fight my way through them than stand by and watch you poison honest men's souls."

She stepped across the room and put out her hand as though to the bell on the table. Kendric watched her sternly. She stopped and looked at him wonderingly. Suddenly she dropped her hand to her side and with the gesture came a swift alteration in her expression. A strange smile molded her lips, an inscrutable look dawned in the dark eyes.

"I knew already that you were a brave man, Jim Kendric," she said. "I was forgetting, losing all clear thought because a man had dismissed me from his presence? Well, of that, more another time. But brave men I need, brave men I must have in that which comes soon. If there is not one way, then there will be another to draw you to my side."

She was going out but stopped as they heard horses in the

yard. She stood still, waiting. Presently there came an unsteady step at the front door. A hand fumbled, the door opened and Twisty Barlow entered. His arm was in a sling, a bandage bound his forehead, his eyes shone feverishly. He stopped on the threshold and stared at them. Kendric spoke quickly.

"Twisty," he said, "do you know who shot you?"

Barlow merely shook his head.

"I did. I was at Bruce's. I did not know you but—"

"But you'd have shot just the same, anyway?" grunted Barlow.

"You got yourself into damned bad company, Barlow. But that's your affair. Just tell me one thing: Was it not at Zoraida Castelmar's orders that you went?"

Barlow's look shifted for an instant to Zoraida's half smiling face. But his hesitation was brief.

"No," he said shortly.

An hour later Kendric gave up waiting for Bruce and went off to his bedroom. On his table were two letters in their envelopes. They were the letters he and Bruce had written, telling of Betty Gordon's captivity.

CHAPTER XII

IN WHICH AN OVERTURE IS MADE, AN ANSWER IS POSTPONED AND A DOOR IS LOCKED

In his bedroom Jim Kendric sat for a long time pondering that night. What had appeared to him the simplest, most straight-away errand in the world had brought him down here, just the time-honored search for treasure. In all particulars the adventure had seemed the usual one, two men undertaking to share whatever lay ahead, expense, danger or loot. And through no fault of his own Kendric saw simplicity altered into complexity. There were Barlow's changed attitude, the desires and ambitions of Zoraida, the absurdity of Bruce West's infatuation, the interference of Ruiz Rios and finally the situation in which Betty Gordon found herself.

"I came down this way to get my hands on buried treasure, if it exists," Kendric at last told himself irritably; "not to work out the salvations of half the souls in Mexico! If the issue becomes complex it is because I am getting turned away from the main thing. What Barlow and Bruce do is up to them; Barlow, for one, ought to know better, and Bruce has got to cut his eye-teeth sooner or later. It's up to me to be on my way."

Which did not entirely dispose of all matters, since it ignored Zoraida and made no place for Betty. The latter, however, he did not bar from his thoughts or even from his plannings: If she said the word and would take the chance with him, he'd find the way to get her safely out of this house of intrigue. He

Jackson Gregory

was constitutionally optimistic enough to decide that. Among the bushes out in the garden a rifle was hidden; slung under his left arm pit was a dependable friend; and in his heart he was spoiling for a row.

Such was his mood, an hour after he had gone to his room, when a rap discreetly announced a soft-footed somebody at his door. He rose eagerly, thinking it would be Bruce or perhaps Barlow. But when he opened the door it was Ruiz Rios who slipped noiselessly into the room, swiftly closing and locking the door after him.

"Not in bed yet, my friend?" smiled Rios. "It is well. I have something to say to you."

Kendric went back to his chair from which he eyed Rios narrowly. The Mexican's look was full of craft.

"Let's have it, Rios. What now?"

"What I said to you earlier in the evening came from the heart," said Rios. "That without my help you cannot leave; that you may have that help. For a price."

His utterance was incisive; his voice, eager and quick, filled the room. Evidently he had no fear of eavesdroppers. Kendric stared at him curiously.

"For a double-dealing gentleman you have considerable assurance," he grunted. "You don't seem to care who hears."

Rios waved an impatient hand.

"I know what I am about," he retorted. "La Senorita Zoraida is in her own rooms where she entertains one of your friends while the other cools his heels in her anteroom. I have assurance, yes; because just now I am the man of the hour! Your destiny and that of your compatriot, Miss Betty, as well as the destinies of your two friends and perchance of yet others, lies in my hand."

"You talk big when Zoraida's eyes are not on you," said Kendric.

Rios stared insolently, then shrugged and made for himself a tiny white paper *cigarita*.

"I talk big because I can, as you say north of the border, 'deliver the goods.' Do you wish to go free?"

"Since you ask it," said Kendric drily, "yes. I've got no stomach for your crowd here."

"And you would like to take with you the pretty little Betty?" Rios's eyes were full of insinuation. Kendric felt an impulsive desire to kick him but for the time kept his head and witheld his boot.

"Speak on, Senor Man of the Hour," he jeered. "Somehow I'm not particularly sleepy yet. If you've really got anything to say let's have it."

"It is this: The treasure you have come so far to find will never be yours. Mine it may be; if not mine, then Zoraida's. On my honor it will never go into your hands or those of Barlow."

"Your honor," laughed Kendric, "fits well in your mouth, Ruiz Rios, but rides light in the scales."

"You mean you would want proof?" Rios was imperturbable. "It may be given you in due time, but only when it is too late for you to make any stock out of it. Now, for what you know, I offer you your own safety and that of Miss Betty. Have I not marked how you look at her?" He laughed in his turn.

"If this is all you have to say," answered Kendric, "suppose you shut the door from the outside?"

Jackson Gregory

For just now, while he had thought of other matters, he had pondered on this one also. Even were he disposed to treat with Rios, the secret was not his to give. Further, once Rios had the knowledge he sought, he would no doubt fail to keep his word. And in any case there was always the possibility of getting away without the Mexican's aid; and if there was treasure, as Rios so plainly believed, it should be worth many times the twenty-five thousand dollars which had been demanded of Betty's father. On top of all this it was sheer nonsense to plan on what Betty might have to say until her word was spoken. Hence Jim was no little pleased to baffle Rios.

"You are thinking of yourself," said Rios sharply. "Not of the girl. Can you not imagine that it might be unpleasant for her, left here over long?"

Then Kendric sought to be as crafty as his visitor.

"Am I responsible for all wandering damsels in distress?" he asked coldly.

"But Miss Betty—"

"Exactly. What the devil is Miss Betty to me? I never saw her until a few hours ago."

"But," insisted Rios, "in some soils some flowers bloom quickly! Love comes when it comes, in a year, in a day, in a moment."

"Love!" Jim's surprise was not altogether feigned. Then he laughed and remembered his craft. He was thinking that already Zoraida suspected him of being too warmly interested; he did not know but that Rios was here now on Zoraida's errand, making pretenses the while he sought to ferret out real emotions. And so for Zoraida's sake should the words be carried to her, he cried as though in high amusement: "Love? What are you thinking of, man?"

He saw that he had puzzled Rios. The Mexican had been convinced of his keen interest in the girl and, further, knew from of old how lightly Jim Kendric held such mere bagatelles as dollars. Kendric drew a certain satisfaction from the situation. But his frank grin died away slowly as Rios went on.

"We are not friends, you and I, senor," he said smoothly. "But just now that matters not, since my personal interests move me to do you a kindness. Of what happens to you later on, I care less than that." He snapped his fingers. "Perhaps you do not fully understand either your own case or that of Miss Betty. You are to be held here indefinitely; unless you decide to throw your lot in with La Senorita Zoraida's and become her man, body and soul, there will come a time, suddenly, when her patience will die and her wrath rise and you will die too. And for Miss Betty—there remains always the puma."

Rios spoke with every sign of sincerity. Kendric, with what he knew of Zoraida to guide his thoughts to a conclusion, was more than half convinced that the man was telling the truth. Rios himself was not above murder; hardly now had the body of Escobar stiffened when he seemed to have forgotten the rebel captain and the deed of violence. And Zoraida was Rios's blood cousin.

"You appear to be sure that there is treasure?" Kendric said.

"Yes. There is no question." Again was Rios unusually frank. "I could lie to you but there is no need. The treasure is beyond your reach; it may fall to my hand. Yes, I am sure."

"What do you know of it? What makes you so confident?"

Rios smiled.

"Again there is no need to lie to you. You have marked that my cousin is a very rich woman? There is no richer in all Mexico. And why? Because she has long been in possession of a portion of the hidden wealth of the Montezumas. A *portion*, mark you? For there is some sign which she has understood to tell her that there is still other hidden treasure. Always, since she was a little girl, has she looked for it, never content with what she has. And if I come first to it—Think, senor!" His eyes brightened, a flush warmed his dusky skin, he lifted his head arrogantly. "It will mean that I, even I, can dictate in some things to Zoraida! It will mean that she must join forces with me. It will mean that she and I together will go far, will rise high. As she will be the one bright star in all Mexico, so will I be the newly risen sun."

"So," muttered Kendric, "you two are tarred with the same stick!"

Now Rios's black eyes were deadly.

"What you know means everything to me," he said, his voice at last sunk to a harsh whisper. "I killed Escobar for less. Remember that, Senor Americano!"

Kendric ignored the threat.

"What of my friend?" he demanded. "Even were I of a mind to talk turkey with you, there is Barlow. Half is his."

"Barlow is touched with madness. Have I not told you he will have none of it? You have eyes, senor. Already my fair cousin has made of Barlow a tame animal like her cat. When she commands, he will speak. Think you he will remember in that dizzy moment that you have claims to be safeguarded? All will go to Zoraida. What you are pleased to call your share, along with his own."

Jim hated to believe that. And yet he did believe. Tonight Barlow had looked at him out of hard, unfriendly eyes; he, himself, had shot Barlow out of a cattle raider's saddle.— Suddenly, startling Rios, Kendric's fist came smashing down on his table.

"Here I've just been deciding the whole game is simple enough," he cried, "and along you come messing it all up again! Clear out. I'm going to sleep."

"And my answer?"

"Talk to me tomorrow, if you've a mind to. Most likely I'll tell you to go to blazes, but that can be said as well after breakfast as now."

Rios accepted his dismissal equably.

"For me there is gold at stake," he said, going out without protest. "For you there is your life and Miss Betty's. I can afford to wait as well as you. *Buenos noches, senor.*"

"Go to the devil," retorted Kendric, and banged the door shut after him.

Though he had not intimated his intention to his visitor, Kendric, holding to his determination to simplify matters, had made up his mind to have a talk with Barlow first of all. Since that could not come until tomorrow, the thing now was to go to bed. He undressed and put out his light. Then he flipped up his window shade. Only when he was about to thrust his head out of the open window to inhale the fragrant night air and have his little "look around," did he discover the bars to any possible escape there; a heavy iron grill had been fastened across the opening. Just how it was secured he could not tell since it had been set in place from outside and though he thrust his hand through the bars he could not reach far enough to locate the staples or hooks which held it in place. He shook it tentatively; it was amply solid.

But the door was open from his room to the bath. He groped his way across the smaller room and found the knob of the door which led to the room Barlow had occupied last night. That door was locked. As he fumbled with it he heard someone stir in Barlow's room.

"Who's there?" he called out. "That you, Twisty?"

There was no answer. He rapped on the door and called again. Then he heard quick steps across the room and a door closed; whoever had been there, listening without doubt to his talk with Rios, had gone.

He came back and passing through his own little sitting-room tried the door to the hall, that through which Rios had departed. Fastened by heavy iron hooks on the other side; he could hear them grate in their staples as he shook the door.

"A man had better be in bed this time of night than rapping at locked doors," he decided. And in five minutes was asleep.

CHAPTER XIII

CONCERNING WOMAN'S WILES AND WITCHERY

When Jim woke next morning his first act was to try doors and window. All were as he had left them last night. But since he was not the man for worry before breakfast he went into his tub singing. When he had splashed refreshingly in the cool water and thereafter had dressed, breakfast was ready for him. For, while he was in his own room he heard the door to the room Barlow had slept in the first night open. And when he went through the bath to see who was there he saw a tray spread on a little table by a window, the coffee steaming. No one was there. He tried the outer door which led to the hall. Locked, of course. So he sat down and uncovered the hot dishes and made a hearty meal.

"They've certainly got the big bulge on the situation," he conceded. "They could starve a man, poison his rolls or bore a bullet into him while he slept, and who outside to know about it?"

Now he had the run of four rooms and could look out into the gardens. Not so bad, he consoled himself. He had his smoke and sat back in his chair, assuring himself that there were advantages in being shut off by himself where he could take time to shape his plans. But as an hour passed in silence—not a sound from any part of the big house all of whose inmates might have been asleep or dead—and another hour dragged by after it, he grew first impatient and then angry. He had found

Jackson Gregory

that all of his planning could be done in five minutes: It resolved itself down to a decision to have a talk with Barlow and then, with or without help from Ruiz Rios, to make a bolt for the open. If Bruce and Barlow would come to their senses and join him, it would all be so simple. Three able-bodied, determined Americans against a handful of Zoraida's hirelings.

The time came when Jim thundered at the doors and called. When only silence followed his echoing voice he hammered at the hardwood doors with the butt of his revolver and shouted, demanding to be a let out. He tried the iron gratings over the windows and found them firm in their places and too heavy-barred to be bent. In the end he gave over in high disgust and waited.

Toward noon, while he was in his own room, pacing restlessly up and down, he heard a door slam. He ran to the bathroom and found that the door leading to Barlow's former quarters was closed and locked. Someone was moving about just beyond the thick panel. He heard the homely sound of dishes on a tray and waited, his hand on the doorknob, meaning to push his way forward once the door was opened. But he heard no other sound, though he waited minute after minute until perhaps half an hour had dragged by. Then he sat on the edge of the tub, grown stubborn, determined not to budge. And so another half hour passed.

An hour was a long time for Jim Kendric to sit or stand still and at the end of it he began pacing up and down again; at first just in the narrow confines of the bath, presently soft-footedly upon the soft carpet of his room. And no sooner had he stepped a dozen paces from the bathroom door than he heard a bolt shot back. He raced to the door that had so long baffled him and threw it open. As he did so he heard the outer hall door slam shut. When he laid hasty hands on it it was barred again.

"Well, there's food, anyway," he muttered. And sat down.

Half way through his meal a thought struck him which gave little zest to the rest of his food. He had walked silently when he left his post; no one waiting in the room where the tray was could have heard him, he felt sure. Then how did that person know the instant he stepped away? He could not have been spied on through the keyhole of the door since no keyhole was there; the fastening on the other side was simply that of primitive bar. But that he had been spied on he was confident. Well, why not? The house was old and no doubt had known no end of intrigue in its time. The walls were thick enough for passageways within them; an eye might be upon him all the time. He did not relish the thought but refused to grow fanciful over it.

The afternoon he spent stoically accepting his condition. As he put it to himself, the other fellow had the large, lovely bulge on the situation. For the most part of the sultry afternoon he sat in shirt-sleeved discomfort at his open window, staring out into the empty gardens and wondering what the other dwellers of the old adobe house were doing. Where were Bruce and Barlow and what lies was Zoraida telling them? And where was Betty? He did not realize that his wandering thoughts came back to Betty more often than to either of his friends whom he had known so many years. But realization was forced upon him that, despite all he had told both Zoraida and Ruiz Rios, he did feel a very sincere interest in her. When repeatedly vague fears on Betty's account disturbed him he told himself not to be a fool and sought to dismiss them for good. What though Zoraida had indulged in wild talk? At least she was a woman and though she held Betty for ransom would be woman enough to hold her in safety. And yet his fears surged back, stronger each time, and he would have given a good deal to know just where and how Betty was spending the long hours of this interminable day.

Finally came dusk, time of the first stars in the sky and lighted lamps in men's houses. And, bringing him infinite relief, a tap at his door and the gentle voice of Rosita saying:

"La Senorita invites Senor Kendric, if he has rested sufficiently, to join her and her other guests at table."

He followed the little maid to the great dim dining-room. Purple-shaded lamps created an atmosphere which impressed him as a little weird; the long table was set forth elaborately with much rich silver and sparkling glass; several men servants stood ready to place chairs and serve; there were rare white flowers in tall vases, looking a bluish-white under the lamps. As Kendric came to the threshold wide double doors across the room opened and Zoraida's other "guests" entered. They were Bruce, stiff and uncomfortable, seeming to be doing his best to unbend toward Betty; Betty herself, flushed and excited; Barlow, morose because of the arm he wore in a sling or because of a day not passed to his liking; and Ruiz Rios, suave and immaculate in white flannels.

When they were all in the room a constraint like a tangible inhibition against any natural spontaneity fell over them. Kendric read in Barlow's look no joy at the sight of him but only a sullen brooding; Betty flashed one look at him in which was nothing of last night's friendliness but an aloofness which might have been compounded of scorn and distrust; Bruce appeared not to notice him.

"Oh, well," was Kendric's inward comment. "The devil take the lot of them."

Zoraida did not keep them waiting. One of the servants, as though he had had some signal, threw open still another door and Zoraida, a splendid, vivid and vital Zoraida, burst upon their sight. She was gowned as though she had on the instant stepped from a fashionable Paris salon. And as though, on her swift way hither, she had stopped only an instant in some barbaric king's treasure house to snatch up and bedeck herself with his most resplendent jewels. Her arms were bare save for scintillating stones set in broad gold bands; long pendants, that seemed to live and breathe with their throbbing rubies, trembled from the tiny lobes of her shell-pink ears. Her throat was bare, her gown so daringly low cut at breast and back that Betty stared and flushed and turned away from the sight of her.

At her best was Zoraida tonight. Life stood high in her blood; zest shone like a bright fire in her eyes. A moment she poised, looking the queen which she meant to become, which already in her heart she felt herself. The inclination of her head as she greeted them, the graciousness which the moment drew from her, were regal.

Even the heavy arm-chair at the head of the table had the look of a throne. Two men drew it back for her, moved it into place when she was seated. Then she looked to her guests, smiled and nodded and in silence each accepted the place given him. Thus Jim Kendric sat at the other end of the table in a chair like Zoraida's. At his right was Betty who, since she averted her face from both him and Zoraida, kept her eyes on her plate. At his left was Ruiz Rios. To right and left of Zoraida sat Bruce and Barlow.

"I am afraid," said Zoraida lightly, embracing them all with her quick smile, "that I have seemed to lack in courtesy to my friends today! But here, *amigos*, when you come to know our land of the sun, you will understand that the long hot days are for rest and solitude in shady places while it is during the nights that one lives." A goblet of wine as yellow as butter stood at her hand having just been poured from an ancient misshapen earthen bottle. She lifted it and held it while the other glasses were filled. "I drink with you, my friends, to many golden nights!"

She scarcely more than touched the yellow wine with her lips and looked to the others. Barlow, still surly, tossed off his drink at a gulp. Bruce drank slowly, a little, and set his glass down. Betty did not lift her eyes and kept her hands in her lap. Ruiz tasted eagerly and his eyes sparkled and widened. Kendric mechanically set his glass to his lips, drank sparingly and marveled. For never had he tasted vintage like this. Its fragrance in his nostrils rose with strange pleasant sensation to his brain; a drop on his palate seemed to pass directly into his blood and electrically thrill throughout his whole body. The draft was like a magic brew; potent and seductive it soothed and at the same time set a delicious unrest in the blood, like that vaguely stirring unrest of youth in springtime.

Barlow, the sullen, alone had drunk deeply. And in a flash Barlow was another man. A warm color crept into his weathered cheeks, he drew himself up in his chair, his eyes shone. Zoraida, looking from face to face, laughed softly.

"What say you, my guests, to Zoraida's wine?" she said happily. "Made for Zoraida a full four hundred years ago, treasured for her in the vaults of the ancient Montezumas, distilled from the olden moonberry which no longer do men know where to find or how to grow! None but the Montezumas themselves and the priests of the great god Quetzel ever drank of it, and they only on great feast days of rejoicing. A taste, Miss Pansy Blossom, would bring back the roses to your pale cheeks. And see my friend Barlow!" Lightly, laughing, she laid her hand for a fleeting instant on his arm. "Already has the moonberry made his heart swell and blossom and filled it with dream stuff like honey!"

Something—the golden liquor in his veins or Zoraida's touch or the look in her eyes—emboldened the sea-faring man. He clamped his big hairy hand down over her slim fingers and cried out, half starting from his chair:

"It's in my mind, Zoraida, that the old Montezumas left more than bottled moonshine after them. To be taken by them that have the hearts for the job. Maybe for you—Yes, and for me!"

Zoraida drew her hand away but the laughter did not die in her eyes or pass away from her scarlet lips. Barlow, holding himself stiff, shot a look that was open challenge at Kendric who returned it wonderingly. Rios touched up the ends of his black mustachios and appeared highly good humored.

"Who knows?" said Zoraida softly, with a sidelong look at Kendric. "At least, spoken like a man, friend Barlow!"

Her mood was one of intense exhilaration. The movements of her supple body in her ample chair were quick and graceful and sinuous, like a slender snake's; she seemed a-thrill and glowing; it was as though for the moment life was for her as a great dynamo to which she had drawn close so that it sent its mighty pristine and vigorous current dancing through her. She lifted her glass and sipped while she still smiled; she saw Barlow's empty goblet and impulsively emptied into it half of her own. Though her back for the time was upon Bruce she seemed to feel his quick jealous frown, for she turned swiftly from Barlow, and her fingers fluttered to Bruce's shoulder. Kendric saw her eyes as she gave them to Bruce in a look that was like a kiss. The boy flushed and when she made further amends by holding to his lips her own glass, he touched it almost reverently.

Kendric, sickening with disgust at what he chose to consider a competition in assininity between his two old friends, turned from them to Betty with some trivial remark. As he spoke he was contrasting her with the splendid Zoraida and had he voiced the comparison Zoraida must have whitened with anger and mortification while Betty flushed up, startled. He would have said; "One is like a poison serpent and the other like a flower." But instead of that he merely said:

"And how have you spent the long day, Miss Betty?"

Betty raised her head and looked at him steadily. A flower? Quickly, even before she spoke, he amended that. A girl, rather; a girl with a mind of her own and a sorching [Transcriber's note: scorching?] hot temper and her utterly human moments of unreasonableness. Her glance meant to cut and did cut. Her voice was serene, cool and contemptuous.

"I do not require to be amused, thank you," she said.

"Amused?" demanded Kendric, puzzled equally by words and expression.

"I am here against my will," she explained. "You are among your chosen friends. To entertain me you need not deny yourself the pleasure of their delightful conversation."

"You know better than that," he said sharply. "If you don't care to talk with me—"

"I don't," said Betty.

Kendric reddened angrily. He opened his lips for the retort he meant to make; then instead gulped down his wine and sat back glowering. After having been fool enough to worry over her all day long to be told to hold his tongue now set him to forming sweeping and denunciatory generalizations concerning her entire sex. Well, he wanted matters simplified and here came the desired solution. Betty could forage for herself, could go to the devil if she liked, he told himself bluntly. Before the night passed he meant to make a break for the open and, thank God, he'd go alone. As a man should, with no woman around his neck. Because a girl had hurt him he chose now to pretend to himself that he was glad to be rid of her.

After that, during the meal, both Jim and Betty sat for the most part silent and Rios, nursing his mustache and watching all that went forward, had little to say. On the other hand Zoraida and Bruce and Barlow made the dinner hour lively with their talk. Skilled in her management of men, Zoraida had never shown greater genius for holding two red blooded, ardent men in leash. She threw favors to each side of her; a tumbled rose from her hair was loot for the sailorman who at the moment was of a mood to forget other greater and more golden loot for the scented, wilting petals; a bracelet coming undone was for Bruce's eager fingers to fasten. And always when she looked at one man with a kiss in her oblique eyes her head was turned so that the other man might not see. Kendric she ignored.

"The same old story of good men gone wrong," philosophized Kendric. "Let a man get a woman in his head and he's no earthly good." And, in his turn, he ignored Betty. Or at least assured himself that he did so. But Betty, being Betty, though for the most part her eyes seemed downcast, knew that the man at her side thought of little but her own exasperating self. She did a good bit of speculating upon Jim Kendric; she was perplexed and uncertain; when he was not observing she shot many a curious sidelong look at him.

"Miss Zoraida is about due to overreach herself," thought Kendric. "She can't drive Barlow and Bruce tandem."

But Zoraida appeared to feel no uneasiness. As the meal went on and meats and fruits were served and other vintages poured and coffee set bubbling over a tiny alcohol flame on the table, her spirits rose and she dared anything. She was sure of herself and of her destiny and of her dominance over the pleasureable situation. Bruce's eyes and Barlow's clashed like knives, but when they met hers softened and worshiped.

At the end of the meal, when they rose, Zoraida cried: "Wait!" At her signal her servants swiftly lifted the table and carried it out through the double doors. Another smaller table was brought in; a man came to Zoraida with a small steel box. She took it laughing, and laughing spilled its contents out upon the table so that gold pieces rolled jingling across the polished top and some fell to the floor. With her own hands she carelessly divided the gold into four nearly equal piles.

"For my guests!" she told them lightly. She took from the servant's hands a deck of cards and tossed it down among the minted gold. "I would watch such men as you four play for the whole stake. And," she added more slowly, her burning look embracing them all but lingering upon Jim Kendric, "I have a curiosity to know who of you in my house is the most favored of the gods!"

"There's a goodly pile there, Senorita," said Barlow who could never look upon gold without hungering. "You mean it all goes to the man who wins? And you don't play?"

"All that," she answered him steadily, "goes to the man who wins. With perhaps much more? Who knows?"

Bruce stepped eagerly to the table where already Barlow was before him with a heap of the gold drawn up to his hand. Ruiz Rios took his place indifferently, affecting a look of ennui. Kendric held back. Betty, aloof from them all, looked about her as though to escape. But at each door, as though forbidding exit, stood one of Zoraida's men.

"You yourself do not play?" Barlow asked of Zoraida.

"This time, my friend," she replied, "I am content to watch."

Content rather, thought Kendric, to amuse herself by stirring up more bad blood among friends. For the look he saw on her face was one of pure malicious mischief. It occurred to him that she had sorrowed not at all over the taking off of Escobar at Rios's hand; he had the suspicion that in her cleverness she discerned looming trouble as a result of encouraging the infatuations of two men like Bruce and Barlow, and that before she would let herself be destroyed by an inevitable jealous rage she meant to set them at each other's throats. Such an act he deemed entirely germane to Zoraida's dark methods.

"Senor Jim does not care to play?" she asked quietly.

Had not Betty chosen to look at him then Kendric's answer would have been a blunt, "No." But Betty did look, and the glance was as eloquent as a gush of stinging words. Without a clue to the girl's thoughts, he merely set her down as the most illogical, impertinent and irritating creature it had ever been his bad lot to encounter. For her eyes told him that he was an animal of some sort of a crawling species which she abhorred. This after he had put in long troubled hours seeking the way to be of service to her!

"Bah," he said in his heart, staring coldly at her until she averted her eyes, "they're all the same." And to Zoraida, "I'll play but I play with my own money."

Zoraida only laughed. His open rudeness seemed unmarked.

"Barlow," said Kendric, "I want a word with you first."

Barlow did not turn or lift his eyes.

"Talk fast then," he retorted. "The game's waiting."

"In private, if you don't mind," urged Kendric.

Now Barlow looked at him sullenly.

"After what happened last night, Kendric," he said heavily, "you and me have got no private business together. Am I the man to take a bullet from another and then go chin with him?"

"You blame me for that?" Kendric was incredulous. Barlow snorted. "Well," continued Kendric stiffly, "at least we've unfinished business between us. You haven't forgotten what brought us down here, have you?"

"Treasure, you mean?" Barlow spat out the words defiantly. "Put the name to it, man! Well, what of it?"

"The understanding was that we stand together. That we split what we find fifty-fifty. Does that still go?"

Barlow pulled nervously at his forelock, his eyes wandering. For an instant they were fixed on the smiling face of Zoraida. Then grown dogged they came back to Kendric.

"Hell take the understanding!" he blurted out savagely. "We stand even tonight, one as close to the loot as the other. It's every man for himself, whole hog or none, and the devil take the hindmost. That's what it is!"

"Good," snapped Kendric. "That suits me." He slammed his little pad of bank notes down on the table and took his chair. "What's the game, gentlemen?"

They named it poker and played hard. Reckless men with money were they all, men accustomed to big fast games. The most reckless of them, Jim Kendric, was in a mood for anything provided it raced. Betty's attitude, Betty's look, had stirred him after a strange new fashion which he did not analyze. Barlow's unreasonable unfriendliness hurt and angered; the jeer in Rios's hard black eyes ruffled his blood. And even young Bruce looked at him with a defiance which Kendric had no stomach for. From the first card played, Jim Kendric, like a pace maker in a race, stamped his spirit upon the struggle.

Betty, seeing that she was not to be allowed to go sat down and for a space made a pretense of ignoring what went forward before her. But presently as the atmosphere grew strained and intense, she forgot her pretense and leaned forward and watched eagerly. Zoraida had a couch drawn up for her, richly colored silken cushions placed to her taste, and stretched out luxuriously, her chin in her two hands.

There are isolated games wherein chance enters which make one wonder what is this thing named chance, and from which one rises at last touched by the superstition which holds so firm a place in the hearts of all gamblers. From the beginning it was Jim Kendric's game. When a jack-pot was opened he went into it with an ace high, though it cost him a hundred dollars to call for cards, which was not playing poker but defying mathematics and challenging his luck. And the four cards given him by Bruce, whose blue eyes named him fool, were two more aces and two queens. And the pot that was close to ten hundred dollars before the sweetening was done, was his. Barlow, who had lost most, glared at him and muttered under his breath; young Bruce merely stared incredulously and looked again at the cards to make sure; Rios, who had kept clear, smiled and murmured:

"Lucky at cards, unlucky in love, senor."

"I prefer the cards, thanks," said Kendric, stacking his winnings. And there was enough of the boy left in him for him to look briefly for the first time at Betty. Zoraida saw and bit her lip.

But though it was borne in upon those who played and those who watched that it was Jim Kendric's game there were the inevitable tense moments when each man in turn had his own eager hope. Bruce, no cool hand at gambling, showed his excitement in his shining blue eyes; Barlow muttered to himself; Rios sat forward in his chair and left off pointing the tips of his mustaches. At the end of the first half hour, though Kendric's heap of winnings was by far the greatest, no man of them was down to bed rock.

And by now Kendric lost patience.

"Make it a jack pot for table stakes," he invited. "One hand for the whole thing!"

"What's the hurry?" demanded Bruce. "You're doing well enough as it is, aren't you?"

"A quick killing is better than slow torture," returned Jim lightly. "And you'll note that I am offering odds. Better than two to one against the flushest of you."

"*Bueno, senor,*" said Rios. "It suits me."

"It's a fool thing to do," growled Barlow. A fool thing for Kendric, but not for him, since his were the biggest losses. He had always loved money, had Twisty Barlow, and could never understand Headlong Kendric's contempt for it and now looked at him as though at one gone mad. Then he shrugged. "Suits me," he said.

"Wait!" Zoraida suddenly leaped to her feet, tossed out her

arms in a wide gesture, her eyes unfathomable and shining with the mystery of a hidden thought. "I am glad to have in my house men like you four! You are *men*! Were it life or death, love or war or wealth, you would play the game the same. Men like you make the blood run hot in the heart of Zoraida who also grips life by the naked throat. Wait. And look."

She whirled and in another moment, as lithe as a cat, had sprung to the top of a serving table half across the room. And there she displayed herself in all her barbaric splendor, posing like a model in an artist's studio, turning slowly, standing at last confronting them, a-thrill with her own daring.

"Would you play for such a stake as never men played for before? For such a stake as kings would risk their crowns for? As such Zoraida offers herself, pledging her word to make the rich gift of herself to the man who wins!"

For a moment all four and Betty with them and the serving men at the doors stared at her and the room was dead still. Through the deep silence cut Zoraida's laugh, clear and sweet as a silver bell. Under their bewildered gaze she preened herself like a peacock, proud of her beauty so boldly displayed before their eyes. Zoraida smiled slowly.

"Is the stake high enough for your play?" she asked gently, in mock humility.

Bruce surged up from his chair only to drop back into it without having said a word. Rios's eyes caught fire and for the first time Kendric guessed that he, too, was in heart bond-servant to his amazing cousin. Barlow tugged at his forelock and muttered.

"Heap all the gold together," cried Zoraida. "Play for it and each man of you pray his favorite god for success. For with it goes Zoraida!"

Betty, looking at her out of round eyes, seemed once more the little girl Kendric had first taken her to be.

"Will you play?" said Zoraida softly.

"Yes! By God, yes!" cried Barlow.

Rios merely nodded and shoved his money to the middle of the table. Bruce started like a man from a dream and with hands that shook visibly thrust forward his own gold. Then all looked to Kendric.

Impulse decided for him and his answer came with no measurable time of hesitation. If he played and lost, as he looked at it, there was nothing to regret. If he played and won, perhaps it would have been Zoraida's own all-hazarding hands which had shown the way to break the chains that bound his two friends to her. It would need something like this to bring both Bruce and Barlow to their senses. It was mostly of Bruce that he thought just then.

"One hand of cards?" said Barlow.

"Rather one card, my friend," said Kendric drily. "We are keeping a lady waiting."

"Oh!" gasped Betty.

A shining pyramid was made of the gold pieces. Then the cards were shuffled and one of the serving men was called forward. He dealt one card to each of the four men, face down, and stepped back. Then the cards were turned over.

All were high cards, not one lower than a ten, yet with no two alike. The one ace—the ace of hearts—lay in front of Jim Kendric.

CHAPTER XIV

CONCERNING A DIFFICULT SITUATION, RECKLESSLY INVITED

For a moment in the heavy silence Jim Kendric sat appalled by what he had done. In the grip of the game he had been swayed by emotion, not tarrying for cold logic during an episode when time raced. He had hoped to win. Thus, since he had discovered that Rios, too, was enamored of his beautiful cousin, he would tease an old enemy, sober Bruce, jolt Barlow—and vex Betty. He had not thought of himself nor of Zoraida.

No one spoke. The first sound was a long shuddering breath from young Bruce; his face was a sick white save for a spot of red in each cheek; his eyes looked like those of a man with a high fever. Kendric sat staring in perplexity at the gold he had won, automatically gathering it toward him. Zoraida stood motionless, displaying herself, awaiting his eyes. And abruptly, when he lifted his head, his eyes went not to her but to Betty.

The girl appeared fascinated and horrified. Jim's eyes pleaded with her. Betty began to twist her hands in an agony of bewildered emotions. Zoraida, waiting for Jim's face to be lifted to her and not one accustomed to waiting on a man, frowned. But swiftly and before anyone but the always watchful Rios saw, she broke the silence with her little cooing laughter. She put out her two white arms toward the men at the table, saying softly:

"Will you help me down, Senor Jim?"

Before Kendric could answer Bruce was on his feet. The blood charged to his face so that the red spots were merged in the crimson flood. The boy looked ready for murder.

"Stop this, Zoraida!" he said excitedly. "Stop it! You are mad. Have you forgotten?—Good God!"

"Betty—" said Kendric, hardly knowing what he would say. He wanted her to understand—

"Don't speak to me!" Betty flung the words at him passionately. "You are an unthinkable beast!"

Bruce heard nothing that was said, saw nothing but Zoraida. He came two steps toward her and then stopped, staring at her.

"Zoraida," he commanded, as one who speaks with love's authority, "you don't realize what you are doing. It is that cursed wine you have drunk or there is just desperation in the air and it has got into you. This hideous jest has gone far enough—too far. Tell them, tell Kendric, that it was all a jest. Nothing more."

"Had you won," said Zoraida sweetly, "what then, Senor Bruce? Would you have been jesting?"

Bruce's lips moved but no words came. Suddenly he whirled from her upon Kendric, his face distorted with rage.

"Damn you!" he burst out.

No longer was it merely a case of murder in his look. The urge to kill had swept into his heart, rushed hotly along his pounding arteries. Before now had Kendric seen men frenzy-lashed, like Bruce, briefly insane with the blood impulse and as Bruce cursed him he knew that he meant to kill him. There were half a dozen paces between the two men and already was Bruce's hand lost under the skirt of his coat. Kendric sprang to his feet and as he did so Bruce whipped out his pistol. There seemed no loss of time between the action and the discharge. But Kendric had been quick and only his promptness saved the life in him that night. As he went to his feet he swept up in his hand a heap of the shining gold pieces and flung them straight into the boy's purpling face. The bullet went by Kendric's head doing no harm beyond splintering the wall behind him. Before Bruce could shake his head and fire again Kendric was upon him, worrying him as a dog worries a cat. Bruce, even in the desperation driving him, and with a gun in his hand, was little more than a stripling in the hard hands at his wrist and throat. A sudden heave and mighty jerk came close to breaking his arm and freed the pistol from his claw-like fingers. Kendric hurled him back so that Bruce staggered half across the room and crashed to the floor. Before he could come to his feet the pistol had been dropped into Kendric's coat pocket.

During the whole time Twisty Barlow had sat like a man bereft of volition, his face puckered queerly, his mouth a little open. He looked at the gold on the table top and at Zoraida; when Kendric had hurled the coins into Bruce's face he looked at the gold rolling across the floor and again back to Zoraida. Rios, having risen quietly, stood with one hand on the back of his chair, one hand at his mustache, looking steadily at his cousin. Even while Kendric and Bruce battled Rios gave them scant attention. He was watching Zoraida as though his life itself depended on his reading her wild heart aright.

Slowly, as though he had been half stunned, Bruce rose from the floor. Once more his face was white and looked sick. He had in his eyes the startled expression of a man rudely awakened from profound slumber. He walked with dragging feet across the room and dropped wearily into a chair. He put his elbows on his knees and his head into his hands.

Zoraida, seeing that Kendric would not come to her, caught up her gown and leaped lightly down, landing softly like a cat.

She put into her eyes what she pleased, a confusion of messages, a swooning passion, a maidenly tenderness, a joy that seemed to peep forth shyly. On tiptoes, as though she would not break the hush of the room, she went to the hall door, smiling a little in her backward look. A moment she whispered to the serving man at the door; then she was gone and they heard only the light patter of her slippers.

The man to whom Zoraida had whispered spoke in an undertone to his fellows. One of them went out swiftly; the others threw wide the three doors and then gathered up the fallen gold. It was replaced in its box and gravely presented to Kendric. He threw back the lid, thrust into his pocket without counting what he deemed equal to the amount he had played and tossed the box back to the servant.

"Divide with your friends," he said shortly, and turned toward Betty. But already, with the doors open, she had sought escape. He saw the whisk of her skirt and marked the erect carriage of her head of brown hair as she went out.

Jim Kendric stood looking about him and cursed himself for a fool. Headlong he had always been, plunging ever into deep waters that were not over clear, but he could not recall the time he had been a greater blunderer. He had no more than decided that the one thing for him to do was to simplify matters than here he went already interfering in other people's business and making a mess of the whole thing. Betty adjudged him being desirous of becoming Zoraida's lover; Bruce sought his death; Rios's eyes were like knives; Barlow still sent his sullen glances from the box of gold in a servant's hands to the door through which Zoraida had passed. Kendric went to where Bruce still sat and put his hand gently on the slack shoulder.

"Bruce, old man—" he said.

But Bruce, though with little spirit in the movement, shook the hand away.

"There's no call for talk between you and me, Jim," he said wearily. "Talk can't change things. Just now I wanted to kill you!" He shuddered.

The man with whom Zoraida had whispered was speaking quietly with Rios. Kendric, seeing them beyond Bruce's bowed head, saw a fire of rebellion burning in Rios's eyes. Then, surprising him when he expected an outburst, Rios merely shrugged his shoulders and left the room. The servant came on to Barlow. Again he whispered. Barlow heard him through stolidly, then for the first time looked long and steadily at Kendric. Kendric guessed from the workings of his face that he was struggling with his own problem. Gradually the sailor closed his mouth until at last the teeth were clamped tight, the muscles at the corners of his jaw bulging.

"Barlow," said Kendric then, "there's too infernally much whispering in corners in this house. Even if we three seem to be at cross purposes now we have been friends—"

"You talk of friendship!" Barlow spoke with cold bitterness. "When here I crawl around with a hole in my shoulder; when West there in his chair has just tried to bore you and got smashed in the face for his trouble? After what's happened tonight, man, you and me are done." He stalked off to the door. But at the threshold he paused long enough to turn and mutter: "We all know what we are after, I guess. Don't fool yourself, Jim Kendric, that everything's landslidin' you [Transcriber's note: your?] way."

Plainly Zoraida's orders had been intended to clear the room save for Kendric. For the servant came to Bruce when Barlow had gone and spoke to him. Kendric tried to catch the words but could not. But he saw Bruce suddenly jerk up his head and watched a slow return of color into the drawn face. Then Bruce, eyeing Kendric with suspicion and in open hostility, quitted him in a silence that was ominous.

Kendric's anger, ever ready like his mirth, burned hot through him. He had shot Barlow in Bruce's quarrel, not knowing Barlow in the dark, and for this Barlow hated him. Bruce had sought to kill him, and for this Bruce hated him. He had sought to befriend Betty, and Betty hated him. He had played fair with them all, and now all of them were set against him.

"Devil take the whole outfit!" he cried out passionately. "From now on, Jim Kendric, you feather your own nest and hit the one-man trail for the open."

The servingman, whom Zoraida's commands had constituted a sort of master of ceremonies, came to Kendric, his look curious but not unfriendly. The box with its gold was still in his hands.

"You will follow me, senor?" he invited. "*La Senorita Reinita* awaits you."

"I'll do nothing of the sort," snapped Kendric. "I am going outside for a smoke and you can tell your lady queen so with my compliments."

But the man stood in front of him, shaking his head dubiously. He looked distressed. In his simple mind orders from Zoraida were orders absolute, and yet such largesse as Jim's bought respect and something akin to affection.

"Later you will smoke outside, senor," he urged. "Now it would be best—oh, surely, best, senor!—to follow me to La Senorita."

Jim shoved by him toward the door. The fellow looked a trifle uncertain, his small calibre brain confused by two contending impulses. But in an instant long habit and an old fear that was greater than his new liking, asserted themselves. He slipped between Kendric and the door and at his glance the other servant joined him. The two glanced at each other and then at Kendric's set and determined face and then looked swiftly down the long hallway behind them. This look was eloquent and Kendric guessed its meaning; that way had their companion gone hastily when Zoraida had left; that way, perhaps, would he be returning presently with others of her hireling pack at his heels.

"Stand aside," commanded Jim. "I'm on my way."

They were stalwart men and they did not stand aside. Rather they stepped closer together, shoulder to shoulder, grim in their stubborn obedience to the orders they had been given. Sick of waiting and words and obstructions, Kendric bore down on them, vowing to go through though they might raise an outcry and double their strength. They were ready for him and stood up to him. But their impulse of obedience and routine duty was a pale weak motive before his rage at eternal hindrance. He charged them like a mad bull; he struck to right and left with the mighty blows of lusty battle-joy, and though they struck back and sought to grapple with him he hurled one of them against the wall with a bleeding mouth and sent the other toppling backward, crashing to the floor in the hall. And through he went, growling savagely. But only to confront the third man returning with half a dozen sullen-eyed half breeds at his heels, only to see beyond them the bright interested eyes of Zoraida.

"Call your hound dogs off," he roared at her. "I'm going through."

Zoraida clapped her hands.

"*Muchachos*," she commanded them, "tame me this wild man! But no pistols or knives, mind you!"

She drew up close to one wall and watched; she might have been an excited child at a three-ring circus. Kendric found time to marvel at her even as he shot by her, hurling the whole of his compact weight into the mass of bodies defying him passageway. And as flesh struck flesh, Zoraida clapped her hands again and watched eagerly.

"One against six—seven," she whispered. "One against nine!" she added, for already the two men who had sought to hold Kendric back from the hallway were up and after him. "He is a mad fool—and yet, by the breath of God, he is a man!"

And a man's fight did he treat her to, carried out of himself, gone for the moment the madman she had named him. It was Jim Kendric's way to fight in silence, but now he shouted as he struck, defying them, cursing them, striking as hard as God had given him strength, recking not in the least of blows received, heart and mind centered alone on the pulsing, throbbing prayer to feel a bone crack before him, to see a head snap back, to feel blood gush forth from a battered face. A man tripped him cunningly from the side and he all but fell. But he struck back with his boot and steadied himself by hurling his toppling body against a resisting body and crashed on. Yes, and through, though they clutched at him and dragged after him! A man hung to his belt and he dragged him four or five steps; then he turned and drove his fist into the man's neck and freed himself and bore on. So he came to the end of the hall and to a locked door and turned with his back to the wall. And again Zoraida's hound dogs were in front of him.

He laughed at them and taunted them and reviled them. They were nine men and upon many of the dark faces were signs of his passing. And as they came closer there was respect as well as caution in their look. They meant to beat him down; in their minds was no doubt of the ultimate outcome, for were they not nine to one? But they had felt his fists and had no joy in the memory. So they drew on slowly.

Kendric watched them narrowly. In the eyes of the nearest man he saw a sudden flickering; it flashed over him that the fellow meant trickery and no fair man-to-man fight. He stood with his back to the door; he saw the approaching man's eyes switch to it briefly. Then it flashed upon Kendric that he was to be attacked from behind—

But even as the thought came and before he could leap aside, the door was jerked open and from behind he felt arms about him. He struggled and strained in a tensing grip. Not just one man was there behind him; two at the very least and maybe three. He heard them muttering. Then the men in front came on in a flying body and with a dozen men piling over him Jim Kendric at last went down. And once down, being the man to know when he had played out his string, he lay still.

"Will *el senor* Jim come with me?" Zoraida was above him, smiling curiously. "Or shall I have him carried along by my men?"

"I'll come," he answered shortly. "Having no choice. Call them off before I stifle."

Zoraida ordered, the men fell back and Kendric rose. She made a quick signal and they filed out through a further door.

"Come," she said to him. She caught up a cloak which had slipped from her shoulders, a thing of silken scarlet, and led the way down the hall.

He followed, ready and eager for a talk with her which would be the last. He fully meant to make a break for the open tonight. And alone. He was assuring himself that he drew a vast pleasure from that consideration—that he was free from now on to play out his own hand in his own way without reference to others. What he did not admit to himself was that he was trumping up an explanation of the fact that, while he was following Zoraida, he was thinking of Betty. He was wondering where Betty had gone in such a flurry, when he should have been asking himself where Zoraida was taking him and for what purpose of her own.

CHAPTER XV

OF THE ANCIENT GARDENS OF THE GOLDEN TEZCUCAN

He supposed that Zoraida was conducting him to the barbaric chamber in which she had received him the other evening. For she led, as the little maid had done, out under the stars, along the rear corridor, into the house again by the same door. Once more in the building they came to that heavy door which in time was thrown open by the evil-looking Yaqui with the sinister weapons at his belt. The man bowed deeply as Zoraida swept by him. Another moment and Zoraida and Jim were in the room which appeared always to be pitch black. But from here on the way was no longer the same.

He heard Zoraida's quiet breathing at his side. She stood a long time without moving, apparently waiting or listening, and he stood as still. Then she put out her hand and caught his sleeve and he followed her again. Their footfalls were deadened by a thick carpet; Kendric could see nothing. Never a sound came to him save that of their own quiet progress. They went forward a dozen steps and Zoraida paused abruptly. Another dozen steps and again a pause. Then he heard the soft jingle of keys in her hands; lock after lock she found swiftly in the dark until she must have shot back five or six bolts; a door opened before them. He could not see it, since beyond was a dark no less impenetrable, but caught the familiar creak of hinges. He heard the door close softly when they had gone through; he heard the several bolts shot back. Then Zoraida left him, groped a moment and thereafter the tiny flare of a match in her upheld hand showed her to him and, vaguely, his surroundings. They stood in a low-vaulted, narrow passageway through what appeared to be rock.

Set in a shallow niche in the wall was a small lamp which Zoraida lighted. She held it high and continued along the passageway. Now Kendric saw that a long tunnel ran ahead of them, walls and ceiling rudely chisseled, the uneven floor pitching gently downward. Herein two men, their elbows striking, might walk abreast; here a man as tall as Kendric must stoop now and then. The tunnel ran straight a score of paces, then turned abruptly to the right. Here was another door with its reenforcement of riveted steel bars and its half dozen bolts and padlocks. Zoraida gave him the lamp to hold, then produced a second bunch of keys and one after the other opened the padlocks. The door swung back noiselessly; they went through, Zoraida closed it and dropped into place the steel bars.

"Doors and bars and locks and keys enough," mocked Kendric, "to guard the treasure of the Montezumas!"

She turned upon him with her slow, mysterious smile.

"And not alone in doors and locks has Zoraida put her faith," she said. "If I had not prepared the way neither you nor another man, though he held the keys, could ever have come so far! I have been before and removed certain small obstructions. Come! I will show you others, Zoraida's true safeguards."

They were in a small square chamber faced with oak on all sides excepting ceiling and floor which were of hewn rock. The panels of the walls, each some two feet wide, had, all of them, the look of narrow doors, each with its heavy latch. Zoraida put her hand to the nearest latch and opened the door cautiously. Kendric saw only a long, very narrow and dark passageway.

"Listen," commanded Zoraida.

He heard nothing.

"Toss something down into the passage," said Zoraida. "Anything, a coin if you have no other useless object upon you."

So a coin it was. He heard it strike and roll and clink against rock. Then he heard the other sound, a dry noise like dead leaves rattling together. Despite him he drew back swiftly. Zoraida laughed and closed the door.

"You know what it is then?"

He knew. It was the angry warning of a rattlesnake; his quickened fancies pictured for him a dark alleyway whose floor was alive with the deadly reptiles and he felt an unpleasant prickling of the flesh.

"If you went on," she told him serenely, "and you chose any door but the right one—and there are twelve doors—you would never come to the end of a short hallway. And, even though you happened to choose the right door, it were best for you if Zoraida went ahead. Come, my friend."

She opened another door and stepped into the narrow opening. Though he had little enough liking for the expedition, Kendric followed. Once more he heard a rustling as of thousands of dry, parched leaves, and was at loss to know whence came the ominous sound. Again Zoraida laughed, saying: "I have been before and prepared the way," and they went on. Then came another door with still other bars and locks. Zoraida unlocked one after the other, then stood back, looking at him with the old mischief showing vaguely in her eyes.

"Open and enter," she said.

He threw back the door. But on the threshold he stopped and stared and marveled. Zoraida's pleased laughter now was like a child's.

"You are the first man, since Zoraida's father died, to come here," she told him. "And never another man will come here until you and I are dead. It is a place of ancient things, my friend; it is the heart of Ancient Mexico."

The heart of Ancient Mexico! Without her words he would have known, would have felt. For old influences held on and the atmosphere of the time of the Montezumas still pervaded the place. He forgot even Zoraida as he stepped forward and stopped again, marveling.

Here was a chamber of colossal proportions and more than a chamber in that it gave the impression of being without walls or roof. And in a way the impression was correct for straight overhead Kendric saw a ragged section of the heavens, bright with stars, and at first he failed to see the remote walls because of the shrubbery everywhere. Here was a strange underground garden that might have been the courtyard to an oriental monarch's palace, a region of spraying fountains, of heavily scented flowers, of berry-bearing shrubs, of birds of brilliant plumage. It was night; the stars cast small light down here into the depths of earth; and yet it was some moments before the startled Kendric asked himself the question: "Where does the full light come from?" And it was still other moments before he located the first of the countless lamps, lamps with green shades lost behind foliage, lamps set in recesses, lamps everywhere but cunningly placed so that one was bathed in their light without having the source of the illumination thrust into notice.

That here, at some long dead time of Mexican history, had been the retreat of some barbaric king Kendric did not doubt from the first sweeping glance. He knew something of the way in which the ancient monarchs had builded pleasure palaces for their luxurious relaxation; how whole armies of slaves, captured in war, were set at a giant task like other captives in older days in Egypt; he knew how thousands, tens of thousands of such poor wretches hopelessly toiled to build with their misery places of flowers and ease; how to celebrate many a temple or palace completed these poor artificers in a mournful procession of hundreds or thousands as the dignity of the endeavor required, went to the sacrifice. Now, standing here at Zoraida's side in this great still place, these thoughts winged to him swiftly, and for the moment he felt close to the past of Mexico.

"What was once the country place of Nezahualcoyoti, the Golden King of Tezcuco," said Zoraida, "is now the favorite garden of Zoraida. For the great Nezahualcoyoti captive workmen, laboring through the days and nights of many years, builded here as we see, my friend. Here he was wont to come when he would have relief from royal labor and intrigue, to shut himself up with music and feasting and those he loved. Here he came, be sure, with the beloved princess whom he ravished away from the old lord of Tepechpan. And here she remained awaiting him when he returned to the royal place at Tezcotzinco. And here were placed, four hundred and fifty years ago, the ashes of the golden king and of his beloved princess—and here they remain until this night. Come, Senor Americano; you shall see something of Zoraida's garden which after Nezahualcoyoti came in due time to be Montezuma's and after him, Guatamotzin's."

Kendric found himself drawn out of his angry mood of a few minutes past, charmed out of himself by his environment. Following Zoraida he passed along a broad walk winding through low shrubs and lined on each side with uniform stones of various colors that were like jewels. These boundaries were no doubt of choice fragments of finely polished chalcedony and jasper and obsidian; they were red and yellow and black and, at regular intervals, a pale exquisite blue which in the rays of the lamps were as beautiful as turquoises. They passed about a screen of dwarf cedars and came upon a tiny lakelet across which a boy might have hurled a stone; in the center, sprayed by a fountain that shone like silver, was a life-sized statue in marble representing a slender graceful maiden.

"The beloved princess," whispered Zoraida.

They went on, skirting the pool in which Kendric saw the stars mirrored. Now and then there was a splash; he made out a tortoise scrambling into the water; he caught the glint of a fish. They disturbed birds that flew from their hidden places in the trees; a little rabbit, like a tiny ball of fur, shot across their path.

Before them the central walk lay in shadows, under a vine-covered trellis. A hundred paces they went on, catching enchanting glimpses through the walls of leaves. Here was a column, gleaming white, elaborately carved with what were perhaps the triumphs of the golden king or some later monarch; yonder the walls of a miniature temple, more guessed than seen among the low trees; on every hand some relic of the olden time. Suddenly and without warning amidst all of this tender beauty of flowers and murmurous water and birds and perfumes Kendric came upon that which lasted on as a true sign to recall the strange nature of the ancient Aztec, a nation of refinement and culture and hideous barbarism and cruelty; a nation of epicures who upon great feast days ate of elaborately-served dishes of human flesh; a people who, in a garden like this, could find no inconsistency, no clash of discordancy, in introducing that which bespoke merciless cruelty and death, a grim token and reminder that a king's palace was a slaughter house as well; a strange race whose ears were attuned to ravishing strains of music and yet found no breach of harmony if those singing notes were pierced through with the shrieks of the tortured dying. Just opposite the most enchanting spot in these underground groves of pleasure was a great pyramidal heap of human skulls, thousands of them.

"The builders," explained Zoraida calmly. "Those who obeyed the commands of the Tezcucan king, who made his dream a reality, who were in the end sacrificed here. Five priests, alternating with another five, were unremitting night and day until at last the great sacrifice was complete. The records are there," and she pointed to a remote corner of the garden where vaguely through the greenery he made out stone columns; "I have seen them and I have made my own tally. Not less than ten thousand captives expired here." It struck Kendric that there was a note of pride in her tone. "Look; yonder is the great stone of sacrifice."

He drew closer, at once repelled and fascinated. A few yards from the base of the heap of skulls was a great block of jasper, polished and of a smoothness like glass. Upon this one after another of ten thousand human beings, strong struggling men and perhaps women and children had lain, while priests as terrible as vultures held them, while one priest of high skill and infinite cruelty drove his knife and made his gash and withdrew the anguished beating heart to hold it high above his head. Again Zoraida pointed; on the stone lay the ancient knife, a blade of "itztli," obsidian, dark, translucent, as hard as flint, a product of volcanic fires.

Kendric turned from stone and knife and human relics and looked with strange new wonder at Zoraida. She claimed kin with the royalty of this ancient order; perhaps her claim was just. He had wondered if she were mad; was not his answer now given him? Was she not after all that not uncommon thing called a throw-back, a reversion to an ancestral type? If in fact there flowed in her veins the blood of that princess of the golden king of Tezcuco who could have smiled at the whisperings of her lord and the tender cadences of music floating through the gardens his love had made for her, while just here his priests made their sacrifices and she, turning her eyes from his ardent ones, now and then languorously watched—was Zoraida mad or was she simply ancient Aztec or Toltec or Tezcucan, born four or five hundred years after her time? Her slow smile now as she watched him and no doubt read at least a portion of what lay in his mind, was baffling; he might have been looking back through the long dead years upon the Tezcucan's princess: in her eyes were tender passion and a glint that might have been a reflection of light from the sacrificial knife.

Speculation aside, here was one point which Zoraida herself had vouched for: since girlhood she had been accustomed to coming here. It would appear inevitable that the atmosphere of the place would have deeply influenced young fancies; that what she was now was largely due to these conflicting influences. What wonder that she saw nothing unlikely in her dreamings of herself as queen of a newly created empire? All that Zoraida was, all that she did, all that she threatened to do, the passion and the regal manner and the look of a naked knife in her eyes, was but to be expected.

Zoraida led on and he followed. Their way led toward the stonework he had glimpsed through the shrubs and vines. Here was a many-roomed building, walls richly carved into records of ancient feasts and glories, battles and triumphs. They passed in through a wide entrance; within the walls were lined with satiny hardwoods, the panels chosen with nice regard to color and grain. Doors opened to right and left and ahead, giving views of other chambers on some walls of which still hung ancient cloths; there were chairs and tables and benches and chests. Zoraida went on, straight ahead and to the doorway of a much larger, high-vaulted chamber. And again was Kendric treated to a fresh surprise.

As she stood in the door and he looked over her shoulder, six old men, evidently awaiting her arrival, bent themselves almost to the floor in a reverential posture that expressed greeting and adoration. Again Kendric's fancies were drawn back into ancient Mexico. They wore loose white cotton robes; their beards fell on their aged breasts; in their sashes were long knives of itztli, like that upon the sacrificial stone. They might have been the old priests who sacrificed for the Tezcucan, their existences prolonged eternally here in an atmosphere of antiquity.

Zoraida spoke and they straightened, and one man answered.

Kendric could not understand a word. Then, shuffling their sandaled feet, the six went out through a door at the side.

"I thought you said," said Kendric, "that since your father's death no man had entered here?"

"And do these six look as though they had come here recently from the outside world?" she retorted, smiling. "The youngest of them, Senor Jim, first came to Nezahualcoyotl's gardens more than sixty years ago. When he was less than a year old, hence bringing with him no knowledge of any other place than this."

"And you mean that they have never gone out from here?"

"Would they thrust their heads through solid rock? Would they tread along corridors carpeted with snakes? Would they grow wings and soar to the stars up there? Not only have they never gone out; they do not so much as know that there is an Outside to go to."

"But you come to them!"

Zoraida laughed.

"And I am a spirit, a goddess to worship, the One who has always been, the power that created this spot and themselves!"

"They are captives and caretakers of a sort?" he supposed. "But when they are dead? Who then will keep up your elaborate gardens?"

"Wait. They are returning. There is your answer."

The six ancients filed back. Each man of them led by the hand a little child, the oldest not yet seven or eight. All boys, all bright and handsome; all filled with worship for Zoraida. For they broke away from the old men and ran forward, some of them carrying flowers, and threw themselves on their knees and kissed Zoraida's gown. And then, with wide, wondering eyes they looked from her to Jim Kendric.

"Poor little kids," he muttered. And suddenly whirling wrathfully on Zoraida: "Where do they come from? Whose children are they?"

"There are mysteries and mysteries," she told him, coldly.

"Stolen from their mothers by your damned brigands!" he burst out.

She turned blazing eyes on him.

"Be careful, Jim Kendric!" she warned. "Here you are in Zoraida's stronghold, here you are in her hand! Is act of hers to be questioned by you?"

She made a sudden signal. The six little boys withdrew, walking backward, their round worshipful eyes glued upon their goddess. Then they were gone, the old men with them, a heavy door closing behind them.

"Again I did not lie to you," said Zoraida. "Since though these have come recently, they are not yet men. Follow me again."

They went through the long room and into another. This time Zoraida thrust aside a deep purple curtain, fringed in gold. Here was a smaller chamber, absolutely without furnishings of any kind. But Kendric did not miss chairs or table, his interest being entirely given to the three young men standing before him like soldiers at attention. Heavy limbed, muscular fellows they were, clad only in short white tunics, each with a plain gold band about his forehead. In the hand of each was a great, two-edged knife, horn handled, as long as a man's arm.

"These came just before my father gave his keys to Zoraida," the girl told him: "There are three more of them who sleep while these guard."

Again Kendric saw in the eyes turned upon them a sheer worship of Zoraida, a wonder at him. Zoraida lifted her hand; the three bowed low. She spoke softly and they withdrew slowly to the further wall, walking backward as the children had done. Then one of them lifted down the five bars across a door, employing a rude key from his own belt. And when he had done so and stepped aside Zoraida with her own keys in five different heavy steel locks opened the way. She swung the door open and Kendric followed her. As in the adobe house here was a place where a curtain beyond the doorway hid from any chance eyes what might lie in this room. Only when the door was again shut and locked did Zoraida push the curtain aside. Another match, another big lamp lighted—and Kendric needed no telling that he was in an ancient treasure chamber.

There were long gleaming-topped tables of hardwood; there were exquisitely wrought and embroidered fabrics covering them; strewn across the tables were countless objects of inestimable value. Vases and pitchers and plates of hammered gold; golden goblets set with rich stones; ropes of silver; vessels of many curious shapes, some as small as walnuts, some as large as water pitchers, but all of the precious metals; knives with blades of obsidian and handles of gold; mirrors of selected obsidian bound around in gold; necklaces, coronets, polished stone jars heaped with gold dust. One table appeared to be heaped high with strange-looking books; ancient writings, Zoraida told him, heiroglyphs on the *mauguey* that is so like the papyrus of the Nile.

"And look," laughed Zoraida. "Here is something that would open the greedy eyes of your friend Barlow."

She opened a cedar box and poured forth the contents. Pearls, pearls by the double handful, such as she had worn that night at Ortega's gambling house, many times in number those which Barlow had declared would make Kendric's twenty thousand dollars "look sick." In the lamplight their soft effulgence stirred even the blood of Jim Kendric.

"When the great Tzin Guatamo knew that he would die a dog's death at the hands of the conquerors," Zoraida said, "he had as much of the royal treasury as he could lay his hands on brought here. The Spaniards guessed and demanded to be told the hiding place. Guatamotzin locked his lips. They tortured him; he looked calmly back into their enraged eyes and locked his lips the tighter. They killed him but he kept his secret."

She had mentioned Barlow, and just now Kendric's thoughts had more to do with the present and the immediate future than with a remote and legendary history.

"So," he said, "while Barlow and I made our long journey south, seeking the treasure of the Montezumas, you already had had it safe under lock and key for God knows how long!"

"Choose what pleases you most, Senor Jim," she said. "That I may make you a rich gift."

But though for a moment the glowing pearls, the gold and silver trinklets held his eyes, he shook his head.

"It strikes me," he said bluntly, "that you and I are not such friends that rich gifts need pass from one to the other of us."

"Then not even all this," and with a quick gesture she indicated all of the wealth that surrounded him, "can move you? Are you man, Jim Kendric, or a mechanical thing of levers and springs set into a man's form?"

"I have never had the modern madness of lusting for gold; that is all," he told her.

"Not entirely modern," she retorted, "since here are ancient hoardings; nor yet entirely mad, since it is pure wisdom to put out a hand for the supreme lever of worldly power. You are a strange man, Senor Jim!"

"I am what I am," he said simply. "And, like other men,

content with my own desires and dreamings."

She studied him, for a while in open perplexity, then in as frank a glowing admiration. That he should set aside with a careless hand that which meant so much to her, but made of him in her eyes a sort of superman.

"The thing to do," said Kendric out of a short silence, "is to open your doors and let me go back to the States. I came here looking for treasure trove; your claim antedates mine and I am no highwayman."

Zoraida seated herself in a big carved chair by the long table whereon lay the ancient writings, folded like fans and protected between leaves of decorated woods of various shapes and colors.

"Let me tell you two things, my friend. Three, rather. You saw the sky just now and thought to yourself that all of my safeguards here would be foolish and unavailing if a man sought the way to make his entrance from above? Be sure the way is guarded there, too. Above us towers Little Quetzel Hill, which is a long dead volcano; the hole you saw was in the bottom of the cone. If a man sought to come to it, first he must climb a steep and dangerous mountain flank. The old kings did not forget so obvious a thing. Captives toiled up there while their fellows burrowed down here; the hazardous way through infinite labor continuing through many years, was made infinitely more hazardous. There are balanced rocks of a thousand tons' weight that are secure in the outward seeming, placed to hurl to destruction the adventurer who sets an unwary foot on them; there is a spring, and it is death to drink of it; there are pits for a man to slide down into and in the bottoms of these pits are countless venomous snakes; there are traps set such as men of our time know nothing of. There have been chance travelers up yonder at infrequent intervals and for every such traveler there has been a death so that the mountain bears an evil name. And, further, should a hardy spirit once win to the hole in the bottom of the volcano's cone and find the way to lower himself hundreds of feet into the gardens, there is always, night and day, one of Zoraida's guards at the spot where he must descend, and that guard, night and day, is armed and eager to grapple with a devil whom he has been told to expect soon or late."

"I have told you," said Kendric, "that I have no wish to steal that which is another's."

"One thing I have told you; here is another. I speak it frankly because I may gain by it and am not in the least afraid of losing, since your destiny lies in my hands! It is that only a portion of the great treasure is here with us; another portion was hidden outside." She put her hand on one of the tinted manuscripts. "The tale is here. The treasure bearers were trapped in the mountains by the Spanish; they had no time to come here. One by one they were killed. They hid much gold where they must. That is the 'loot' of which your friend Barlow speaks; that is the treasure which the Spanish priests knew of and held accursed. And that, Senor Jim, I would add to what I have here!"

She amazed him. Her eyes glittered, the fever of gold lust was in her blood. With all this hers—his eye swept the wealth-laden tables and chests—she still coveted gold, other gold!

"The third thing," said Zoraida sharply, "that you may understand why I mention to you the second, is this: You will never go free until I say the word! And I shall never say the word until you and I have brought the rest and placed it here!"

So there was other treasure! Like this, rich, wrought vessels, fine gold, pearls perhaps! And Zoraida did not yet know where it was; Barlow had had enough sense to keep his mouth closed. Jim Kendric's thoughts flew back and forth rapidly; the strange thing was that at a time like this the vision which shaped itself, vivid and clear cut in his mind, was of little Betty Gordon with a double string of pearls around her throat!

"Of what are you thinking?" demanded Zoraida sharply. She had been watching him keenly. "There is a look in your eyes—"

For an instant she almost dared think that that look was for her; Jim flushed. Zoraida's black brows gathered, her eyes went as deadly cruel as ever were the eyes of her ancient forebears though they watched the priests at the sacrificial stone.

"You think of her!" she cried angrily. She stamped upon the stone floor, she clenched her hands and lifted them high above her head in a sudden access and abandon of rage. "You think that, having made mock of me, you shall turn to her? Fool! Seven times accursed fool! I will show you the doll-faced, baby-eyed girl—and you will see, too, what fate I have reserved for her. To cross the path of Zoraida means—But what are words? You shall see!"

With a strange sick sinking of his heart Kendric followed her, forgetting the treasure about him.

CHAPTER XVI

HOW TWO, IN THE LABYRINTH OF MIRRORS, WATCHED DISTANT HAPPENINGS

An oppression such as he had never known fell upon Kendric. Nor was the depressing emotion an emanation alone of his growing dread on Betty's account; the atmosphere of the place through which he moved began to weigh him down, to crush the spirit within him. They left the treasure chamber which was six times doubly locked after them. They went through the ancient empty rooms and out into the gardens. Kendric, looking up, saw the small ragged patch of sky and felt as though upon his own soul, stifling him, rested the weight of the hollow mountain. To him who loved the fresh, wind-swept world, the open sea with its smell of clean salt air, the wide deserts where the sunshine lay everywhere, this pleasure grove of a long dead royalty was become musty, foul, permeated with an aura of a great gilded tomb. His sensation was almost that of a drowning person or of one awaking from a trance to find himself shut in the narrow confines of a buried coffin. The air seemed heavy and impure; he fancied it still fetid with all the blood of sacrificial offerings which the ravening soil had drunk.

But he knew that now was no time for sick fancies and he shook them off and bent his mind to the present crisis. Zoraida was retracing the steps which had led them here; she had spoken of Betty. It was likely then that they were returning through the long passageways to the house. Dark hallways to thread, the dark mind of his guide to seek to read.

Now, while darkness outdoors was well enough, the black gloom of a maze at any corner of which Zoraida might have placed one or a dozen of her hirelings, had little lure for him. She did not mean to let him go free; she had kept him all day immured in his own room; she would no doubt seek to lock him up again.

"It's tonight or never to make a break for it," he decided as he followed her.

They were passing the block of jasper, the ancient stone of sacrifice. Zoraida went by first; Kendric was passing when an impulse prompted him to put out a sudden hand for the keen edged knife of obsidian. He slipped it into his belt and hid the haft with his coat. If it came to an ambush, to an attack in the dark, a revolver bullet might fly wild while the wide sweep of a knife blade would somehow find a sheath in something more palpable than thin air.

They went on, returning along the way they had come. When the gardens of the golden Tezcucan were behind them and a door barred Kendric experienced a sense of relief, even though the tunnels were ahead of him. He kept close to Zoraida, prepared for any sort of trickery and with no desire to have her whisk suddenly through a door somewhere and slam it in his face. His one urgent prayer was for a breath of the open; just then the consummation of human happiness seemed to him to be freedom on horseback somewhere out in the mountains with the whole of the wide starry sky generously roofing the world. He thought of Betty—and he thought, too, of the six little boys doomed to count themselves happy back yonder where at most the sun shone down upon them a few minutes of the day.

Never once did Zoraida turn, not once did she speak as they hastened on. What little he saw of her face where there was lamplight showed him hard set muscles. At last they were again in the house which was hushed as though untenanted or as though its occupants were asleep or dead. He could fancy

Bruce in some remote room, tricked by some false message of Zoraida's, eagerly expecting her, hungering for her lying explanations; he could picture Barlow, glowering, but awaiting her, too. Well, the time had passed when he could largely concern himself with them and what they did and thought. Tonight he must serve himself, and Betty. If she would listen to him.

Presently he saw where it was that Zoraida was conducting him. He remembered the dim ante-room in which they paused a moment while Zoraida fastened the door behind them; then, the curtain thrown aside, they were again in that barbaric, tapestry-hung chamber in which, the first night here, he had been brought before her. As before the ruby upon the thin crystal stem shone like a burning red eye.

Now, for the first time since they had turned away from the golden Tezcucan's treasure chamber, was Kendric given a full, clear view of Zoraida's face. During their progress many thoughts had come and gone swiftly through his mind; now as they two stood looking steadily at each other, he realized clearly that one matter and one alone had occupied her. No abatement of cruelty had come into her long eyes; no flush of color had swept away the cold whiteness of her cheek. She was set in a merciless determination, relentlessly hard; the colorless face resulted from a frozen heart. Before now Kendric had seen murder staring out of a man's widened eyes; now he saw it in a woman's.

For the instant only she had looked at him as though she were probing into his secret thought and there swept over him the old, disquieting sensation that each thought in his mind lay as clear to her look as a white pebble in a sunlit pool. Then her eyes passed on, beyond him. He turned and saw the hangings parted at that spot where Zoraida had appeared to him that other time; one of the brutish, squat forms which Kendric remembered, stood in the opening.

Zoraida spoke with the man swiftly, her voice hard and sharp.

A quick change came into the heavy, thick-lipped face; the stupid eyes brightened; the face was distorted as by some hideous anticipation. Zoraida ended what she had to say; the man spoke gutturally, nodding his head. Then he dropped the curtain and was gone.

Zoraida went to her black chair with the crystal balls for feet and sat stiffly, her ringed fingers tapping restlessly upon the wide arms. Presently the man returned, carrying a wide flat box. Thereafter, while Zoraida watched him impatiently, he occupied himself after a fashion which Kendric found inexplicable. From the box the man took a number of rectangular mirrors, fine clear glass framed with thin bands of ebony. Deftly, into a grove made in the back of each mirror, he slipped the end of a tall ebony rod. Then he rolled back the heavy rug from two thirds of the floor. The floor was of stone, laid fancifully in colored mozaic; here and there, seemingly placed utterly at random, were smooth round holes in the stone blocks. Into each hole the haft of one of the rods was thrust so that when the man stepped back to survey his handiwork there was a little forest of mirrors on glistening stems grown up in apparent lack of design, like young pines on a tableland.

Then Zoraida rose and went from one of the glasses to another, turning them a little to right or left, adjusting painstakingly, seeming to read the meaning of some fine lines scratched in the stone floor. Her eyes were like a mad woman's. She herself moved her chair, shoving it from the rug to the bare floor, careful that each supporting crystal sphere rested exactly upon a chosen spot. Her retainer handed her a small stool; she placed it and, since it was near the spot where he stood, Kendric made out the four crosses where the four legs were to go. Then Zoraida went swiftly back to her chair.

As she sat down she called again sharply to the squat brute who served her. His broad ugly teeth showed white in his animal grin; he ran across the room and swept back the curtains draping the wall. They were laced to rings along the upper edge and the rings ran on a long rod. As they were whipped back they disclosed no ordinary wall but a great expanse of mirror extending from floor to ceiling, from corner to corner. When two other walls were exposed they too resolved themselves into clearly reflecting surfaces.

"Clap-trap again," muttered Kendric, beginning to feel a strange dread in his heart and growing angry with it and determined that Zoraida should not guess.

"Be seated," commanded Zoraida sternly. "If you would see what amusement is being offered a friend of yours!"

One by one the lamps were being put out by the hasty hand of the fellow whom Kendric began to long to strangle; he could hear a low guttural gurgling sort of noise rising from the thick throat, issuing from the monstrous mouth. Zoraida did not appear to hear but sat rigid, waiting. At last, when all but one opaque shaded lamp were extinguished and the room was cast into shadowy gloom, Kendric, impelled by environment, a curious dread and perhaps the will of Zoraida, sat down on the stool.

"Clap-trap, you say!" scoffed Zoraida. "Watch the first mirror!"

At first the mirror reflected nothing save the shadowy room and a vague, half-seen line of other mirrors. But while Kendric watched there came a swift change. Somewhere a lamp had been lighted—several lamps, for there was a brilliant light. He saw reflected what appeared to be a small room with a door in one wall. He saw the door open and a man come in; it was either the man who just now had obeyed Zoraida's commands or his twin-fellow. The man began hooking together what appeared to be several frames of steel bars. Working swiftly he shaped them into a steel cage hardly larger than to accommodate a man standing. Kendric's heart leaped and then stood still. He remembered words which Juanita, terrified by idle threat from him, had spoken.

He sat like a man in a trance. The dim mirrors seemed unreal. What he saw elsewhere—was it a reflected reality or was his mind under the spell of Zoraida's? Was she through hypnosis projecting a lying image into his groping consciousness? Absolutely, he did not know. He drew his eyes away from the vision of that room and turned them questioningly upon Zoraida. Stern she was and rigid and white, a dim figure in that dim light save alone for her eyes; they burned ominously, glowing like a cat's.

A quick shifting of the image in the glass jerked back his straying attention. The man had completed his brief labors with the steel frames which now made a strong cage; he shook the bars with his hand as though trying them, and they were firm in their places. He opened a section which turned on hinges so that a narrow door swung back. Then he drew away and across the room. And now the remarkable thing was that though he moved several paces, still he remained in full view at the center of the mirror.

Plainly in a complicated series of reflectors there were mirrors which were being turned as the man moved, cunningly and skilfully adjusted to his slow progress; otherwise would he have passed out of the scope of Kendric's vision. As it was, the cage slid away out of view, an uncanny sort of thing since it had the appearance of gliding under a will of its own.

Presently, however, the man opened a door in the wall and was gone. For an instant the mirror darkened; then the light flashed back and Kendric was treated to a broken procession of images which set him marveling. First he saw straight into the heart of the gardens of the golden Tezcucan; he saw the sacrificial stone; he saw one of the old men approach it and pass by; he saw the treasure chamber. Again he stared at Zoraida, again the fear was upon him that she had mastered his mind with hers, that what he fancied he saw was but what she willed him to imagine. For he could not ignore the long tunneled distance they had traversed, the dark passageways, the heavy doors with their massive locks. And yet his reason told him that to a mind like Zoraida's as he began to believe it, a brain filled with ancient craft and perhaps a strain of madness, actuated by such dark impulses as certainly must abide there, the actual physical accomplishment of this sort of parlor magic was a thing in keeping. There would be small tube-like holes through walls, angled with reference to other mirrors; there would be scientific arrangement; there would be, somewhere in the great house, a sort of operating room, a room of mirrors with a trained hand to manipulate them. Perhaps, with modern reflectors, she but improved on some fancy of an ancient king who sought to guard himself against treachery or his hoardings against the hand of his treasurers.

Again and again, as Kendric sat watching, the mirrors darkened and grew bright again, with always a new image. He saw the room in which he had spent a long day immured and knew then that had Zoraida been of the mind she could have sat here in her private room and have observed every move he made. He saw still another room and in it Bruce pacing up and down, up and down, swinging suddenly to look eagerly at his door; he saw Barlow's back as Barlow stared out of a window —somewhere.

"Thus Zoraida knows what goes forward in her own house," said Zoraida, speaking for the first time. Kendric, struck with a new thought, looked about the room everywhere, seeking to locate the necessary opening in the wall through which came the reflections from mirrors in other places. But the great glasses covering three of the walls presented what appeared to be smooth, unbroken surfaces; where the fourth wall was tapestry-draped there was no sign of an opening; neither floor nor ceiling, places offering no detail but blurred with vague shadows, showed him what he sought.

"Watch closely!" said Zoraida.

Again it was the small room of the steel cage. The savage-looking man in the short tunic was there again. He looked watchful, tense, not altogether at his ease. In one hand was a heavy whip; in the other a pistol. Kendric thought of the animal trainers he had seen at circuses. The man's eyes were on the door through which he had come. So vivid were old images bred now of associations of ideas that Kendric had no doubt of what small head with fierce eyes would appear next; he could prevision the lithe puma, in its quick nervous movements, the lashing of the heavy tail and the glint of the teeth. And so when he saw what it was that entered, he sat back for a moment limp and the next sprang to his feet. It was Betty.

Betty clothed strangely and with a face dead white, with eyes to haunt a man. She wore a loose red robe, sleeveless, falling no lower than her ankles; her bare feet were in sandals. Her hair was down; about her brows was a black band that might have been ebony or velvet; into it was thrust a large white flower.

Betty was speaking. Kendric had dropped back into his chair, having lost sight of her when he stood. He saw that she was speaking swiftly, supplicatingly; her hands were clasped; all this he could see but no slightest sound came to him. He could not tell if she were near or far. He began to realize the exquisite torture which Zoraida might offer a man through her mirrors.

He saw the squat brute's wide grin that was as hideous as the puma's could be; all of the teeth he saw and they were glistening and sharp, unusually sharp for a human being. And then he saw Betty pushed forward though she shrank back at first with dragging feet and though then, suddenly galvanized, she fought wildly. But two big hands locked tight on her arms and as powerless as a child of six she was thrust into the steel cage, the door snapped after her. She stood looking wildly about her; her lips opened as she must have screamed; she dropped her face into her hands. Kendric saw the white flower fall.

Again the man looked to the door through which he and then Betty had entered. And now came the puma. It ran in, snarling; it was looking back over its shoulder as though someone had whipped it into the room. It saw another enemy armed with whip and pistol and sidled off with still greater show of dripping fangs. All this in dead silence so far as Kendric was concerned; never the faintest sound coming to him. The whip was flung out and snapped, and there was no sound; the puma's teeth clicked together on empty air, and no sound; Betty, looking up, shrieked, and no sound. They looked to be so close to Kendric that he felt as if with one stride he could hurl himself among them; and yet he knew that they might be shut off from him by innumerable walls and locked and barred doors. He saw Betty so plainly that until he reasoned with himself he felt that she must see him.

"A puma will not attack a human being." Kendric sought to speak as though merely contemptuous of Zoraida's entertainment. "They are cowardly brutes."

"The puma," said Zoraida, "is starving. Further, he has been driven mad by men who whipped and then appeared to run, frightened of him. Watch."

The man threatening the puma slipped out through the door behind him. The door closed. Betty and the animal were alone. The great cat lay down and looked at her with its hard, unwinking eyes, only its slow tail moving back and forth like a bit of mechanism clock-regulated. Presently the puma lifted its head and began a horrible sniffing; it lifted itself gradually from the floor; it drew a step nearer Betty's cage and sniffed again. Kendric could see Betty draw back the few inches made possible by the narrow confines of the cage, could see that again she screamed.

"A little fresh blood has been sprinkled on the floor of the cage," said Zoraida. "A little of it is on the gown she wears. It will not be overlong to watch. Are you growing impatient?"

"Are you mad?" he burst out. "Good God, do you mean to let this go on?"

"Am I mad?" Her eyes, slowly turned to his, looked it.

"Perhaps. Who that is mad knows he is mad? And who, my friend, is sane? Do I mean to let this go on?" She laughed at him, and the sound was as hard as the tinkle of bits of jangling glass. "You have but to be patient to know."

The puma sniffed again, again drew closer. Betty was tight pressed against the far bars shutting her in, and even so had the great cat thrust a claw forward she could not withdraw beyond the reach of the ripping talons. The cat circled her. Always Betty turned with it, her eyes upon its eyes, her eyes that were large and fixed with terror.

"A puma is patient, more patient than a man," said Zoraida. "It may be an hour; it may be all night before it strikes. It may be a night and a day, and still another night and day. Its hunger does not diminish as time passes! Or," and she shrugged with a great showing of her indifference, "it may strike now, at any moment. That is one of the things that makes the moment tense for that white-faced little fool in there. Imagine when she is worn out, if it lasts that long; when sleep will no longer flee because of terror; and when I command that the light shall be extinguished where she is! You see, she must be thinking all those things."

The sweat broke out on Kendric's forehead, he felt as though ice ran in his veins. If he only knew where all this was going on! Was it above him or below, to right or left? Ten steps or a hundred yards away?

"By God—" he shouted. But only Zoraida's merciless laughter answered him.

"I had to choose between this and the ancient stone of sacrifice," she told him. "Have I not chosen well?"

The puma had been still. Now again it moved and its feet had quickened, it glided with ever-increasing swiftness, it came close to the steel bars, it showed more of its sharp, tearing, dripping teeth.

"Betty!" shouted Kendric. "I—"

He knew that Betty could not hear, that he could do nothing. Nothing? As the thought framed he leaped to his feet and in the grip of such a rage as even he had never known, hurled himself across the few paces between him and Zoraida.

"You have the way to stop this damned thing!" His hands, like claws, were thrust before her face. "You will stop it."

Even in his headlong rage there were cool cells in his brain. He saw the quick significant look Zoraida shot over his shoulder and turned; there behind him stood one of the squat brutes who did her bidding. Kendric saw something in the man's hand but did not reck whether it was gun or knife or club or something else. He whipped about and struck. As the man staggered under the unexpected blow, Kendric snatched up the heavy stool on which he had been sitting and struck again, so swift that the blow landed while the figure was yet staggering backward. The man fell, stunned, and then, as quick as light, before Zoraida could lift a hand, Kendric was upon her again.

"Call off your cat!" he shouted at her.

She lifted her head defiantly.

"Never has man dictated to me!" she cried angrily. "Here I dictate. If you dared put a hand on me—"

He saw her own hand creeping out toward the table. What it sought he did not know; a hidden bell, perhaps. Or a dagger. He remembered her swift attack upon Ortega. He seized her wrist, his fingers locked hard about it; she struggled and he held her back in her chair. Suddenly she relaxed and shrugged and laughed at him.

"You add to the entertainment!" she mocked him. "For, mind you, while you make large commands, the puma draws nearer and nearer. If you will, between your great commands, but glance into the mirror—"

"I say you can put a stop to that infernal torture," he said fiercely. "And you will!"

"Yes?" she sneered at him. "And you will make me, perhaps? You, a common adventurer will dictate to Zoraida!"

For the moment he felt powerless in face of her cold taunting. But there was too much at stake for him to yield now to a feeling of powerlessness. One hand was on her wrist; the gripping fingers of the other shut about the haft of the ancient obsidian knife. The old knife of sacrifice. His face was white and stern, his eyes no whit less deadly than Zoraida's.

"You threaten my life?" she gasped. "*You*?"

He made no answer. He was beyond speech. Slowly he lifted the great knife, slowly as in a dream he set the thin point against the soft flesh of Zoraida's throat. As a tremor shook his hand Zoraida whipped back.

"You would not dare! You would not dare!"

His hand was steady again. He held her still, and the point of the knife crept a hair's breadth closer to the life within her. A little more and it would have slipped into the skin it was pricking.

"You could not do it," she whispered.

Then he spoke.

"I can do it." His lips were dry, his voice very harsh. "You have said that you know me for a man of my word. Well, then, I swear to you that little by little I'll drive that knife in unless you set that girl free."

Still she sought to brave it out, sought to defy him; her eyes, on his, told him that his will was less than hers, and that this could never be. But Kendric knew otherwise. It was given him to know that if Betty died, he did not care to live. Like men of his stamp it was unthinkable to him that he should lift his hand against a woman. But woman for the moment Zoraida was not. Fiend, rather; reincarnated savage; a thing to stamp into the earth. What he had said he meant. He was giving her time because on her rested Betty's fate. He pressed the knife a little deeper. So steady was his hand, so stiff Zoraida's body, so gradual the increased pressure, that the knife point made in the white flesh a tiny, shadow-filled dimple.

Now came into Zoraida's eyes a swift change, a look which in all of her life had never been there until now. A look of terror, of realization of death, of frantic fear. She sought to speak, and words failed her. The knife pressed steadily. A piercing scream broke from her.

CHAPTER XVII

HOW ONE WHO HAS EVER COMMANDED
MUST LEARN TO OBEY

Suddenly Zoraida had become as docile as a little frightened child. She shivered from head to foot. She put her two hands to her throat where just now the point of the knife had been.

"Quick!" said Kendric.

She rose in haste. A vertigo was upon her like that dizzy weakness of one very sick, seeking prematurely to rise from bed. She had experienced a shock from which she could rally only gradually; she looked broken. Her eyes appeared to see nothing about her but stared off into the distance through a veil of abstraction.

"We will have to go," she said tonelessly. "There is no other way."

They passed by the inert figure on the floor and out, Kendric with his left hand always on her arm. Again the knife was hidden under his coat, but his fingers did not release it.

"Quick," he said again.

So Zoraida, obedient in this strange new mood governing her, making no effort to shake off his hand having no thought to gainsay him, hastened. In perhaps five minutes they were unlocking the last door, and Kendric heard beyond the whining of the puma. Kendric had had time for thought during this brief interval which had seemed much longer; for the present both his safety and Betty's would undoubtedly depend upon his keeping Zoraida with him. So now, as he flung open the door, he carried Zoraida along into the room.

At first he did not see the cat lying close to the cage; he saw only Betty. A little color had come back into her cheeks; he saw the look in her eyes before it changed and knew that to Betty had come the time when hope is given up and when death is faced. She had passed beyond tears and pleading and crying out. It was given Kendric then to learn that when the crisis had come it found in the girl's heart a courage to sustain her. Her face was set, her attitude was no longer cringing. In such tender breasts as Betty's have beat the steady hearts of martyrs.

When she saw Jim Kendric and Zoraida standing before her she stared incredulously. She was in a daze. Her first wild thought, reflecting itself unmistakably in her wide eyes, was that they had come to taunt her, he and she side by side. Then her faltering gaze left Zoraida and ignored her and went, full of earnest questioning, to Jim's face. Suddenly, at what she saw there, the red blood of joyousness ran into Betty's cheeks. At moments like this it is with few words or none at all that perfect understanding comes. In a flash his look had told her all that it would require many fumbling spoken words to repeat one-half so eloquently.

The puma had sprung to its feet but stood its ground. The murderous eyes were everywhere at once, on Betty, on Jim, on Zoraida, most of all on Betty; the quivering nostrils widened and sniffed; the tawny throat shook with a series of low growls. Jim's foot stirred; the cat's teeth came together with a snap.

With little wish as Kendric had to create a disturbance just now, it was beyond his power to withhold his hand as he saw Betty draw back against the walls of her cage. In his pocket was

Bruce's weapon. Kendric jerked it out, and before Zoraida's cry could burst from her lips and before her hand struck his arm, he drove a bullet into the puma's skull between the hard evil eyes. The animal dropped in its tracks, with never another whine.

As the puma went down, Zoraida winced as though in bodily pain, as though it had been her flesh instead of her cat's that had known the deep bite of hot lead. She looked from the twitching animal to Kendric like one aghast, like one stupefied by what she had seen, who could not altogether believe that an accomplished act had in reality taken place. There was horror in her look; she recalled to him vividly though fleetingly a South Sea island priest whom he had seen long ago when the savage's idol had been overthrown and cast down into a mud puddle under the palm trees. At that moment Zoraida might well have been sister to the idolater of the South Seas or some ancient Egyptian priestess stricken dumb at the sight of sacred cat violated.

But there was Betty. Jim jerked open the door of the cage. Betty stumbled through and somehow found herself in his arms. They closed tight about her. The two turned to Zoraida. She, white-faced and silent, watched them with smoldering eyes. And into those eyes, as for a space Betty's heart fluttered against Jim Kendric's breast, came for the first time since the knife had been withdrawn from her throat, a quickening of purpose, a glint as of a covered fire breaking through.

"Come, Betty," said Jim quickly. "We are going to clear out of this, you and I. Right now!"

He noted a slight restless stirring of Zoraida's foot and stepped to her side, his hand again on her arm.

"We are not through with you yet," he told her. "Miss Gordon will want some clothes."

"In her room," agreed Zoraida. "Come."

Jackson Gregory

Had she delayed her answer the fraction of a second he might have followed her, suspecting nothing. But as it was he remarked on her eagerness; Zoraida was passionately set on treachery and he sensed it.

"No," he answered. "From here we go straight out into the open." Zoraida had yielded to the pressure on her arm as though to continue in her new role of implicit obedience. But now his distrust was wide awake. There may have been a slight involuntary stiffening of her muscles, hinting at rebellion; there was something which warned him in the look she sought to veil. "What clothes Betty needs you can give her. Here and now."

"Oh!" cried Betty, with a look of abhorrence and a shudder. "I couldn't—"

"It can't be helped," he retorted. And to Zoraida: "She'll want shoes and stockings."

The look he had then from Zoraida was one of utter loathing and at last of unhidden lust for his undoing. But after it she bestowed on him a slow contemptuous smile and again she obeyed. Her little shoes she kicked off; she drew off her stockings and he handed them to Betty.

"Zoraida goes barefooted at a man's command!" A first note of laughter was in Zoraida's voice. "What more? Am I to disrobe in a man's presence?"

"Your cloak," he muttered. "We'll make that do."

The cloak Betty accepted and threw about her shoulders. The shoes and stockings she held a moment, looking at them with repulsion in her eyes; they were too intimate, they had come too lately from Zoraida and in the end she threw them down.

"My sandals will do," she said. "I can't wear her things."

Kendric picked them up and thrust them into his pocket.

"Later, then," he said. "God knows we can't be choosers. Now," and again he confronted Zoraida, "you will show us the way. Clear of the house. And we'll want horses. One thing, mind you: It is in my thought that if we allow you to hold us here we'll both be dead inside a few hours. I've no desire for that sort of thing. The issue is clear cut, isn't it?"

Zoraida merely lifted her brows at him.

"If it becomes a question of your life or ours," he told her sternly; "I'd naturally prefer it to be yours! Is that plain enough? For once, young woman, it's up to you to play square. Now, go ahead."

They went out silently through the door which had given them entrance into this ugly room, Zoraida leading the way, Kendric holding close at her side and allowing her the sight of the obsidian knife held under his coat with the point within an inch of her side, Betty close behind him. Kendric felt a crying need of haste. For a few minutes he knew that the fear of death had been heavy on the spirit of Zoraida, paralyzing her will, freezing up the current of her thought. But she was still Zoraida, essentially fearless; her characteristic fortitude would not be long in reinstating itself in her heart; the mental confusion was swiftly being replaced by the activity of resurging hatred. He must be watchful of every corner and door, most of all watchful of her.

Thus it was Kendric's hand, once bolts were shot back, that threw open each door, as he held himself in readiness to spring forward or back. But as appeared customary here the house seemed deserted. He thanked his stars that the fellow he had struck down in Zoraida's room had fallen hard. Not even the dull explosion of the pistol just now had brought inquiry; no doubt the thick walls had deadened the sound. After what seemed a long time they came into the wide dimly-lighted hall. The door giving entrance to the *patio* was open; under the stars the little fountain played musically.

"Out this way," commanded Kendric. "Then around to the front of the house. And if we meet anyone, Zoraida, you'd best think back a few minutes before you start anything."

There was no one in the *patio* and they went through swiftly and out at the far side into the garden. Kendric filled his lungs with the sweet air that was beginning to grow cool. The glitter of the stars was to him like a hope and a promise. Never had he been so sick of four walls and a smothering roof. Now the musty gardens of the golden king seemed to him infinitely far away, a thousand times farther removed than the dancing lights in the heavens.

With his hand gripping Zoraida's forearm they skirted the house. Presently they came to the front driveway and Zoraida must have wondered as he forced her to go with him to a clump of bushes. He stooped, groped about a moment, and then straightened up with a little grunt of satisfaction; the rifle was in his hands.

"Now the horses," he said, and the three walked out into the starlight and toward the double gates. "Whatever you will say will go with the men out there. And be sure you say we are to be allowed to go for a ride."

Zoraida did not answer and Kendric wondered, not without uneasiness, what she would say. His grip tightened on her arm. She did not appear to notice.

The watch towers on either side of the gate were lighted as usual. From one came the low drone of two men's voices; the other was silent. No other sound save that of the rattle of bit-chains as a horse somewhere shook its head.

A man appeared from nowhere, with the air of having suddenly materialized out of the atmosphere. He came close, made out that one of the three was Zoraida and backed away, sweeping off his hat. They came to the gates which the newly risen figure threw open; they went through, Kendric having the air of a man lending his arm to a lady, Betty with the cloak drawn close about her, following. They were out! Now nearer than ever came the friendly stars, sweeter than ever was the night air. Kendric looked swiftly about, taking note of the darkness lying close to the earth, thanking God that there was no moon. If one could keep for a little in the shadow of the wall, if then he could get clear of the house and out into the fields lying at the rear, it was but a short run to the mountains—

They had turned and already were under one of the watch towers, the one whence came the men's voices. The saddled horses stood, tethered to rings set in the wall. Zoraida turned toward Kendric and in the starlight her eyes shone strangely, bright with mockery. But tonight was Jim Kendric's, and he was still bent on playing out his hand.

"*Que hay, amigos*?" he called familiarly to the men in the square tower, his voice sounding careless and indifferent. "La Senorita is here. She wants horses."

A head appeared at the little opening that served for window above, a hat was doffed with exaggerated deference, a second uncovered head was thrust out. Kendric stepped back half a pace so that they could see plainly that it was Zoraida.

"*Bueno*," said one of the two men. "*Viva la Senorita*!"

Already Kendric was undoing the two tie ropes. He regretted the necessity of stepping two paces from Zoraida's side, but realized that inevitably that necessity must come soon or late and he lost no time grieving over it. The horses were at hand, saddled and bridled; Betty was with him; the night was too dark for eyes to watch from a distance; the two men within Zoraida's call were still up in the tower. He was taking his chance now and he knew it; Zoraida's period of obedience and inactivity was no doubt near at end. Well, his luck had befriended him thus far and for the rest it was up to Jim Kendric. And they were out in the open!

Thus he was ready for Zoraida's outcry. He saw her whip back so as to be beyond the sweep of his arm, he heard her crying out wildly, commanding her retainers to stop the flight of her prisoners, shrieking at them to shoot, to shoot to kill!

"Betty!" cried Jim. "Quick!"

Then he saw that Betty, too, had been ready. Just how she managed it, encumbered as she was with Zoraida's cloak, he did not know. But she was already in one of the saddles.

"Jim!" she cried wildly. "Run!"

He went up to the back of the other horse, his rifle in his hand. And as he struck saddle leather his horse and Betty's shot forward and away. He heard Zoraida's scream of command, breaking with rage. He heard men's voices shouting excitedly; there came the well-remembered shrilling of a whistle and then drowning its silver note the popping of rifles.

"There'll be a dozen of them in the saddle and after us!" Jim shouted at Betty. "Swing off to the right. We've got to make for the mountains. Ride, girl! Ride, Betty! Ride for all that's in it!"

He glanced over his shoulder. Only a flare here and there as a rifle spat its red threat, that and a blur of running figures. As yet no horseman following them. That would take another minute or two. He looked at Betty. She rode astride and well; no need to bid her make haste. She leaned forward in the saddle, the loose ends of her reins whipping back and forth regularly, lashing her horse's shoulders. He looked ahead. There the mountains rose black and without detail against the sky. He looked up; the stars were shining.

Abruptly, as though at a command, the rifles ceased firing after them. And, instead of the explosions which had concerned Kendric little, came another sound fully to be expected by now and of downright serious import. It was the scurry and race of hoofs, how many there was no guessing. Pursuit had started and it was certain that the numbers of the pursuers would swell swiftly until perhaps a score of Zoraida's riders were on their track. Kendric settled down to hard riding, drawing in close to Betty's side.

"We got a couple of minutes on them," he called to her. "That means we're ahead of them between a quarter and a half mile. In the dark that's something."

Betty made no answer. They sped on. He tried to see her face but her hair was flying wildly. He wondered if her terror were freezing the heart in her. His own sensation at the moment was one of a strange sort of leaping gladness. After prison walls, this rushing through the night was like a zestful game. He felt that he had that even break which was ever all that he asked. If only Betty could feel as he did.

His horse stumbled and then steadied and plunged on. The ground underfoot was rapidly growing steeper and more broken. The first slopes of the mountains were beneath them. The horses, though urged on, were not making their former speed. Now and then dry brush snatched and whipped at the stirrups; here and there a pine tree stood up black and still.

And then Kendric knew that the riders behind were gaining on them. Zoraida's men would know every trail even in the dark, would know all of the cleared spaces, would thus avoid both brush and steeps. Kendric turned in the saddle. He made out dimly the foremost of the pursuers and heard the man's shout to his companions.

"Betty," called Kendric.

"Yes?" she answered, and it struck him that perhaps he had imagined her terror greater than it actually was; for her voice was quite clear and even sounded untroubled. "What is it?"

"In ten minutes or so they'll overhaul us. They know the way and we don't. Further, we're apt to get a spill over a pile of rocks."

"Yes, Jim," she answered. And still her voice failed to tremble as he had thought it must.

"The old dodge is all that's left us," he told her. "When I say the word, pull up a little and slide out of the saddle. Let your horse run on and you duck into the brush."

"And you?"

"I'm with you, of course." And presently, when they were in the shadows of the ever-steepening mountain side, he called softly: "Now!"

Until then he had never done Betty's horsemanship justice. He saw her bring her mount down from a flying gallop to a sliding standstill, he saw her throw herself from the saddle, he saw the released animal plunge on again under a blow from the quirt which Betty had snatched from the horn, the whole act taking so little time that it hardly seemed that the horse had stopped for a second's time. Kendric duplicated her act and ran toward the spot where she had disappeared. In another moment his hand had closed about hers, was greeted by a little welcoming squeeze, and he and Betty slipped side by side into the thicker dark at the mouth of a friendly canon.

CHAPTER XVIII

OF FLIGHT, PURSUIT, AND A LAIR IN THE CLIFFS

Straightway Jim Kendric began to understand the real Betty. He broke a way through the bushes for her, confident that the noise of their progress was lost in the increasing beat of hoofs and rattle of loose stones. They stumbled into a rocky trail in the bottom of the canon and made what haste they could, climbing higher into the mountain solitudes. The pursuit had swept by them; they could hear occasional shouts and twice gunshots. They came to a pile of tumbled boulders across their path and crawled up. There was a flattish place at the top in which stunted plants were growing. Here they sat for a little while, hiding and resting and listening. Hardly had they settled themselves here when they heard again the clear tones of Zoraida's whistle. Not more than fifty yards away they made out the form of Zoraida's white horse.

There was a little sound from where Betty sat, and Jim thought that she was sobbing. "Poor little kid," he had it on his lips to mutter when the sound repeated itself and, amazed, he recognized it for a giggle of pure delight. This from Betty, sitting on a rock in the mountains with a crowd of outlaws riding up and down seeking her!

"You're about as logical an individual as I ever knew," was what he said. And with a grunt, at that.

"I never claimed to be logical," retorted Betty. "I'm just a girl."

Jackson Gregory

Even then, while they whispered and fell silent and watched and listened, he began to understand the girl whom he was to come to know very well before many days. She did not pretend at high fearlessness; when she was afraid she was very much afraid, and had no thought to hide the fact. Tonight her fright had come as near killing as fright can. But then she was alone and there was no one but herself to make the fight for her. Now it was different. Since Jim had come she had allowed her own responsibility to shift to his shoulders. It was instinctive in her to turn to some man, to have some man to trust and to depend upon. Jim was looking out for her and right now, while Zoraida and her men searched up and down, Betty clasped her arms about her gathered-up knees and sat cozily at the side of the man whose sole duty, as she saw it, was to guard her with his life. So Betty, close enough to touch the rifle across Jim's arm, could giggle as she pictured Zoraida rushing by the very spot where they hid.

"You're not afraid, then?" asked Jim.

"Not now," whispered Betty.

They did not budge for half an hour. During that time Kendric did a deal of hard thinking. Their plight was still far from satisfactory. No food, no water, no horses, and in the heart of a land of which they know nothing except that it was hard and bleak and closely patrolled by Zoraida's riders. That they could succeed now in eluding pursuit for the rest of the night seemed assured. But tomorrow? Where there was one man looking for them now there would be ten tomorrow. And there were the questions of food and water. Above all else, water.

At last, when it was very still all about them, they moved on again. They climbed over the rocks and further up the canon. Here there were more trees and thicker darkness, and their progress was painfully slow. They skirted patches of thorny bushes; they went on hands and knees up sharp inclines. They stopped frequently, panting and straining their ears for some sound to tell them of a pursuer; they went on again, side by side or with Kendric ahead, breaking trail.

"We'll have to dig in somewhere before dawn," said Jim once while they rested. "Where we can stick close during daylight tomorrow."

Betty merely nodded; all such details were to be left to him. It was his clear-cut task to take care of her; just how he did it was not Betty's concern. So they went on, left the canon where there was a way out, made their toilsome way over a low ridge and slid and rolled down into the next ravine. And here, at the bottom, they found water. A thin trickle from a spring, wending its way down to the larger stream in the valley. They lay down, side by side, and drank. Then they sat back and looked at each other in the starlight.

"Betty," said Jim impulsively, "you're a brick!"

"Am I?" said Betty. And by her voice he knew that she was pleased.

"We're not as far from the house as I'd like," he said presently. "But it will take time to locate a decent hiding place, and we've got to stick within reach of water."

To all of this Betty agreed; personally she'd like to be a thousand miles away from this hideous place, but they would have to make the best of things. That willingness of hers to accept conditions without bemoaning her fate was what had drawn from him his impulsive epithet.

"The thing to do, then," said Kendric, getting up "is to look for a likely place to spend a long day. And it may be more than one day."

Then Betty made her suggestion, offering it timidly, as though she were entering a discussion in which, rightly, she had no part:

"Up yonder," and she pointed to the abrupt ridge cutting black across the stars, "are cliffy places. It's not too far from water. There ought to be hiding places among the broken boulders. And," she concluded, "we might be able to peek out and look down and see what was happening."

No; he had not done her justice. He looked toward her, wondering for a moment. Then he said briefly: "Right," and they drank again and began climbing.

It was Betty who, fully an hour later, found the retreat which they agreed to utilize. Kendric was somewhere above her, making a hazardous way up a steep bit of cliff, when Betty's voice floated up to him.

"I think I've got it," were her words, guarded but athrill with her triumph. "Come see. It's a great hole, hid by bushes. I don't like to go poking into it alone. You can't tell, there might be a bear or a snake or something inside."

He climbed down to where she stood at the edge of a little level space, her gown gathered in a hand at each side, her pretty face thrust forward as she sought to peer into the dark before her. He saw the clump of bushes but not immediately the hole of which she spoke, so was it covered and hidden. But at length he made out the irregular opening and, thrusting the bushes aside with his rifle barrel, judged that Betty had done well. Here was a perpendicular cleft in the rock, one of those cracks which not infrequently result from the splitting of gigantic masses of rock along a well-defined flaw. In some ancient convulsion this fissure had developed, the two monster fragments of the mountain had been divided, one had slipped a little, and thereafter through the ages they had stood face to face, close together. Kendric could barely squeeze his body through; he found the space slanting off to the side; he groped forward half a dozen steps, encountered an outjutting knob of stone, slipped by it, and found that the split in the cliff now slanted off the other way and widened so that there was a space five or six feet across. How far ahead the fissure extended he could form no idea yet. He turned back for Betty and bumped into her just inside the entrance.

"It's just the place for us tonight," he said. "Though how in the world you stumbled onto it gets me."

"The bushes grew close to the rocks," Betty explained. "I was thinking that we could creep back of them and find a little space where, with the brush on one side and the cliff on the other, we'd be hidden. And I found this hole."

"The air gets in and it's clean and fresh," he went on. "We couldn't hope for better."

"The walls are so close," whispered Betty, with a little shudder. "They give one the feeling they're going to press in and crush you."

"They widen a bit in a minute." He groped on ahead, came again to the outthrust knob and pressed by. "Here we turn a little to the right and here's room for a dozen people."

Betty hurried and stood close to him. In vain her eyes sought to penetrate the absolute dark; no slightest detail of floor or wall was offered save vaguely through the sense of touch.

"It's dark enough to smother you," she whispered. "I wonder what's ahead of us? I wish we dared have a light!"

He was silent a moment.

"Maybe we do dare," he said thoughtfully. "The crookedness of this place ought to shut off any glow from the outside. Let's go on a little further and we'll try."

He went on slowly, feeling a cautious way with his feet, his hand on the wall of rock at his side, Betty pressing on close behind him. Thus they continued another dozen paces or so. Then they stopped because they could find no means of continuing; so far as they could tell by groping with their hands the fissure narrowed again until it was no wider than the original entrance, and its irregularities presented difficulties to blind progress.

"Stand here," said Kendric. "Close to the rock. Here's a match. I'll slip back to the mouth of the place and we'll see if there's any glow gets that far."

"Hurry, then," said Betty, with a little shiver, fingers finding his and taking the match.

Appreciating her sensations he hurried off through the dark. He rounded the turn, called softly to her to strike the match and went on again until he was near the entrance. So still was it that he heard the scratching of the match against the sole of her sandal. But no flare of light came out to him.

"Did you light it?" he asked.

"Yes. Couldn't you see it?"

"Not a glimmer. Wait a minute and I'll bring in some stuff for a fire."

The match burned down until it warmed her fingers and went out. In the dark she waited breathlessly. A sigh of relief escaped her when she heard him coming.

He went down on his knees and made a very small heap of the dry leaves and twigs he had scraped up. When he set fire to it and straightened up they watched the flames eagerly. There was scarcely more light than a candle casts but even that faint illumination brought something of cheeriness with it. They looked about them curiously. They could see dimly the passageway along which they had come; they could make out its narrowing continuation on into the mass of the mountain. They looked up and saw an ever dwindling space merging with darkness and finally lost in utter obscurity. Underfoot was debris, rocky soil worn away from the cliffs throughout the ages, here and there fallen slivers and scale of rock. Shadows moved somberly, misshapen and grotesque, like brooding spirits of evil stirring in nightmare.

Kendric threw on a little more fuel and, to make doubly sure, went outside again, standing in the open beyond the fringe of bushes.

"Never a flicker gets through," he announced when he returned. "A man would have to come close enough to hear the wood crackle or smell the smoke to ever guess we had a fire going. And even the smoke is taken care of." They tilted back their heads to see how it crept lazing up and up until it was dissipated among the lofty shadows. "If we can manage water and food," he went on, "I think we would be safe here a year. The lazy devils taking Zoraida's pay can't make it up this way on horseback, and they're not going to climb on foot up every steep bit of mountainside hereabouts, looking for us."

"A year?" gasped Betty.

"I hope not." He became conscious of a sudden sense of relief after all that the night had offered and his old joyous laughter shone in his eyes. "But there may be wisdom in sticking close for a few days. Until they decide we've gone clear."

It was the time, inevitable though it may be long delayed, of relaxing nerves and muscles. Betty sat down limply, her hands loose in her tap, her eyes drawn to their fire, looking tired and wistful. Kendric, looking at her, felt a hot rush of anger at Zoraida for being the cause of their present condition. Betty lifted her head and caught the expression molding his face. She was wrapped about with her red gown and Zoraida's cloak; her ankles were bare; then were scratches on them; her sandals looked already worn out; her hair was tumbled and snarled. She shook it loose and began combing it through with her fingers, then twisting it up into two loose brown braids.

"IL we do have to stay a while," said Betty, gathering her courage in both hands, looking up at him an managing a smile, "I'll show you how I can cozy the place up. Tomorrow, while you're doing the man's part and finding us something to eat, I'll show you what a housekeeper I can be. Why, I can make this just like home; you'll see."

While he was doing the man's part! In her mind, then, it was all simplified and reduced to that. His, naturally, was to be the task of furnishing food, for nothing was clearer than that they must eat and that filling the larder was Jim's affair and not Betty's. Where he was to get food and how and what kind of food it might be was to be left to him. There was Betty for you, quite content to leave such matters where they properly belonged—in a man's hands. But he might rest assured that whatever he brought in, be it a handful of acorns or pine nuts or the carcass of a lean ground squirrel, would be, in Betty's eye, splendid!

"Somehow," he burst out, "in spite of Zoraida and all the bandits in Mexico, we'll carry on!"

"Of course," said Betty.

He saw that she was leaning back against the rocks, that her whole body drooped, that she looked wearied out.

"I'm going out for some boughs, the softest I can find handy," he said. "We'll have to sleep on them. And while I'm doing that I've got to figure out a way to bring some water up here. We don't know what's ahead and we'd be in hard luck bottled up here all day tomorrow with nothing to drink. Lord, I'd give a lot for a tin bucket!"

He made a little heap of dead wood close to her hand so that she could keep her fire going, and put down on the other side of her his rifle and the long obsidian knife, planning to use his pocket knife for the work at hand.

"You won't go far?" asked Betty.

"Only a few steps," he assured her. "I'll hear if you call. And you have the rifle handy."

He was going out when Betty's voice arrested him.

"It's the housekeeper's place to have the buckets ready," was what she said.

"What do you mean by that?" he asked.

"I'll show you when you come back. You'll hurry, won't you?"

"Sure thing," he answered. And went about his task.

Now Jim Kendric knew as well as any man that there is no bed to compare with the bed a man may make for himself in the forestlands. But here was no forest, no thicket of young firs aromatic and springy, nothing but the harsher vegetation of a hard land where agaves, the *maguey* of Mexico, and their kin thrive, where the cactus is the characteristic growth. He'd be in luck to find some small pines or even the dry-looking sparse cedars of the locality. These with handfuls of dry leaves and grass, perhaps some tenderer shoots from the hillside sage, with Zoraida's cloak spread over them, might make for Betty a couch on which she could manage to sleep. It was too dark for picking and choosing and his range was limited to what scant growth found root on these uplands close by.

When he returned with the first armful of branches he informed Betty cheerily that outside her fire was hidden as though a sturdy oak panel shut their door for them. Betty was bending busily over her cloak and still thus occupied when he brought in the second and third trailing armful of boughs. He stood with his hands on his hips, looking down at her curiously. And as at last Betty glanced up brightly there was an air of triumph about her.

"The bucket is ready for the water," she said.

He came closer and she held out something toward him, and again he adjusted his views to fit the companion whom he was growing to know. She had spoiled a very beautiful and expensive cloak, but of it she had improvised something intended to hold water. Not for very long, perhaps; but long enough for the journey here from the creek, if a man did not loiter on the way. With the ancient sacrificial knife she had hacked at a stringy, fibrous bit of vegetation growing near the mouth of their den; she had managed a tough loop some eight or ten inches in diameter. Then she had ripped a square of silk from the cloak which she had shaped cunningly like a deep pocket, binding it securely into the fiber rim by thrusting holes through the silk and running bits of the green fiber through like pack thread. The final result looked something less like a bucket than some strange oriole's hanging nest.

"It *will* hold water," vowed Betty, ready for argument. "I've worn bathing caps of a lot poorer grade of silk and never a drop got through. Besides I put a thickness of silk, then a layer of these broad leaves, then another piece of silk, to make sure."

"Fine," he said. "Yes, it will hold water for a while. But it's a long time from daylight until dark, and I'm afraid—"

"As if I hadn't thought of that!" said Betty. "I knew that if I looked around I'd find something. I thought of your boots, of course; and I thought of your rifle barrel. But you'll need the boots and may need the gun. Come and I'll show you our reservoir."

She put a handful of leaves and twigs on the fire for the sake of more light, and led the way toward the narrowing fissure further back in their retreat. Here she stopped before a great rudely egg-shaped boulder five or six feet through that lay in a shallow depression in the ground.

"Our water bottle," said Betty.

He supposed that she referred to the depression in the rock floor, since the boulder did not fit in it so exactly as to preclude the possibility of the big rude basin holding water. The word "evaporation" was on his lips when Betty explained. She had hoped to find somewhere a cavity in a rock that would hold their water supply; she had noted this boulder and a flattish place at its top. There her questing fingers had discovered what Kendric's, at her direction, were exploring now. There was a fairly round hole, a couple of inches across. The edges were surprisingly smooth; Kendric could not guess how deep the hole was.

"Poke a stick into it," Betty commanded.

Obeying, he learned that the hole extended eighteen inches or more. Here was a fairly regular cylinder let into a block of hard rock that would contain something like two quarts of water— certainly enough to keep the life in two people for twenty-four hours.

"We'll make a plug to fit into the mouth of it," he said, catching her idea and immediately was as enthusiastic over it as Betty. "And while we're out getting the water we'll find something for straws. There are wild grasses, oats or something that looks like oats, in the canon."

The night was well spent; dawn would come early. And with the dawn, they had no doubt, the mountain trails would fill with Zoraida's men, questing like hounds. Hence Betty and Jim lost no more time in making their trip down the steep slope to the trickle of water. They drank again, lying side by side at a pool. Then Jim filled Betty's "bucket" and they returned to their place of refuge. Kendric arranged the boughs for Betty and made her lie down. By the time he had carved and fitted a plug into their "water bottle" Betty was asleep.

CHAPTER XIX

HOW ONE WHO HIDES AND WATCHES MAY
BE WATCHED BY ONE HIDDEN

But Kendric himself did not sleep. He sat by their dead fire and watched the gradual thinning of the darkness about him as the vague light filtered in from the awakening outside world. He looked at Betty sleeping, only to look away with a frown darkening his eyes. She would sleep heavily and long; she would awake refreshed and—hungry. He was hungry already.

"It's open and shut," he told himself. "It's up to me to forage."

And it was as clear that there was always a risk of being seen as he left their hiding place. That risk would increase as the day brightened. Hence, since he must go, it were best not to tarry. He found in his pocket a stub of pencil and an old envelope. On it he wrote a brief message, placing it on the ground near her outflung hand, laying Bruce's pistol upon it.

"I'm off to fill the larder. Stick close until I come back. If I'm long gone it will be because I can't help it. But be sure I'll be back all right and bring something to eat. Jim."

He left her, not without uneasiness, but eager to hurry away so that, if all went well, his return might be hastened. He took the rifle and slipped cautiously through the bushes, stopping to make what assurance he could that he was not being seen, crawling for the most part across the open places, keeping as much as possible where boulders or trees hid him. He had already made his tentative plans; he made his way down into the bed of the ravine and thence upstream. Swiftly the light increased over the still solitudes. The sun was up on the highlands, the canons only were still dusky.

He found a place where he could stand hidden and see the cliff-broken slope where Betty was. Here he stood motionless for a long time, watching. For he knew that if by chance someone had seen him and had not followed it was because that someone had elected rather to seek the girl. At last, when the stillness remained unbroken and he saw no stirring thing, he expressed his relief in a deep sigh and went on.

His plan was to work his way up the ravine until at last he topped the ridge and went down on the further side. From his starting place he had roughly picked out his way, shaping his trail to conform to those bits of timber which would aid in his concealment. Once over the ridge he would press on until several miles lay between him and Betty. Then, if he saw game of any sort or a straying calf or sheep, he would have to take the chance that a rifle shot entailed. If his shot brought Zoraida's men down on him, he would have to fight for it or run for it as circumstances directed.

He was an hour in cresting the first ridge. Before him lay a wild country, broken and barren in places where there were wildernesses of rock and thorny bush; in other places scantily timbered and grown up in tough grasses. A more unlikely game country he thought that he had never seen. But the land hereabouts was not utterly devoid of water and always, as he went on, he sought those canons where from a distance he judged that he might come to a spring. Even so he was parched with thirst before he found the first mudhole. And before he drew near enough to drink he sat many minutes screened by some dusty willows, his eye keen either for watering game or for Zoraida's hirelings who would be watching the waterholes.

But, when at last he came on, he found nothing but a jumble

Jackson Gregory

of tracks. Ponies had watered here and had trampled the spring into its present resemblance to a mudhole. He found a place to drink, and drank thirstily, finding no fault with the alkali water or the sediment in it. He washed his hands and face in it, wet his hair and went on.

There came three more spurs of mountain to cross, all unlikely for game, each one hotter and dryer than the others. Twice he had seen a coyote; he had seen two or three gaunt, hungry-looking jackrabbits. They had been too far away to draw a shot, gray glimmers through patches of sage. He had seen never a hoof of wandering cattle. And he realized that during the heat of the day there was small hope of his sighting any browsing animal. He would probably have to wait until the cool of evening and then, if he made his kill, return to Betty in the dark. And, though he keenly kept his bearings, he knew that if he mistook a landmark somewhere and got into a wrong canon, he'd have his work cut out for him finding her at night. Well, that was only a piece of the whole pattern and he kept his mind on the immediate present.

He estimated that he was ten miles from camp. Ahead of him stretched still another ridge, a little higher than the others but a shade less barren; there were scattered pines and oaks and open grassy places. From the top of this ridge, half an hour later, he glimpsed a haze of smoke rising from the little valley just beyond. And when he came to a place whence he could have an unobstructed view he saw a scattering flock of sheep, a tiny stream of water and a rickety board shack. It was from this shelter that the smoke rose. It was high noon and down there the midday meal was cooking.

Food being cooked right under his nose! All day he had been hungry; now he was ravenous. So strong was the impulse upon him that he started down the slope in a direct line to the house, bent upon flinging open a door and demanding to be fed. But he caught himself up and sat down in the shade, hidden behind some bushes, and pondered the situation. The sheep straggled everywhere; he might wait for one of them to wander off into the bushes and then slip around upon it and make it his own with a clubbed rifle. Or he might go to the house, taking his chance.

While he was waiting and watching he saw a man come out of the cabin. The fellow lounged down to the spring for a pan of water and lounged back to the house; the eternal Mexican cigaret in his lips sent its floating ribbon of smoke behind him. Ten minutes later the same man came out, this time to lie down on the ground under a tree.

"Just one *hombre*," decided Kendric. "A lazy devil of a sheepherder. There's more than a fair chance that his *siesta* will last all afternoon."

At any rate, here appeared his even break. He sprang up, went with swinging strides down the slope, taking the shortest cut, and reached the cabin by the back door. The Mexican still lay under his tree. Kendric looked in at the door. No one there, just a bare, empty untidy room. It was bedroom, kitchen and dining-room. In the latter capacity it appealed strongly to Kendric. He went in, set his rifle down, and rummaged.

There was, of course, a big pot of red beans. And there were *tortillas*, a great heap of them. Kendric took half a dozen of them, moistened them in the half pan of water and poured a high heap of beans on them. Then he rolled the tortillas up, making a monster cylindrical bean sandwich. A soiled newspaper, with a look almost of antiquity to it, he found on a shelf and wrapped about his sandwich which he thrust into the bosom of his shirt. All of this had required about two minutes and in the meantime his eyes had been busy, still rummaging.

There was a box nailed to the wall with a cloth over it. In it he found what he expected; a lot of jerked beef, dry and hard. He filled his pockets, his mouth already full. On a table was a flour sack; he put into it the bulk of the remaining beef, some coffee and sugar, a couple of cans of milk. Then he looked out at the Mexican. The man still lay in the gorged torpor of the afternoon *siesta*.

"What will he think?" chuckled Kendric, "when he finds his larder raided and this on the table?"

This was a twenty dollar gold piece, enough to pay many times over the amount of the commandeered victuals. Kendric took up sack and rifle, had another mouthful of *frijoles* and beef, and went out the way he had come. And, all the way up the slope, he chuckled to himself.

"Enough to last Betty and me a week," he estimated. "And a place to get more if need be. That hombre will pray the rest of his life to be raided again.—And never a shot fired!"

He ate as he went, enough to keep life and strength in him but not all that his hunger craved. For he thought of Betty hungering and waiting in that hideous loneliness of uncertainty, and had no heart for a solitary meal. But in fancy, over and over, he feasted with her, and beans and jerked beef and coffee boiled in a milk-can made a banquet.

He hastened all that he could to return to her, though he knew that speeding along the trail could hardly bring him to her a second earlier. For he would, in the end, be constrained to wait for the coming of night before he climbed again to their camp. He realized soberly that Betty must not again fall into Zoraida's hands; that the result, inevitably, would be her death. Were Zoraida mad or sane, she was filled with a frenzy of blood lust. There was danger enough without his increasing it for the sake of coming an hour sooner with food. In one day Betty would not starve and fast she must.

But there was satisfaction in drawing steadily closer to her. He traveled as cautiously as he had come, he stopped in many places of concealment whence he could overlook miles of country, he followed not the shortest paths but the safest. And the sun was still high when he came to the last ridge and looked down the canon and across and saw the cliffs of home.

In his thoughts it was home.

All day long, save for the herder, he had seen not a single soul. Now he saw someone, a man at a distance and upon the side of the canon opposite the spot he and Betty had chosen. Kendric had been for ten minutes lying under a tree on the ridge, his body concealed by an outcropping ledge of rock over which he had been looking. The man, like himself, was playing a waiting game. But just now he had stirred, moving swiftly from behind a tree to a nearby boulder. Thus he had caught Kendric's eye. And thus Kendric was reassured, confident after the first quick sinking of his heart, that the other had not seen him.

The man, too far away for Kendric to distinguish detail of either costume or features, was hardly more than a slinking shadow. But almost with the first glimpse there came the quick suspicion that it was Ruiz Rios. He saw something white in the man's hand; a handkerchief since the gesture was one of wiping a wet forehead. And on that slender evidence Kendric's belief established itself. Zoraida's vacqueros would not carry white handkerchiefs; if they carried any sort at all they would probably be red or yellow or blue; or, if white originally, they would not be kept so snowy as to flash like that one. And the gesture itself, once the thought had come to him, was vaguely suggestive of that slow grace in every movement that was Rios's. The man might be anyone, conceivably even Barlow or Brace; but in his heart Kendric knew it was Rios.

Lower than ever Kendric crouched in the shelter of the rock; steady and unwinking and watchful did his eyes cling to the distant figure. He made out after a long period of motionlessness another gesture; the man's hands were up to his face; he was shading his eyes or studying the mountainside with field glasses.

The latter probably.

The afternoon dragged on and for a long time neither man moved. At last Rios, if Rios it was, withdrew a little, slipped behind a tree, passed to another and disappeared. Kendric did not see him again though he kept alert every instant. At last came the time when the sun slipped down behind the ridge and the dusk thickened and the stars came out. Kendric rose, stiff and weary, and began his slow, tedious way down into the canon. His long enforced stillness during which he had not dared doze a second, had served to bring a full realization of bodily fatigue and need of sleep. No rest last night; today many hard miles and little nourishment; now every nerve yearned for a safe return to camp for a sight of Betty, for the opportunity to throw himself down on a bed of boughs and rest.

Though it was dark when he started to climb the steep toward camp he relaxed nothing of his guarded precautions. Urged by impatience as he was, eager to know if all was well with Betty, his uneasiness for her growing with every step toward her, he crawled slowly and silently through bushes and among boulders, he stopped frequently and listened, he forced himself to a round about way rather than take the direct. All this in spite of his keen realization that for Betty the time must be dragging even as it dragged for him. Betty hungry, frightened and lonely was, above all, uncertain.

But at last he came to the opening in the rocks. He squeezed through, his heart suddenly heavy within him as the stillness of the place smote him like a positive assurance that Betty was gone. He went on, his teeth set hard. If Betty were gone, by high heaven, there would be a rendering of accounts! And then, even before the first glimmer of her little fire reached him, he heard her glad cry. She came running to meet him, her two hands out, groping for his. And he dropped rifle and provision bag and in the half dark his hands found hers and gripped hard in mighty rejoicing.

"Thank God!" said Betty.

And Jim Kendric's words were like a deep, fervent echo: "Thank God."

CHAPTER XX

IN WHICH A ROCK MOVES, A DISCOVERY IS MADE AND MORE THAN ONE AVENUE IS OPENED

In the light of Betty's fire Jim hastily poured forth the contents of his bag and never did a child's eyes at Christmas time shine like Betty's. She had hungered until she was weak and trembling and now such articles as Jim displayed were amply sufficient to elicit from her that little cry of delight. Tortillas and beans, meat and coffee and sugar and milk—it was a banquet fit for a king and a queen!

"The only thing," cautioned Kendric, "is to go slow. It's a course dinner, Miss Betty. And first comes a bit of milk."

He ripped open a can with his pocket knife, poured out half of the thick contents into the silk-water bag and diluted the remainder with water. Thereafter he watched Betty while she forced herself, at his bidding, to eat and drink sparingly. And he noted that during his absence she had been busy working on her wardrobe. Using both the red garment and the cloak, employing in her task the obsidian knife and strips of green fiber, she had made for herself a garment which it would have been hard to classify and yet which was astonishingly becoming. As much as anything Kendric had ever seen it resembled a stylish and therefore outlandish riding habit. She wore Zoraida's shoes and stockings.

"I washed them with sand and water first," said Betty around a corner of her sandwich. "And I let them air all day."

"No visitors?" said Kendric. "No sign of anyone on our trail?"

Betty assured him that she had been unmolested, that the terrible stillness of the mountain had been unbroken. And she sought to tell him how long the day had been.

"I know," he said. "It was long enough for me, and I was out in the open and stirring. It must have been a slice of torment for you here alone all day, not even knowing if I'd ever get back or have any food when I came."

"I knew you'd come," said Betty. "But it was lonesome and shivery."

He told her of his day and finally of the man he had seen across the canon. Further, of his suspicion that it was Ruiz Rios. Betty shuddered.

"He is a terrible creature," she said. "I'd rather it was anyone else. Do you think he has an idea we're here?"

He stretched out by the fire, helped himself to a bit of the dried beef and told her his thoughts.

"I know just about how Rios would reason things out. And, oddly enough, it strikes me that though he began with a false premise he has come pretty close to reaching the right conclusion. You see, he knows that I came down here with Barlow looking for treasure. He knew Captain Escobar was ahead of him on the same trail and when he could get nothing further out of Escobar he killed him. But he did know in a general way where we expected to find the stuff. So, when you and I skip out and don't head straight back to the gulf, he's pretty sure I'm still making a stab at getting the treasure. And it has happened that you and I, blundering along in the dark, have hit on this spot which is not far from the place where the treasure is supposed to be. So Rios hides in the brush with a pair of glasses and keeps his eye peeled for us. I think that's the whole explanation of his being out yonder. And I think that's all he knows."

"It's enough." Betty shook her head dubiously.

"Of course," he admitted, "this is just a guess on my part. He may know more than I think.—During the day," he added, "and just now while I lay out yonder waiting for dark, I've had a lot of time to think things out. First, it strikes me as best to hide out here one more day and then, tomorrow night, to make a break for the outside. Personally, I don't know that I'd be fit for much tonight; it's a good stiff hike to where we left the *Half Moon* and I won't be able to keep awake much longer. Then by tomorrow night, even if Zoraida is as keen as ever to get us back, I doubt if her men's enthusiasm for vigilance will have lasted at the first heat. There'll be a better chance for us to slip through."

Here, again, the responsibility in Betty's way of thinking was his and she accepted his plan without challenge.

"Another thing I've been thinking of," he went on, "is that queer, smooth hole in that boulder; where we've our water stored. What have you made of it?"

"A reservoir," she answered lightly, her spirits risen swiftly with his coming and a taste of food. "What else?"

"Rios is hard set in his belief that there's ancient treasure nearby. So is Barlow. So, evidently, was Escobar. If so, what more likely place than where we are? That hole didn't make itself after that regular fashion. I don't see just what it has to do with the case, I'll admit. But somebody made it a long time ago and didn't do it just for the fun of the job. I've a notion that it has its bearing on the thing. Somehow."

"It isn't big enough to hold much treasure," said Betty. "Maybe they didn't finish it?"

But from this they went to other matters. Kendric merely decided that while they spent a long tomorrow of inaction he would look into the matter. There was no great temptation to tarry for treasure and the incentive to be on the way, traveling light, was sufficiently emphasized. But there was a quiet day to be put in tomorrow, if all went right, and he was not the man to forget what had brought him southward.

"We'll both go to sleep," he said presently, "and not do any worrying about what the other fellow may be doing. With our fire out and a lot of dead limbs scattered about the entrance to crack under a man's foot, they'll not surprise us tonight, even if they should know where we are. Tomorrow we'll keep a watch over the ravine. And tomorrow night I hope we'll be on the trail toward the gulf. Now do you want to slip out with me for a goodnight drink of water? Or would you rather wait here for me?"

Betty was on her feet in a flash.

"I've done enough waiting today to last me the rest of my life!" she cried emphatically. "I'll go with you."

So again, and as cautious as they had been last night, they made their way down the steep slope and drank in the starlight. They tarried a little by the trickle of water, heeding the silence, breathing deep of the soft night, lifting their eyes to the stars. The world seemed young and sweet about them, clean and tender, a place of infinite peace and kindness rather than of a pursuing hate. They stood close together; their shoulders brushed companionably. Together they hearkened to a tiny voice thrilling through the emptiness, the monotonous vibrating cadences of some happy insect. The heat of the day had passed with the day, the perfect hour had come. It was one of those moments which Jim Kendric found to his liking. Many such still hours had he known under many skies and out of the night had always come something vague and mighty to speak to something no less mighty which lay within his soul. But always before, when he drank the fill of a time like this, he

Jackson Gregory

had been alone. He had thought that a man must be alone to know the ineffable content of the solitudes. Tonight he was not alone. And yet more perfect than those other hours in other lands was this hour slipping by now as the tiny voice out yonder slipped through the silence without shattering it. Certain words of his own little song crept into his mind.

"Where it's only you
And the mountainside."

That "you" had always been just Jim Kendric. After this, if ever again he sang it, the "you" would be Betty.

"Shall we go back?" he asked quietly.

He saw Betty start. Her eyes came back from the stars and sought his. He could see them only dimly in the shadow of her hair, but he knew they were shining with the gush of her own night-thoughts. They scooped up their water then and went back up the mountain. Their fire was almost down and they did not replenish it. They went to their beds of boughs and lay down in silence. Presently Jim said "Good night." And Betty, the hush of the outside in her voice as she answered, said softly "Good night."

They were astir before dawn. Fresh water must be brought before daylight brightened in the canons. This time Jim went alone to the creek and when he got back Betty had their fire blazing. Betty made the breakfast, insisting on having her free unhampered way with it.

"There are some things I can do," said Betty, "and a great many I can't. It happens that I know what things are beyond me and those that are within the scope of my powers. One thing that I can do is cook. And I have camped before now, if you please."

So, when Jim had brought her firewood and had placed the various articles of their larder handy for her and had offered his services with jack-knife to open a can or hack through a bit of beef, he stood back and fully enjoyed the sight of Betty making breakfast. He enjoyed the prettiness of her in her odd costume of blouse, scarlet sash and knickerbockers, silk stockings and high heeled slippers; the atmosphere of intimacy which hovered over them, distilled in a measure from the magic of a camp fire, certainly aided and abetted by the homey arrangement of Betty's brown hair; the aroma of coffee beginning to bubble in a milk tin; the fragrance of an inviting stew in the other tin wherein were mingled *frijoles* and "jerky." Ruiz Rios might lurk around the next spur of the mountain; Zoraida might be inciting her hirelings to fresh endeavor; much danger might be watching by the trail which in time they would have to follow—but here and now, for the few minutes at least, there was more of quiet enjoyment in their retreat than of discomfort or of fear of the future.

"Let's go camping some time," said Jim abruptly. "Just you and me. We'll take a pack horse; we'll load him to the guards with the proper sort of rations; we'll strike out into the heart of the California sierra—where there are fine forests and little lakes and lonely trails and peace over all of it."

Betty looked at him curiously, then away swiftly.

"Breakfast is ready," she announced.

He sipped at his coffee absently; his eyes, looking past Betty, saw into a hidden, cliff-rimmed valley in those other, fresher mountains further north, glimpsed vistas down narrow trails between tall pines and cedars and firs, fancied a lodge made of boughs on the shore of a little blue lake. He'd like to show Betty this camping spot; he'd like to bring in for her a string of gleaming trout; he'd like to lie on his side under the cliffs and just watch her. He had whittled two sticks for spoons; he ate his stew with his and forgot to talk.

And Betty, watching him covertly, wondered astutely if over the first meal she had cooked for him Jim Kendric wasn't readjusting his ancient ideas of woman. For some hidden reason, or for no reason at all, her silence was as deep as his.

After breakfast, however, it was Betty who started talk. They sought to plan definitely for tonight. Kendric told her of the way he and Barlow had come, of the *Half Moon* awaiting his and Barlow's return, of his determination to make use of the schooner if they could come to it. Barlow's plans were not at Kendric's disposal; the sailor might be counting on the vessel and he might not. At any rate he and Betty could slip down the gulf in it and either take ship at La Paz, sending it back up the gulf then, or steer on to San Diego. Of course he would seek to get in touch with Barlow; he could send a message of some sort. But after all Barlow had taken the game into his own hands and had said that it was now each man for himself.

"We can make the trip during the night, if we can make the get-away," he told her. "We'll have to take a roundabout way at first, edging the valley along the foothills on this side until we're well past the ranch house, then cut across the shortest way and pick up the trail on the other side. We can take enough water in our milk tins to last us, especially since we're traveling in the cool."

"And if," suggested Betty, "the *Half Moon* isn't there? Or if Zoraida has set some of her men to watch for us there?"

Naturally he had thought of that. If they came to the gulf and a new problem of this sort offered itself, then it would be time to consider it.

"We'll just hope for the best," he answered, "and try to be ready for what comes."

Carefully they conserved each tiny fragment of food, using the flour sack for cupboard. They went cautiously to the entrance of their hiding place and for a long time crouched behind the bushes, watching the canon sides, seeking for a sign of Rios as they fancied Rios was seeking them. And during the quiet hours they explored the place in which they were.

First they considered the odd hole in the big boulder, seeking to find some logical reason for its being, asking themselves if it could have any connection whatever with the ancient hidden treasure. Clearly it was the result of human labor. Therefore it appeared to have its relation to an older order of civilization since it was not conceivable that a modern man had taken such a task upon himself. But its meaning baffled.

"It could be a sign, like a blazed tree or a cross scratched on a block of stone," said Kendric. "But it could mean anything. Or nothing," he was forced to admit.

It was only in the late afternoon, after a long period of inactivity and silence, that an inspiration came to Kendric. Meantime they had poked into every crack and cranny, they had scraped at any loose dirt on the ground, they had gone back and forth and up and down over every square inch of the place repeatedly. And Kendric thought that he had given up when the last idea came to him. He went quickly back to the boulder. Betty watched him interestedly.

"I thought we'd given that up," she said.

He had both hands on the boulder, his fingers gripping the edge of the baffling hole, and was seeking to shake the big block of rock. Betty came to his side.

"You think that it was made as a hand-hole? That you can turn the rock over?"

"It does move—just a little," he said. He put all of his strength into a fresh attack. The boulder trembled slightly—that was all.

"I'll bet you my half of the loot that I've got the hang of it, Miss Betty," he announced triumphantly.

"Wait and see."

He began looking about him for something.

"If I only dared slip outside for a minute," he said. Then his eye fell on the rifle. "We'll have to make this do. I run a risk of jamming the front sight but I guess we can fix that."

He protected the sight as well as he could by wrapping his handkerchief about it. The muzzle of the gun he thrust down into the hole in the rock.

"Get it now?" he asked. "If that hole wasn't made to allow a lever to be inserted, then tell me what it *was* made for. And here's even the place to stand while a man uses it! I'll double the bet!"

That excitement which always gets into any man's blood when he believes that he is on the threshold of a golden discovery, already shone in his eyes. He stepped to a sort of shelf in the cavern wall close to the boulder, so that now his feet were on a level with the top of the rock he meant to move. So he could just reach out and grasp the butt of the rifle. Betty stood by, watching with an eagerness no less than his own. Gradually he set his force at work on his lever, trying this way and that. And then—

"It's moving!" cried Betty. "The rock is turning!"

And now it turned readily, his leverage being ample to the task.

"Look under the rock as it tips back," he told Betty. "See if there isn't a hole under it. Big enough for a man to go through!"

"Yes!" answered Betty after a breathless fashion. "Yes. A little more. Oh, come see. It looks almost like steps going down!"

"I'll have to force it back a little farther," he returned. "Maybe it will balance there. If not we'll have to get loose stones and wedge under it."

He pried it further and further until at last it would not budge another inch. He loosened his grip a trifle on the rifle-lever and the rock began to settle back into its former place. But Betty had seen and already was bringing fragments of stone to block under the edges.

"Now," she called. "Come see."

He jumped down; the boulder, wedged securely, lay on its side. He went to Betty and from what they saw before them they looked into each other's eyes wonderingly.

"The tale was true," he said with conviction. "You and I have found the way to the treasure."

In the floor was an opening a couple of feet square. Very rude, uneven steps led down, vanishing in a forbidding black dark. Kendric lay flat and looked down. Little by little he could penetrate a bit further, but in the end there lay a region of impenetrable darkness into which the steps merged.

"You're going down *there*!" gasped Betty.

"*Am* I?" he laughed. "You wouldn't want us to skip out tonight without even having looked into it, would you?"

"N-o." But she hesitated and even shuddered as she too lay down and peered into the forbidding place.

"We'll not take any chances we don't have to." He got up and began immediately to make his few preparations. "Here's the rifle; I'll leave it handy for you in case our friend Rios should surprise us. I'll take a handful of stuff with me to burn for a torch. And we'll have another look out into the canon to begin with."

He drew out the rifle and gave it to Betty. He placed other stones with the ones she had slipped under the edges of the boulders. And finally he went to look out into the canon.

"No one in sight," he reported. "And now, here goes."

He sat down at the edge of the opening in the floor, set a match to his crude torch, grinned comfortingly up at Betty and wriggled over and set his foot to the first step. As he did so there came to him an unpleasant memory of the fashion in which Zoraida had guarded her own secret places with rattlesnakes; he wondered if any of the ugly brutes lived down here? As it happened the thought had its influence in saving him from mishap later. For, though he came upon no snakes, he went warily and thus avoided another danger.

His torch burnt vilely and smoked copiously. But what faint light it afforded was sufficient. Step by step he went down until feet and legs and then entire body were lost to Betty above; she had set the rifle aside and was kneeling, her hands clasped in her excitement. Now she could see only his head and the torch held high; he looked up and smiled at her and waved the faggot. Then she saw only the dimly burning fire and the hand clutching it. And dimmer and dimmer grew his light until she strained her eyes to catch a glint of it and could not tell if it were being extinguished for want of dean air or if he were very, very far below her.

"Jim!" she called.

"All right," his voice floated back to her.

He had reached the bottom of the stone stairway; his feet shifting back and forth informed him that he was on a rock floor that was full of inequalities and that pitched steeply ahead of him. His fire was almost out, deteriorating into a mere smudge curling up from dying embers. The air was bad, thick and heavy; breathing was difficult. He looked up and made out the dim square by which Betty knelt. He could go a little further without danger, since if the air grew worse he could still turn and run back up the steps? The floor seemed to be pitching still more steeply. Fearful of a precipice or a pit and a fall, he went down on his hands and knees and crept on. Thus he held his poor torch before him and thus he made a first discovery. The smoke was drifting steadily into his face. And that meant a current of air.

Still crawling, he pressed forward eagerly, sniffing the air. But he relaxed none of his caution; the floor underneath still pitched steeply and, it seemed to him, grew steeper. Then his light began to brighten; the embers glowed and when he blew on them, broke again into flame. He looked up; he could not see the square of light above now. Evidently he was passing into some sort of wide tunnel or lengthy chamber. Dimly he could descry walls on either side of him. Ahead was only black emptiness; underfoot the uneven floor seeming to grow smoother and to slant still more abruptly downward.

"I'd better go easy," he told himself grimly. "If a man started sliding here I wonder where he'd land!"

Decidedly the air was better. He filled his lungs and stopped where he was, moving his torch above his head, lowering it, peering about him on all sides. At last he made out that a dozen steps further on there was a level space about which the walls were squared so as to give the effect of a small room. He drew nearer step by step and again was forced to kneel and then feel his way forward with his hands for the floor under him grew steadily steeper so that it was difficult to keep from sliding down the incline. When he saw his way sufficiently clearly he did slide the last three or four feet. And now, as again his torch flared and the air freshened in his nostrils, he saw that which put an eager excitement in his blood. The small room had every appearance of an ancient storeroom. He saw objects piled on the floor, objects of strange designs, cups and pitchers and vessels of various shapes. He caught one up and it was heavy. He clanked two together and the mellow, bell-like sound had the golden note.

"Solid gold," he muttered. And as something upon one of the vessels—it was a drinking goblet of ornate design—caught the light and shone back at him like imprisoned fire, "Encrusted with precious stones!"

He put the things down and looked further. There was a big chest. As his foot struck it it burst asunder and tumbled its contents to the floor. From the disordered heap there shone forth from countless places the colorful glow of jewels. He passed to another chest, a smaller one placed as in a position of honor upon a square tablet of rock. He held his torch close and looked in; he thrust in his hand and withdrew it filled with pearls. Even he, no connoisseur like Barlow, would have staked his life on their genuineness. They were of many sizes but more large ones among them than small; their soft, rich loveliness dimmed even those of Zoraida's wearing.

"A man could carry a million dollars out of here in his hands!"

He went on. But what he held in his hand he thrust into his pocket as he went. The remembrance of Zoraida's rattlesnakes came to him abruptly. Thus he moved with renewed caution and thus he was saved from a misadventure. For even so he almost stepped to a fall. Between two heaps of tumbled articles was a square hole, sheer and black, several feet across. He stooped over it. The air came up with a rush. At first he could see only a little way. Then he made out that the shaft went straight down only a few feet and then slanted away in a great chute like the floor down which he had already come, only so much steeper that he knew had he fallen there would have been no return possible for him. To what eventual landing place would he have plunged? For a moment or so his eyes strained in vain into the gloom. Slowly faint and then growing detail rewarded him. It was but a small section offered him because of the angling of the tunnel. But before a watch could have ticked ten times he knew into what place he would have fallen, into what regions his glance had penetrated. The light was dim down yonder but he knew that he was looking down into the gardens of the golden king of Tezcuco.

"Another way into the hidden place, and one that Zoraida herself knows nothing of," he thought. "If a man took this drop and then the slide, he'd land with the breath jolted out of him but there is shrubbery to fall on and it wouldn't kill him. But in there he'd stay! There would be no climbing back up the slippery chute."

He withdrew and looked about him again. Expecting pitfalls, he took no single step without making sure first. He crossed the chamber and upon the further side he came to a second pit and a second tunnel. This like the first was steep and smooth; this also gave him a glint of light at the further end. The light was dim; he made out that the distant mouth of the tunnel was obscured by a tangle of brush and scrub trees.

"Another underground garden?" he wondered. "Or the outside world?"

He filled his lungs with the air flowing upward. He fancied that it had a fresher, sweeter smell, that there was the wholesomeness of sunlight in it.

"It would be a joke," was his quick thought, "if there were a way out for us here while Rios watches the canon above!"

It was then that there came to him, faint from far above, Betty's scream. He whirled and ran. Again he heard her screams, echoing wildly. As he stumbled on there came to him the muffled sound of a rifle-shot.

Jackson Gregory

CHAPTER XXI

HOW ONE RETURNS UNWILLINGLY WHITHER HE WOULD WILLINGLY ENTER BY ANOTHER DOOR

Again and again as he ran Kendric shouted to Betty that he was coming. Then at last, after an agony of fear and silence, he heard her call in answer. He stumbled but ran on. When he came where he could see the square of light marking the hole which led to the level where she was, he caught his first glimpse of Betty. She was standing by the opening, tense to the finger tips that were tight about the rifle. He sped up the steps and to her side. And he was treated to the sight of Ruiz Rios, lying white-faced on the floor, a hand at his shoulder and that hand dyed red. Beside him, where it had fallen, was his revolver.

"I—I shot him!" Betty gasped.

"And serves him right," cried Kendric heartily. He took the gun from her hands and strode over to Rios while, at last, Betty's face was hidden by her shaking hands. "So you're on the job, are you?"

Rios looked sick and miserable. But slowly, as he lifted his black eyes to the man standing over him the old evil fires played in them. He stirred a little and lay back.

"My shoulder is broken," he groaned.

"You're in luck to be alive," Kendric told him sternly. "What do you want here?"

"I'll bleed to death!" Quick fright sent a shiver through him. "For the love of God stop the blood for me."

Kendric could scarcely do less than look at the wound. Presently he straightened up with a grunt of disgust.

"It's only a flesh wound," he said coolly. "The bone isn't even touched and it's a clean hole. You'll last for a lot of devilment yet."

Rios sat up. He felt of his hurt with tender fingers and slowly the fear went out of his look and his old craft and hate came back.

"You've found the treasure—here," he said. "You will have to talk with me before you touch it, senor."

"You talk big, Rios," snapped Kendric angrily. "It strikes me that you are just now in no position to dictate. You should thank your stars if, presently, we let you go about your business. Whether or not we have found treasure does not concern you."

So intent was he upon Rios, so occupied with considering what was to be done with him, that he did not note who it was who had come to stand in the narrow cleft between them and the entrance from the canon side. But Betty, her hands dropping from her horrified face saw.

"Oh," cried Betty. "We are lost!"

Then he saw that following Rios had come Zoraida and that she stood and looked at them, her eyes filled with mockery and triumph.

"Who is it that speaks of what shall be done with that which rightfully is Zoraida's?" she demanded, her voice ringing out boldly. "And you two, who thought to escape me, I have you in a trap!"

Kendric swung his rifle about so that the muzzle was towards her. His eyes hardened.

"If we have to shoot our way out of this, we're going free," he told her shortly.

Zoraida's only answer came quickly, unexpectedly, before he could step forward. Her hand went to her bosom; out came her silver whistle; a blast shrilled forth from it, loud and penetrating.

"Twenty of my men, all armed, hear that," she said defiantly. "They are just below. Listen and you will hear them coming."

The sound, first of men's voices somewhere outside, then of rattling stones under running feet, told that Zoraida spoke truly. Kendric heard and for an instant was struck motionless with indecision. The entrance was narrow and he could make a fight for it—there was Betty to think of, behind him but in the path of glancing bullets—there was Rios, wounded but treacherous—there was Zoraida—there was the treasure below and he had no mind to see it snatched from under his eyes—

Then the one chance presented itself to him, clear and imperative.

"Rios," he commanded, "down you go through that hole or I swear to God I'll blow your brains out! Quick! And Zoraida, you with him." He sprang upon her and dragged her with him, shoving her toward the opening in the floor. He took time then to whirl and fire one shot along the narrow way which Zoraida's men must come, confident that they would pause, if only for an instant. "Down, Rios. Down, Zoraida!"

A sort of fury looked out of his eyes and even Betty drew back from him fearfully. He grasped Rios by the shoulder and the Mexican seeing the look in his eyes made no resistance. Had he fought back he would have been killed and he knew it. He went down the steps. Zoraida would have held back but again Kendric's hand, rough on her arm, sent her forward and, rather than fall, she was forced to Rios's heels. Kendric fired again along the cleft. Then he began knocking loose the stones which held the lever-rock back. When only one stone kept the boulder in place, he called sharply to Betty:

"Down we go with them. Then I'll knock that stone out from below and we'll have time to breathe before they come on us."

"But," exclaimed Betty, "can we lift it again from below?"

"God knows," he returned. "I think so. But I don't know that we'll have to; I think there's another way out. Hurry."

Voices were calling excitedly from without. Plainly the men taking Zoraida's pay would in time steel themselves to making an entrance, but just as plainly they saw death in store for some of them and hesitated. It struck Kendric that their delay would give him time for one other thing and that that other thing would mean much more time gained later on. He scooped up handful after handful of dirt and poured it into the lever-hole in the boulder, filling it even with the surface. Thus, it would not be readily detected and might never be noted. Then, snatching up his rifle and the bag of food, he ran down the steps with Betty. A thrust with his rifle barrel, and a quick jerk back, knocked the wedge stone free and saved him his gun. The boulder toppled back into place; the stairway and tunnel below were plunged into absolute darkness.

Kendric caught Betty's hand.

"This way," he told her. "It's straight going and no danger for a while. Rios, Zoraida! Stand where you are and wait for us or I'll start shooting wild. Where are you?"

"Here," growled Rios, his voice indicating that he had gone no great distance.

"And Zoraida?"

Zoraida did not answer. Kendric went on a step or two and then struck a match. By its short-lived light he made out Zoraida standing close to Rios. Then the flame burned out.

"Straight ahead," commanded Kendric. When there was no sound of a step being taken, he drew Betty's hand through his arm so as to have both of his hands free and went forward.

"I can hardly breathe," whispered Betty. He felt her hand tighten on his arm. "It is getting terribly steep underfoot—"

He came to where Rios was and set the rifle barrel in the small of his back. Rios cursed bitterly but moved on. Kendric's hand found Zoraida's arm and gripped it tightly.

"We're all together in this," he said sharply. "And don't start your old favorite knife act. This is no time for foolery."

Zoraida moved on. But again she set her whistle to her lips and thereafter she called out loudly to her men, commanding them to follow swiftly.

"They won't hear you," said Kendric. "And they couldn't obey you this time anyhow. Hurry; we'll all stifle if we don't get out of this foul air. Rios, give me some matches; mine are getting short."

Rios, without comment, having as little love as another for the uncertainty of the dark about him, did as he was commanded. He also saved half of his box and began striking them himself. And thus they went on, all of them save Kendric wondering. Making the last, steepest descent, they stood huddled together in the treasure chamber.

"Here," said Kendric, releasing Zoraida, "we have fresh air. Here we can talk. And, if we are sensible people, a new day can begin for all of us here."

Ruiz Rios's wound must have been even less severe than Kendric had supposed it. For now the Mexican seemed utterly to have lost consciousness of it. He was striking fresh matches; he stooped and picked up something at his foot; a little gasp broke from him. He tossed it down, caught up something else.

"Gold!" he muttered. "Gold everywhere!"

Zoraida looked about her, seeming unmoved. Her eyes followed Rios contemptuously, roved away about the room, tarried only briefly with the heaped-up treasure, sped to Kendric and to Betty.

"You are fools, fools!" she taunted them. "All thanks, Senor Kendric, for having led me straight to that for which I have been looking all my life."

Rios had come back to her side, both hands full.

"Zoraida," he said swiftly, "let us talk reason as the American says. We have this!" He held up his hands; his eyes gloated. "Let them have their lives and go, so that they take nothing in their hands. Look at this! Here—"

His words trailed off abruptly in a scream of terror. He had moved only a trifle as he spoke, he had taken a step backward between the two high heaps of treasure where the pit was. He was falling—he threw out his arms, clutching wildly. In a flash he was gone from sight. But not alone. For his hand, seeking to save him, had caught at Zoraida and she was snatched back, overbalanced, drawn down with him. Her scream rose above his cry of terror. Both vanished and Jim and Betty stood alone, looking into each other's wide eyes.

"Do you think—they are dead?" faltered the girl.

Jackson Gregory

They went to the hole and looked down. The view which Kendric had seen before slowly disentangled itself from the darkness. They saw nothing of those who had fallen.

"It would mean the short fall here," said Kendric musingly, "the steep slide and no doubt another drop at the end. We wouldn't be able to see them at first. But someway, I don't believe they are dead!"

He did not explain then; it would take too long and they had their own salvation to work out. But here was his thought: Zoraida had dropped back into the gardens of the golden king. He did not believe she would be able to climb up this way again. And he did not believe that she would have with her the many keys needed to open the way she knew. It impressed him that here might be the judgment of a just God—Zoraida immured for all time in the heart of ancient Mexico. Zoraida with her priests and young men and children whom her stern decree had imprisoned here. Zoraida and Ruiz Rios together in the place of hidden treasure.

CHAPTER XXII

REGARDING A NECKLACE OF PEARLS AND CERTAIN PLANS OF TWO WHO WERE MEANT TO BE ONE

From afar, reaching them only faintly, came the sounds of men's voices, Zoraida's men clamoring above, mystified and with ample cause.

"It may be our chance is now, not tonight," said Kendric. "Although it's but a little way from the house some of them, if not all, will have ridden; their horses will be down in the canon. If we can slip out this way and come to the horses while they're looking for us up there—"

"This way?" Betty for an instant wondered if he meant to follow Zoraida and Rios.

"There is another way," he told her. "Come.—But first, we'll not go empty handed."

He began a quick rummaging among the ancient chests.

"Hurry," pleaded the girl. "What do we want with treasure? They may find us at any second. Oh, hurry!"

"Coming," he answered. "But here are wings to fly with." She saw him putting a number of small objects into his pockets. He moved to another point and she could not see what he was

Jackson Gregory

doing, could only guess that still he was stuffing something into the provision bag and further cramming his pockets. Just then there was in Betty's soul no thirst for wealth, just the mighty yearning for the open country and flight and the peace of safety afar.

"Here I am." Jim was again at her side. He caught her arm. "This way."

He led her to that other pit giving entrance to the second tunnel. At another time Betty might have hesitated to slip down into it; now she was eager for anything that gave the vaguest hope of flight. For the faint far voices still clamored and she feared that the hounds that hunted in Zoraida's wake might find the secret of the boulder and roll it back with many hands and rush down upon them.

But Kendric held her back while he first went down. He gripped the edges of the pit with his hands and lowered himself to the length of his arms and dropped. It was but a short fall and he landed safely and steadied himself and managed to save himself from going down the slide by clutching at the rock wall. Betty handed down the rifle and bag, then lowered herself and he caught her in his arms. And then, in no little uncertainty and not without grave dread of what dangers they might encounter, they went on.

The slide was steep and yet by going very guardedly, lying face down at times and inching down cautiously, they made a slow descent. The tunnel grew steadily smaller as they progressed; their bodies shut off the light. The terrible thought presented itself to Kendric that when they came to the outlet it might be too small for them to pass through; and that to return up the tunnel was a task which would present its difficulties. So, when they came to a place where Betty could cling on and keep from slipping, he called to her to wait while he went on.

The time had come when his rifle was an encumbrance; he needed both hands to keep from slipping. He had had the forethought to turn the muzzle downward, since Betty was above him. Now he craned his neck and sought to peer down along his body. Far away, somewhere, was a glint of sunlight, small but full of promise. He saw, as he had seen before, a tangle of brush. He wondered if it were a clump of bushes on a little flat? Or if they were shrubs clinging to some steep face of cliff? When at last he came to the mouth of this chute—if it were wide enough for a man's body to pass through—would the man have reached safety or would he be precipitated through space and down a fifty foot fall of rock?

"The bushes ought to stop the rifle," he decided. "At any rate the time has come when I need both hands." And he let it slide past him and sought to watch it as it clattered along the incline. But he saw nothing of it in the dim passage until it struck the fringe of bushes. Then it crashed through and was gone—without telling him how and where! The bag, a knot tied in it, he sent down after the gun.

His misgivings were considerable but he went on. He called out to Betty: "It looks all right. Hold on till I call," and began inching downward again. With his feet he sought to judge the slope below him. It seemed to be growing steeper. Still he went on and down. He caught at any unevenness in the rock he could lay hand upon, lowering himself to the length of his arm, groping for handhold and foothold everywhere. Then a handhold to which he had entrusted his weight betrayed him, the tiny sliver of stone scaled off and he began to slip. He clutched wildly but his body gained fresh momentum. He heard Betty shriek above him. He had a vision of himself plunging down the cliffs. Then he knew that he had struck the bushes, had broken through, was rolling down a steep slope, rolling and rolling.

The breath jolted out of him, he was brought up with a jerk in another clump of bushes, wild sage in a little level space. He hastily jumped up and began to scramble back up toward the tunnel's mouth. He could not see it from below, he could see only the patch of brush which, since it was directly above him, must conceal it. He saw his rifle where it stood on end, the muzzle jammed between two rocks. He wanted to call to Betty but did not dare, not knowing how close some of Zoraida's men might be. Betty could not hold on there forever; she would slip as he had done or, frightened terribly, by now she might be seeking frenziedly to make her way back to the treasure chamber.

But as it happened Betty was to make the descent with less violence than Kendric's. She had thought that surely Jim had been snatched away from her to a broken death below; she had gone dizzy with sick fear; she had struggled for a securer grip—and she, too, had slipped. Down she sped, half fainting. But somewhere her wide sash caught and held briefly, letting her slip again before her fingers could find a hold, but breaking the momentum of her progress. So, when she was shot out into the open, a few yards above Kendric, the brush all but stopped her. And then, as she was slipping by him, Kendric caught her and held her.

Betty sat up and stared at him incredulously. Then there came into her eyes such a light as Jim Kendric had never seen in eyes of man or woman.

"I thought you were dead," said Betty simply. "And I did not want to live."

He helped her to her feet and they hurried down the slope. He caught up his rifle, merely grunted at the discovery of a sight knocked off, found near it the bag of food and treasure, and led the way down into the canon. A glance upward showed him no sign of Zoraida's men.

"There are the horses," whispered Betty.

Down in the bed of the ravine were a dozen or more saddled ponies. They stood where their riders had left them, their reins over their heads and dragging on the ground.

Daughter of the Sun   257

"Run!" said Kendric. "If we can get into saddle before they see us we're as good as at home!"

Hand in hand they ran, stumbling along the slope, crashing through the brush. But as they drew nearer and the ponies pricked up their ears they forced themselves to go slowly. Kendric caught the nearest horse, tarrying for no picking and choosing, and helped Betty up into the saddle. The next moment he, too, was mounted. He looked again up the mountainside. Still no sign of Zoraida's men. A broad grin of high satisfaction testified that Jim Kendric found this new arrangement of mundane affairs highly to his liking.

"We'll drive these other ponies on ahead of us," he suggested. "Until they're a good five miles off. And then we'll see how fast a cowpony can run!"

So, herding a lot of saddled horses ahead of them, reins flying and soon putting panic into the animals, Jim and Betty rode down into the valley. They looked down to the big adobe house and saw no one; the place slept tranquilly in the late afternoon sun. They passed the corrals and still saw no one. If any of her men had not followed Zoraida, they were lounging under cover. The maids would be about the evening meal and table setting, in the *patio* or in the house.

Straight across the valley they drove the ponies and there, in the first foothills scattered and left them. Then they settled down to hard riding, both praying mutely that when they came to the gulf and the beach they would find the *Half Moon* awaiting them.

The stars were out when they came to the beach where only a few days ago Kendric and Barlow had landed. And there, at anchor, rode the *Half Moon*. They saw her lights and they made out the hulk of her. Kendric shouted and fired his rifle. Almost immediately came an answering hail, the melodious voice of Nigger Ben. They saw a lantern go down over the side, they watched it bob and dance and made out presently that it was coming toward them. They heard Nigger Ben's voice, chanting monotonously, as he pulled at the oars of the small boat.

"Howdy, Cap'n, howdy!" cried Ben joyously. He took in the small figure which had dismounted at Kendric's side and ducked his head and included her in his greetings with a "Howdy, Miss." And then, looking in vain for another member of the party: "Where's Cap'n Barlow?"

"Let's get on board, Ben," answered Kendric. "I'll tell you there."

So they stepped into the dingey and pushed off and rowed back to the *Half Moon*.

"There's a gent here says he's a frien' of your'n, Cap," said Ben. "Ah dunno. Anyhows, he's been here all day an' we're watchin' he don't make no mischief."

They went up over the side and Kendric showed Betty straightway to the cabin that was to be hers. Then he turned wonderingly to Ben. He could only think of Bruce, since it wasn't Barlow—

And Bruce it was. The boy came forth from the shadows, standing before Kendric looking at once dejected and defiant and shamefaced.

"I was a damn' fool, Jim," he said bluntly. "Forget it, if you can, and take a passenger back to the States with you. Or tell me to go to hell—and I guess I'll tuck my tail between my legs and go."

Kendric's hand went out impulsively and he cried with great heartiness:

"Forget it, boy.—What about Barlow?"

"Barlow's like a crazy man," said Bruce. He spoke quickly as though eager to get through with what he had to say. "After that cursed game of cards he got the same sort of a message I got; we were to wait, each in his own room, for—for her." He hesitated; Kendric understood that it hurt him even to refer to Zoraida. "We waited a long time. Then something happened which I know little about; I guess you know all of it. At any rate, when she burst in on us—we had gotten tired waiting and were in the *patio*—she, too, was like one gone mad. We had heard the shooting outside but when we started to run out some of her men threw guns on us and held us back. She came running in, terribly excited. When I tried to speak she cursed me, called me a fool, told me that she had never loved any but one man and that that man was—was you. Then she swore that she was going to see you dead and Betty Gordon dead with you. I guess I came to my senses a little at that."

"And Barlow?" insisted Kendric. Bruce had paused, was staring off into the night, seemed to have forgotten to go on.

"I had two words with Barlow when she left us. He looked ready for murder and just snapped out that he was going to stay until he lined his pockets. Rios came in. He told us you were on the run, trying to make it down here. He offered to get me and Barlow clear; he seemed anxious to have us both gone. He promised us we'd be dead in twenty-four hours if we stayed; he tipped his hand enough to say that there was loot to be had and he meant to have his half and didn't care what happened to us so long as we got out of the way. I came, hoping that you'd break through and get here. I told Barlow I was coming. He just shrugged his shoulders at that and said he'd stay; if we could square for the rent of the *Half Moon* in San Diego we could have her. Otherwise, for God's sake to sink her in the ocean and let the old man know. And off he went, looking for—for her."

"You've had a hard deal, Bruce." Kendric put a kindly hand on the boy's shoulder. "But you'll come alive yet. I've made a haul today; just how big I won't know until we get home. But enough, I'll gamble to stake you to a new start. Now, let's get going. And good luck to poor old Barlow. It's his game to play his way."

They slipped out into the gulf, Nigger Ben and Philippine Charlie content to accept the explanation Kendric gave them of Barlow's absence. Bruce, taciturn and moody, went to the stern and stood looking back toward the black line of the receding coast until long after darkness blotted it out. Kendric went to Betty's cabin and rapped.

"Will you come for a moment to the main cabin?" he asked.

When she came he had a lamp on the table. He shut the door and locked it. Then, without a word between them, he began emptying his pockets. She saw him pile up a great number of little square bars that clanked musically.

"Solid gold," he said gravely.

Then he poured forth the pearls. There was strings and loops, necklaces and broad bands made of many strings laced together. They shone softly, gloriously there in the swaying cabin of the *Half Moon*. The finest of them all fashioned into a superb necklace he threw with a sudden gesture about Betty's throat.

"And on top of all that—we're headed for home!" said Kendric.

"Home!" Betty's eyes shone more gloriously than the pearls.

"And thus ends our little camping trip. Tell me, Betty, haven't you any desire for a real camping trip in our own mountains? That place that I know, where the little hidden valley is and the lake—"

"Tell me about it," said Betty.

Pearls and gold heaped on the table, pearls about Betty's throat, and they talked of pack and trail and a little green lodge to be made of fir boughs.

Jackson Gregory

Choose from Thousands of 1stWorldLibrary Classics By

A. M. Barnard
Ada Leverson
Adolphus William Ward
Aesop
Agatha Christie
Alexander Aaronsohn
Alexander Kielland
Alexandre Dumas
Alfred Gatty
Alfred Ollivant
Alice Duer Miller
Alice Turner Curtis
Alice Dunbar
Allen Chapman
Alleyne Ireland
Ambrose Bierce
Amelia E. Barr
Amory H. Bradford
Andrew Lang
Andrew McFarland Davis
Andy Adams
Angela Brazil
Anna Alice Chapin
Anna Sewell
Annie Besant
Annie Hamilton Donnell
Annie Payson Call
Annie Roe Carr
Annonaymous
Anton Chekhov
Archibald Lee Fletcher
Arnold Bennett
Arthur C. Benson
Arthur Conan Doyle
Arthur M. Winfield
Arthur Ransome
Arthur Schnitzler
Arthur Train
Atticus
B.H. Baden-Powell
B. M. Bower
B. C. Chatterjee
Baroness Emmuska Orczy
Baroness Orczy
Basil King
Bayard Taylor
Ben Macomber
Bertha Muzzy Bower
Bjornstjerne Bjornson

Booth Tarkington
Boyd Cable
Bram Stoker
C. Collodi
C. E. Orr
C. M. Ingleby
Carolyn Wells
Catherine Parr Traill
Charles A. Eastman
Charles Amory Beach
Charles Dickens
Charles Dudley Warner
Charles Farrar Browne
Charles Ives
Charles Kingsley
Charles Klein
Charles Hanson Towne
Charles Lathrop Pack
Charles Romyn Dake
Charles Whibley
Charles Willing Beale
Charlotte M. Braeme
Charlotte M. Yonge
Charlotte Perkins Stetson
Clair W. Hayes
Clarence Day Jr.
Clarence E. Mulford
Clemence Housman
Confucius
Coningsby Dawson
Cornelis DeWitt Wilcox
Cyril Burleigh
D. H. Lawrence
Daniel Defoe
David Garnett
Dinah Craik
Don Carlos Janes
Donald Keyhoe
Dorothy Kilner
Dougan Clark
Douglas Fairbanks
E. Nesbit
E. P. Roe
E. Phillips Oppenheim
E. S. Brooks
Earl Barnes
Edgar Rice Burroughs
Edith Van Dyne
Edith Wharton

Edward Everett Hale
Edward J. O'Biren
Edward S. Ellis
Edwin L. Arnold
Eleanor Atkins
Eleanor Hallowell Abbott
Eliot Gregory
Elizabeth Gaskell
Elizabeth McCracken
Elizabeth Von Arnim
Ellem Key
Emerson Hough
Emilie F. Carlen
Emily Bronte
Emily Dickinson
Enid Bagnold
Enilor Macartney Lane
Erasmus W. Jones
Ernie Howard Pie
Ethel May Dell
Ethel Turner
Ethel Watts Mumford
Eugene Sue
Eugenie Foa
Eugene Wood
Eustace Hale Ball
Evelyn Everett-green
Everard Cotes
F. H. Cheley
F. J. Cross
F. Marion Crawford
Fannie E. Newberry
Federick Austin Ogg
Ferdinand Ossendowski
Fergus Hume
Florence A. Kilpatrick
Fremont B. Deering
Francis Bacon
Francis Darwin
Frances Hodgson Burnett
Frances Parkinson Keyes
Frank Gee Patchin
Frank Harris
Frank Jewett Mather
Frank L. Packard
Frank V. Webster
Frederic Stewart Isham
Frederick Trevor Hill
Frederick Winslow Taylor

Friedrich Kerst
Friedrich Nietzsche
Fyodor Dostoyevsky
G.A. Henty
G.K. Chesterton
Gabrielle E. Jackson
Garrett P. Serviss
Gaston Leroux
George A. Warren
George Ade
Geroge Bernard Shaw
George Cary Eggleston
George Durston
George Ebers
George Eliot
George Gissing
George MacDonald
George Meredith
George Orwell
George Sylvester Viereck
George Tucker
George W. Cable
George Wharton James
Gertrude Atherton
Gordon Casserly
Grace E. King
Grace Gallatin
Grace Greenwood
Grant Allen
Guillermo A. Sherwell
Gulielma Zollinger
Gustav Flaubert
H. A. Cody
H. B. Irving
H.C. Bailey
H. G. Wells
H. H. Munro
H. Irving Hancock
H. R. Naylor
H. Rider Haggard
H. W. C. Davis
Haldeman Julius
Hall Caine
Hamilton Wright Mabie
Hans Christian Andersen
Harold Avery
Harold McGrath
Harriet Beecher Stowe
Harry Castlemon
Harry Coghill
Harry Houidini

Hayden Carruth
Helent Hunt Jackson
Helen Nicolay
Hendrik Conscience
Hendy David Thoreau
Henri Barbusse
Henrik Ibsen
Henry Adams
Henry Ford
Henry Frost
Henry James
Henry Jones Ford
Henry Seton Merriman
Henry W Longfellow
Herbert A. Giles
Herbert Carter
Herbert N. Casson
Herman Hesse
Hildegard G. Frey
Homer
Honore De Balzac
Horace B. Day
Horace Walpole
Horatio Alger Jr.
Howard Pyle
Howard R. Garis
Hugh Lofting
Hugh Walpole
Humphry Ward
Ian Maclaren
Inez Haynes Gillmore
Irving Bacheller
Isabel Cecilia Williams
Isabel Hornibrook
Israel Abrahams
Ivan Turgenev
J.G.Austin
J. Henri Fabre
J. M. Barrie
J. M. Walsh
J. Macdonald Oxley
J. R. Miller
J. S. Fletcher
J. S. Knowles
J. Storer Clouston
J. W. Duffield
Jack London
Jacob Abbott
James Allen
James Andrews
James Baldwin

James Branch Cabell
James DeMille
James Joyce
James Lane Allen
James Lane Allen
James Oliver Curwood
James Oppenheim
James Otis
James R. Driscoll
Jane Abbott
Jane Austen
Jane L. Stewart
Janet Aldridge
Jens Peter Jacobsen
Jerome K. Jerome
Jessie Graham Flower
John Buchan
John Burroughs
John Cournos
John F. Kennedy
John Gay
John Glasworthy
John Habberton
John Joy Bell
John Kendrick Bangs
John Milton
John Philip Sousa
John Taintor Foote
Jonas Lauritz Idemil Lie
Jonathan Swift
Joseph A. Altsheler
Joseph Carey
Joseph Conrad
Joseph E. Badger Jr
Joseph Hergesheimer
Joseph Jacobs
Jules Vernes
Julian Hawthrone
Julie A Lippmann
Justin Huntly McCarthy
Kakuzo Okakura
Karle Wilson Baker
Kate Chopin
Kenneth Grahame
Kenneth McGaffey
Kate Langley Bosher
Kate Langley Bosher
Katherine Cecil Thurston
Katherine Stokes
L. A. Abbot
L. T. Meade

L. Frank Baum
Latta Griswold
Laura Dent Crane
Laura Lee Hope
Laurence Housman
Lawrence Beasley
Leo Tolstoy
Leonid Andreyev
Lewis Carroll
Lewis Sperry Chafer
Lilian Bell
Lloyd Osbourne
Louis Hughes
Louis Joseph Vance
Louis Tracy
Louisa May Alcott
Lucy Fitch Perkins
Lucy Maud Montgomery
Luther Benson
Lydia Miller Middleton
Lyndon Orr
M. Corvus
M. H. Adams
Margaret E. Sangster
Margret Howth
Margaret Vandercook
Margaret W. Hungerford
Margret Penrose
Maria Edgeworth
Maria Thompson Daviess
Mariano Azuela
Marion Polk Angellotti
Mark Overton
Mark Twain
Mary Austin
Mary Catherine Crowley
Mary Cole
Mary Hastings Bradley
Mary Roberts Rinehart
Mary Rowlandson
M. Wollstonecraft Shelley
Maud Lindsay
Max Beerbohm
Myra Kelly
Nathaniel Hawthrone
Nicolo Machiavelli
O. F. Walton
Oscar Wilde

Owen Johnson
P.G. Wodehouse
Paul and Mabel Thorne
Paul G. Tomlinson
Paul Severing
Percy Brebner
Percy Keese Fitzhugh
Peter B. Kyne
Plato
Quincy Allen
R. Derby Holmes
R. L. Stevenson
R. S. Ball
Rabindranath Tagore
Rahul Alvares
Ralph Bonehill
Ralph Henry Barbour
Ralph Victor
Ralph Waldo Emmerson
Rene Descartes
Ray Cummings
Rex Beach
Rex E. Beach
Richard Harding Davis
Richard Jefferies
Richard Le Gallienne
Robert Barr
Robert Frost
Robert Gordon Anderson
Robert L. Drake
Robert Lansing
Robert Lynd
Robert Michael Ballantyne
Robert W. Chambers
Rosa Nouchette Carey
Rudyard Kipling
Saint Augustine
Samuel B. Allison
Samuel Hopkins Adams
Sarah Bernhardt
Sarah C. Hallowell
Selma Lagerlof
Sherwood Anderson
Sigmund Freud
Standish O'Grady
Stanley Weyman
Stella Benson
Stella M. Francis

Stephen Crane
Stewart Edward White
Stijn Streuvels
Swami Abhedananda
Swami Parmananda
T. S. Ackland
T. S. Arthur
The Princess Der Ling
Thomas A. Janvier
Thomas A Kempis
Thomas Anderton
Thomas Bailey Aldrich
Thomas Bulfinch
Thomas De Quincey
Thomas Dixon
Thomas H. Huxley
Thomas Hardy
Thomas More
Thornton W. Burgess
U. S. Grant
Upton Sinclair
Valentine Williams
Various Authors
Vaughan Kester
Victor Appleton
Victor G. Durham
Victoria Cross
Virginia Woolf
Wadsworth Camp
Walter Camp
Walter Scott
Washington Irving
Wilbur Lawton
Wilkie Collins
Willa Cather
Willard F. Baker
William Dean Howells
William le Queux
W. Makepeace Thackeray
William W. Walter
William Shakespeare
Winston Churchill
Yei Theodora Ozaki
Yogi Ramacharaka
Young E. Allison
Zane Grey